UNH⊙LY ⊙RDERS

∞ ∞ ∞

MYSTERY STORIES
WITH A RELIGIOUS TWIST

EDITED BY SERITA STEVENS

INTRIGUE PRESS

Philadelphia

ISBN 1-890768-28-6

First Printing, November 2000

Library of Congress Cataloging-in-Publication Data
Unholy Orders: mystery stories with a religious twist/edited by Serita Stevens.
    p. cm.
    ISBN 1-890768-28-6 (hardcover)
    1. Detective and mystery stories, American. 2. Detective and mystery
    stories, English. 3. Religious fiction, American. 4. Religious fiction,
    English. I. Stevens, Serita, 1949-

PS648.D4 U56 2000
813'.087209382--dc21
                                                  00-033458

10 9 8 7 6 5 4 3 2 1

INTRODUCTION

Praiseworthy is he who contemplates the needy. (Psalms 41:1)

Like many others, I had seen the evening news reports showing the horrendous conditions that Romanian orphans lived under: lack of food or medical care, few toys and even scarcer attention.

Naively, I thought all the kids would find good homes. But when 20/20 did a follow up a few years later, I saw this was not the case. Thousands upon thousands of infants remained without homes.

As a single woman I had a hard time getting approved by the authorities. Finally in 1995, I headed to Romania for my daughter. I had only seen one photo of her and knew very little about her health condition. Seeing close-up the cold impoverished buildings, I knew something more had to be done for those abandoned children. Babies lined up in metal cribs, the lead paint nearly eaten off. Stacked like so many packages, children lay in their own urine, numb to the pain of life, numb to the flies that settled on them. They stared into space. Their hope of redeeming homes dissipated.

My daughter's birth mother and two year old brother lived in a single room shack: no water, no heat, and no electricity. Realizing she could not care for another child, the mother had abandoned Alexzandra.

At the age of nine months—and weighing only nine pounds—my daughter could not stand, sit, roll over or talk. Like many of the others in the orphanage, she had been fed only rice water or soaked bread, but despite the inadequate care, her alert eyes followed me everywhere. Somehow she attracted the attention of the adoption agency.

Today, with love, she is articulate and an ice skater.

In 1996, Hearts for Romania was founded by my friend Diana and in 1997, I joined her as a board member. In that time, we have learned a great deal more about the extent of the problem, the intricacies of providing aid and the critical need for fast response. Romanian law says a baby must be left for six months before it can be considered abandoned and released for adoption. By the time a home is found, the child may be eight months or older—and those are the lucky ones. Eight months without human touch scars a child for life. Those who survive their infancy without being placed are tossed out on the street to survive best they can.

So in 1999, to prevent more children from becoming "unadoptables," we started a sister charity, Hugs and Hopes for Romania, opening private foster homes where the kids would get individualized attention. Hugs and Hopes' first private children's home for the orphaned and abandoned is to open soon in Craiova.

The authors of the wonderful stories in this collection have generously directed that their royalties be contributed to Hugs and Hopes-Romania (IRC 501(c)3 status pending). Our goal is to help the orphaned children of Romania become valuable members of their society, so that Romania can stand on its own. As the bible says, *that which is rejected becomes the cornerstone.* While other charitable organizations can help kids while they are in the institutions, we aim to take the kids out of the institution and provide a family atmosphere for the first time in their young lives.

For more information about Hugs and Hopes
contact Serita Stevens:
4829 Whitsett Ave #201, Valley Village, CA 91607.
Email: seritas@earthlink.net

CONTENTS

❦ ❦ ❦

ANNE PERRY

⸿⸿ ⸿⸿ ⸿⸿

Anne Perry was born in 1938 in Blackheath, London. She suffered from respiratory problems and as a result spent some of her childhood in the Bahamas and in New Zealand. Following a particularly tragic event, she returned to England and then lived in the United States for some years where she worked at a variety of jobs, and later joined the Church of Jesus Christ of the Latter-Day Saints (Mormons). Since her first book was published in 1979, she has sold in excess of six million books worldwide; her work has been translated into seven languages. Her first book was dramatized and broadcast in England and the U.S. last year and the first book in the Monk series is currently being adapted for feature film. None of her books has ever been out of print.

THE REVEREND COLLINS' VISIT

BY ANNE PERRY

Henry Rathbone sat in the armchair in his bedroom with a blanket around him and stared out of the window and across the front garden to the pleasant street beyond. A young woman walked by, her long muslin skirts swinging. She had a green coat on, like the spring green of the trees, and a hat at a rakish angle. A hansom cab passed her at a brisk trot, harness jingling, and the driver turned a little on his box to admire her.

She pretended not to notice, but she strode even more jauntily, and Henry found himself smiling.

He sneezed, and felt as if his head were full of glue. His eyes stung too much to enjoy reading, and he had laid his book on contemporary philosophy aside. He enjoyed learning what other people thought, and one day he intended to write a book on philosophy himself . . . probably. His son Oliver, one of the finest barristers in England, did not believe him, and perhaps he was right. There was still so much to consider before one came to any unalterable conclusions.

A carriage drew up at the house next door, to the left, and a young couple alighted and went in . . . making afternoon calls, no doubt. It was the hour for it. The man walked uprightly, with a slight limp. Henry wondered if he had been a soldier, wounded in the recent war in the Crimea. He had a military bearing.

He sneezed again. There was something particularly vicious about an early summer chill. His head ached, his nose was sore, his chest hurt, and nothing tasted or smelled as it should. Even his beloved pipe was no comfort at all. Not that he ever kept it alight for long, but it was a pleasant thing to hold.

His housekeeper had suggested a mustard bath for his feet, no doubt intending to be helpful. What on earth use could that be? The cold was in his head! But he was wretched enough to try almost anything, even if only to give him the feeling he was fighting the thing.

Someone else came round the corner on the far side of the street, staring straight ahead of him like a man fulfilling a purpose. As he passed opposite, Henry recognized him, as much by his gait as anything. It was unmistakably his friend the Reverend John Collins, vicar of the local church. He had long ago abandoned any idea of persuading Henry to join his flock, but they had remained occasional friends, enjoying a comparison of treasures found in old shops: curios, mostly paintings or political cartoons. Collins had a nice sense of humor.

Henry watched as he crossed the road opposite and continued on to the next corner, almost out of sight, then turned in and went up to the front door of old Mrs. Chatterton's house. He rang the bell and a moment later was let in: Henry could not see by whom, but probably the butler. Mrs. Chatterton ran a large establishment. Rumor had it she was more than comfortably off. Rumor also had it that she was extremely poorly, and was not expected to live a great deal longer. But since she was in her eighties, that was not surprising.

Time dragged interminably when there was nothing to do. The weeds were growing in the garden. He could see them if he stood up. Perhaps the definition of a weed was something that was in the wrong place, and grew faster than anything else.

Half a dozen more vehicles passed, and then the Reverend Collins came out of Mrs. Chatterton's and walked back the way he had come, home toward the vicarage. He had just reached the corner opposite when a stout man, accompanied by a woman with a striped coat and a very fine hat, crossed from just beneath the trees to the right, and spoke to him.

Collins nodded several times, then he pointed toward the

street that turned off at right angles.

The man seemed uncertain. He said something more. It appeared he was asking directions. The woman moved closer to them both so she might also hear what the vicar was saying. A gust of wind blew against them and she put up her hand to steady her hat, its broad brim rocking, ribbons bright in the sun.

Collins nodded again, and walked a few paces with them in the direction he had pointed. The man turned and shook his hand warmly. The woman smoothed down her skirt, which was billowing out, then they both walked away. Collins came back to the corner again, and continued on his journey home, a slight spring in his step now, the tight hunch to his shoulders gone. In a few moments he was out of sight.

Henry wandered downstairs and made himself a cup of tea. It was hot, which eased his throat and chest, but like everything else at the moment, it tasted wrong.

He was pleased to see the large white and orange cat from next door wander in. He did not know what they called it, but he had named it Humphrey. He could not speak to it without addressing it as something. He gave it some milk, and later at suppertime shared his scrambled eggs, to Humphrey's great pleasure.

In the morning his housekeeper, Mrs. Stack, complained about it vociferously. As always he nodded politely, and the moment she was out of the room again, forgot about it. Mrs. Stack was a good woman, and necessary . . . whereas Humphrey he genuinely liked.

Mrs. Stack made him a hot luncheon, which he enjoyed, and thanked her for it sincerely. She was well satisfied, because she did not know that Humphrey had decided to spend the afternoon curled up in the bed asleep, and Henry let him.

A little after three o'clock Henry was back in his chair to see the vicar walk along the street again and go in to visit Mrs. Chatterton. Several other people passed by: a maid with a little girl in a frilly dress and a blue sash around her waist; a courting couple; an elderly man with bushy white whiskers; Mr. Lethbridge from the house on the opposite corner. He had recently come home after being in India. The Mutiny had ended that for him. He had lost too many friends. He called in and talked with Henry sometimes.

At quarter to four the vicar emerged from Mrs. Chatterton's and walked as far as the edge of the footpath opposite. He was just stepping out to cross when a youth of about twenty came running along the road and swerved around the corner, lost his balance, and knocked straight into the Reverend Collins.

They both fell heavily into the road.

Henry started forward in alarm.

A middle-aged man appeared from the near side of the street and ran across to them, ignoring the youth, who was already climbing to his feet, and reaching for Collins, who was obviously stunned and bruised. He assisted him up, offering his arm to bear the vicar's weight as he stood, dusting down his extremely rumpled coat, and all the time asking anxious questions, presumably as to his welfare.

Collins kept shaking his head, and after straightening his tie, pushing his hand through his hair and smoothing his own coat and trousers again, he hesitated for a moment. Then waving aside any further help he went on his way, limping slightly.

The man turned on the youth with considerable anger and—Henry assumed—berated him for his thoughtless behavior. It was several minutes before the youth went away. From what Henry could see of his expression and the slump of his shoulders, he felt considerably chastened.

It was another long evening. Not having taken his usual exercise, either by walking or gardening, or any other useful activity, Henry was tired without being sleepy. He listened to the rain pattering on the window and looked at Humphrey now stretched out across the middle of the bed, purring as he moved very slightly and drifted from one dream into another. He envied him, but quite without wishing to rob him of his evident pleasure.

The next day started damp. By eleven the sun broke through and every leaf and blade of grass sparkled. Horses' backs steamed a little as they sped by, and carriage wheels sent up a spray of water and mud.

Henry was definitely feeling better. Mrs. Stack complained about Humphrey, who now left muddy paw prints on the floor. Actually he left them on the bed also, but Henry doubled the blanket over so she would not see them.

She offered to make a mustard bath for Henry's feet, but again he declined. It was very good of her, but the worst was past. She warned him not to go out yet, and he was quite happy to agree, especially since it looked as if it would almost certainly rain again.

He read for a little while, and must have dozed off to sleep for a half hour or so. When he woke up the sun was shining fitfully, and he saw the vicar again, this time already leaving Mrs. Chatterton's and walking home. That was three days in a row now. She must be failing quite rapidly.

Henry watched as Collins walked along the footpath on the far side of the road. There was a child on the corner just ahead of him; from this distance he seemed about five or six years old. Henry wondered why he was out alone. He seemed to be looking for something, peering into the hedge of the nearest garden. Then he got down on his hands and knees, making a fine mess of his trousers in the mud.

Collins reached him and stopped. Apparently he spoke to him, because the boy looked up, then pointed into the hedge, and resumed his search even more eagerly.

Collins hesitated a moment, then squatted rather awkwardly to help him.

Henry smiled. The vicar was a kindly man. Without the slightest effort a dozen instances of small services came to mind: a word of encouragement; the patience to listen to a story told for the umpteenth time; misplaced criticism accepted without retaliation. It did not surprise him that Collins should now take with the utmost seriousness a child's lost toy. Henry felt his own knees cracking as he watched Collins assist the search.

A buxom woman came along the street at a pace little short of a run. She was dressed in a striped blouse under the crisp, white apron of a maid, which all but covered her skirt. She stopped level with the child and began speaking volubly. Henry could not hear at this distance what she was saying, but from her gestures—and as Collins rose to his feet—she seemed to be apologizing profusely for the child's behavior, and then admonishing him for involving the vicar in his loss.

The boy submitted without a struggle, and said something to Collins, while his maid kept a firm hold on his shoulder.

Collins shook his head and raised one hand slightly as if to indicate that it was all no trouble at all.

The maid looked him up and down, perhaps commiserating with his slightly crumpled trousers, and pointed to what may well have been mud. Then she took a corner of her clean, starched apron and brushed him down very carefully in a couple of places. She stepped back and surveyed her work, and was satisfied.

Collins thanked her, tipped his hat, and with a word to the boy, went on his way.

The maid and the child returned in the direction from which she had come, and once again the street was empty for a while.

Humphrey stretched and decided it was tea-time, so Henry abandoned his book and went downstairs to get them both something. In the event he found that Mrs. Stack had left him a shepherd's pie, which he shared with Humphrey, who then washed himself appreciatively, and sauntered outside for a walk.

The following day it rained steadily all morning, and Henry spent it reading and making notes, which he then could not decipher. If anyone came or went along the street, he did not notice them. Mrs. Stack gave him a lecture on laundry, and muddy paw prints.

Henry apologized, without promising to do anything about it.

In the afternoon Humphrey returned, wet, and made himself comfortable on the bed and went to sleep.

Henry found himself watching to see if Mr. Collins went along to see old Mrs. Chatterton again today. At just before half past three he saw the familiar figure walking along determinedly, leaning forward into the brisk wind that was swaying the branches, and probably quite chilly after the rain. He seemed like a man bent on a purpose he did not look forward to.

Henry could sympathize with him. Even a vicar must find it difficult to know what to say to the dying, particularly a disagreeable old woman as Mrs. Chatterton was reputed to be. According to several opinions Henry had heard, she was very well gifted with the world's goods and had no intention of parting with any of them lightly, even at the call of the Almighty. She would not go with a good grace.

When the Reverend Collins could be seen returning again at five o'clock, his step was lighter and he walked as if he were glad to be on his way. Not once did he look behind him, and his feet fairly flew over the paving stones.

Therefore he was brought to an abrupt halt when the young constable stepped out in front of him, just past the crossing, and put a hand on his arm. However he did not seem alarmed, until a moment later when Henry saw the constable begin to tap Collins' pockets in a purposeful fashion.

Collins took a sharp step backward and even from the upstairs window on the opposite side of the street, Henry could see the complete consternation in every angle and gesture of his body.

Henry started forward. What on earth could be going on? Had the constable lost his wits? His behavior was offensive and inexplicable.

Henry was about to turn away and go downstairs and out over the road to do something about it, when the constable pulled his hand up in a sharp movement, obviously holding something. He opened his hand in front of the vicar, showing it to him, then took it away again quickly, put it in his own pocket, grasped Collins extremely firmly by the elbow and more or less marched him away.

Horrified, Henry took off his old cardigan, put on a clean shirt and a tie and his best jacket, polished boots (even if decidedly old—he prided himself in being able to keep a pair of boots for at least ten years, if not more) and went out.

He called first at the vicarage, where Mrs. Collins was unaware of anything amiss. Henry said merely that he hoped the reverend would call by one evening for supper and a chat, and left in a hurry to go to the local police station, which was a far longer walk. His head was still thumping and his nose uncomfortably blocked. He had not had a good stiff walk for several days, and it was farther than he had anticipated; nevertheless that mattered not at all. He must find out what had happened to Collins, and assist if possible.

He was quite breathless when he arrived, and strode into the police station and up to the desk.

"Yes, sir?" The sergeant looked at him enquiringly.

"Is the Reverend Collins in here?" Henry asked him.

"And why would you want to know that, sir?" the sergeant replied. He was a mild man, not easily rattled. All manner of people passed through his domain. People would be surprised if they knew some of them, and the reasons that brought them here.

Henry was a very truthful man; it was his discipline in life science to allow no equivocations. But he was also emotional, and partisan, although he would have been indignant to hear anyone say so.

"Because I witnessed an incident in which he was involved," he replied. "And I may have evidence which is pertinent to it." That was true, he may have, although he could bring none to mind at the moment.

"Ah . . . well." The sergeant was open to reason. "If you wait here, sir, I'll go and inquire. Constable Kendall is handling that matter. Who shall I say, sir?"

"Henry Rathbone."

"Right you are, Mr. Rathbone." The sergeant disappeared, and Henry was left to stare around at the wanted posters and local notices until he returned just over five minutes later, and indicated that Henry should go with him.

It was not Constable Kendall who received him in a small room stacked with books and papers, with one wooden table and two chairs, and a window looking onto an alley; it was a sad, overweight sergeant looking profoundly unhappy.

"Come in, Mr. Rathbone," he said gloomily, pushing a hand up over his head as if to brush back hair, except that he had none. "What is it you know about this miserable business?"

Henry was momentarily nonplussed. He sat down on the rather rickety chair opposite the sergeant and thought what he was going to say.

The sergeant waited patiently.

"I saw your constable search the pockets of the vicar, and then arrest him!" Henry said rather more angrily than he had intended.

The sergeant shook his head. "No choice, sir. Found the jewelry on 'im. Don't know what 'e did with the other pieces, but 'e was red 'anded with that one. Pretty thing, diamonds and pearls, it was. Worth a fair penny."

"That's ridiculous!" Henry protested. "You don't seriously imagine that the vicar would steal jewelry from a dying woman, do you? One of his parishioners!"

"Don't like to sir, but the evidence is there," the sergeant said unhappily, his watery blue eyes full of misery. "Took a piece every time 'e called. 'E was alone with the old lady in 'er bedroom, as was fittin' for talkin' to the dyin', I suppose. If you can't talk confidential to the vicar, then 'oo can you? The maid found something gone each time." He shook his head. "No one wanted to think it was the vicar, but after the third time, there wasn't much choice. So they called us, and we were ready for 'im the fourth time. Found the piece in 'is pocket." He shook his head again. "You tell me some other explanation for that, sir, an' I'll be an 'appy man. I don't know what the world's comin' to, an' I don't think I want to, an' that's a fact."

Henry was stunned. It was not possible—not Collins. Even if he were desperate; and everyone knew clergymen were not generously paid—even so, Collins would not steal!

Never! Least of all from a dying woman, even one as disagreeable as Mrs. Chatterton . . . or as wealthy. The most he would do would be to try and persuade her to donate a little more generously, and even that would go against his grain.

"I don't believe it!" he said uselessly.

"Got to!" The sergeant was a man who faced facts. "The thing was in his pocket. He must 'ave got rid of all the others, but in time we'll find what 'e did with them. He hasn't had a chance to do much."

Henry's mind raced. "He's been to see Mrs. Chatterton four times this last week, and each time he visited her alone in her room?"

"That's right. Poor old lady is too ill to get out of 'er bed," the sergeant agreed.

"But she didn't see him take anything?" Henry persisted.

"Light's kept low and curtains closed. She's dyin', sir!"

"And after each visit the maid found something gone, some piece of jewelry?"

"That's right."

Pictures scattered and reformed in Henry's mind, like the brightly colored fragments in a kaleidoscope. Suddenly it made sense. He leaned forward over the table, his voice earnest.

"Each time he left Mrs. Chatterton's house there was a piece of her jewelry in his pocket, Sergeant, and each time he arrived at his own house there was not! I saw it, without realizing what it was. The piece was taken from the jewel box before he arrived, placed in his coat pocket while it was hanging in the hall and he was upstairs, and very skillfully removed from his pocket while he was on the way home. Each time it happened opposite my window." He sniffed as if to add weight to the point. "I have had a bad cold, Sergeant, and stayed largely in my room. I watched the street, and I observed it."

Hope lit the sergeant's pale eyes.

Henry then described the incident with the couple who inquired for directions, the youth who had bowled the vicar over, and the middle-aged man who had come to his assistance, and then the boy with the lost toy, and his buxom maid.

The sergeant whistled. "The same man and woman!" he said with admiration. "Oh, very neat, sir! Yes, very tidy little trick there! Put away the poor vicar, and no suspicion attached! I think we'd better 'ave a closer look at Mrs. Chatterton's household, and see if any of them have family in a dodgy way o' business. Sounds like Bert and Maisie 'Oskins, to me. Big, 'andsome kind o' woman, was she? Favors stripes?"

"Yes! Yes, she does!" Henry agreed eagerly.

The sergeant nodded, beginning to smile. "I think you could 'ave got it, sir! And that makes me a very 'appy man. I like Mr. Collins, I do, and so does the wife. I was dreadin' 'avin' to tell 'er. Wouldn't know 'ow to begin. She'd be that terrible upset." He climbed heavily to his feet, his smile growing broader by the minute.

Henry stood up too.

"Well now," the sergeant said cheerfully. "I'll send in a constable ter take all that down, an' I'll go an' tell your Mr. Collins as he's free to go! I dare say he'll be thankin' yer himself. That's an 'orrible cold yer've got there, sir. Would you like a nice hot cup o' tea? And perhaps a drop a something in it, like?"

Henry relaxed and smiled back at him. "Thank you, that would be excellent," he accepted.

ROCHELLE KRICH

∞ ∞ ∞

Rochelle Krich was named by the *L.A. Times* as one of ten women writing "superior crime fiction." She won the Anthony Award for her first suspense novel *Where's Mommy Now?* which was filmed as *Perfect Alibi* with Teri Garr. Her series character, LAPD Detective Jessica Drake, debuted in *Fair Game* and returned in *Angel of Death*. Both novels were nominated for the Agatha Award. Her stand-alone mysteries include *Till Death Do Us Part, Nowhere To Run, Speak No Evil*, and *Fertile Ground*. Ms. Krich's works have been published in Britain, Germany, Holland, Iceland, Japan, and France.

WIDOW'S PEAK

BY ROCHELLE KRICH

Rose loved the cinnamon camphor trees. Tall and graceful, they lined both sides of a path wide enough for the passage of a single lane of cars and formed a bright green canopy of fluttering leaves. Ribbons of sunlight, winding their way through the wide, heavy branches, striped the path and the headstones of the graves.

"Over there." Rose pointed twenty feet ahead to her left.

Followed by her daughter and granddaughter in a silent processional, she crossed the path and walked gingerly on the narrow strip of sidewalk, steadying herself with her cane as she stepped around tent-shaped slabs of concrete cracked and raised by the trees' tenacious, clawlike roots.

Rose liked the silence of the cemetery, the peaceful solemnity that banished idle chatter and allowed her to be alone with her thoughts. She would have come more often to visit with her late husband, Herman, but was dependent for transportation on her daughter, Adele, who dutifully prayed at her father's grave every year between Rosh Hashanah and Yom Kippur and on his *yahrzeit*, the anniversary of his death. Herman and Adele had chided Rose for refusing to take driving lessons, but she had been too nervous.

They were standing in front of the grave now, and she read the few words chiseled into the black granite below the Star of David. HERMAN GREENBERG, BELOVED HUSBAND, FATHER, GRANDFATHER. What he would have given to see Shoshana standing under the *chuppah*, the wedding canopy, Rose thought, blinking back tears.

She stole a sidelong glance at her granddaughter. Everyone said Shoshana looked exactly like the young Rose in the sepia-toned photo on the baby grand piano in Adele's living room, and the old woman had to admit the resemblance was striking. As a girl Rose had the same large, ocean blue, almond-shaped eyes; the same thin nose and full, cupid-bow lips; the same heart-shaped face and high forehead accented with a widow's peak. An odd phrase, widow's peak. There was no Yiddish equivalent, as far as Rose knew. She had been unnerved when she'd first heard it, a few months after immigrating to America, and though she'd been assured that it wasn't prophetic, looking back she sometimes wondered.

Rose sighed, though not for the youth that had slipped away, leaving her face crisscrossed with deep lines, the mottled skin on her neck and hands stretched and sagging. She was comfortable with her face and body. She sighed for the satin-gowned young woman who had stood over fifty years ago under an outdoor *chuppah* in a small Polish town; sighed for the nervous, black-frocked, deep-brown-eyed young man, rocking back and forth on the heels of his new shoes, who had been her husband for one night before German soldiers had broken down their door and snatched him away, never to be seen again.

Years later, having miraculously survived the labor camps where she had been interned throughout the war, she stood in a friend's cramped Washington Heights apartment with Herman Greenberg, also a survivor, under a black-and-white-striped prayer shawl supported by four poles. The next day, and for days and weeks and months afterward, she half expected tragedy to invade her home again. Only after their first anniversary did she relax her guard, but even then the knowledge that happiness was a sly seducer never left her completely.

This was not to say that Rose was a morbid woman.

Though she wished fervently that Herman were still alive, she was grateful for the years they had shared, the dreams realized, for the tenderness and passion, the laughter and the arguments, all of which had brought tears to her eyes. She was grateful, too, that she could visit Herman's grave. There had been no burial for Yossel Goronowicz, no grave, no evidence that her first husband had died, save for the report from a female cousin who had seen him near death in Buchenwald. The rabbis, bending over backward to free countless young widows like Rose, whose husbands' bodies would never be found, had in many cases accepted testimony from one female eyewitness where usually that of two males was required.

There were no graves for Rose's parents, either, or her siblings or grandparents. Only memories and a few faded, crackled snapshots she had managed to hide underneath the lining of a shoe.

Rose looked again at her granddaughter. The twenty-year-old bride-to-be, looking like a schoolgirl in a long-sleeved blue blouse and gray pleated skirt, her thick, glossy dark brown hair pulled into a ponytail, had taken out a prayer book and was gently swaying while reciting psalms. She was more pious than Rose, who, bereft of family and faith, had abandoned and then gradually returned to a less stringent form of the Orthodox observance of her parents. More pious, too, than Rose's daughter and son-in-law, Marvin, who had been unprepared and somewhat discomfited when their daughter, inspired by the religious instruction they'd provided her through high school and during a year in an Israeli all-girls seminary, had surpassed them in creed and practice and had chosen for a husband a man who would study the Torah and someday teach it.

The girl was an angel, Rose thought. A beautiful angel, inside and out. This young man she was marrying in three days—pious, smart, kind, charitable, from a respected Orthodox London family—was getting gold.

"I can't believe Daddy's been gone eight years. Can you?" Adele sniffled and wiped her red-rimmed eyes with her fingers.

"Sometimes it feels like it was yesterday," Rose said. "Sometimes, like a hundred years." She patted her daughter's hand.

"Do I say anything special, Grandma?" Shoshana asked. She had finished praying and was standing on the other side of her mother.

Rose shook her head. "Not that I know. You just invite *Zeideh* to your wedding. His *neshamah* will come." His soul.

The girl nodded.

"Did you know, *sheifeleh*, the rabbis say that at every wedding, there are two *chuppahs*. One, God willing, you'll be standing under with your *chosson*," Rose said, using the Hebrew word for bridegroom. "The other one we can't see, but it's there." She smiled. "All your relatives who are in heaven will be standing under it, rejoicing with you. *Zeideh*, too."

And my parents, Rose thought, and grandparents. And their ancestors. So many souls, crowding under one canopy.

A sudden breeze ruffled her thin blouse. She shivered and was overwhelmed by blessing, a time of bliss and a reminder that catastrophe was just around the corner.

She had felt this same disquiet for weeks before Adele's wedding twenty-four years ago, exacerbated when, days after spraining her ankle at a friend's wedding, Adele was involved in a car accident. She had been bruised but not seriously injured. Still, Rose had made Herman run to the rabbi, who checked the mezuzahs on all the doorposts and reported that one of the rolled parchments had a letter missing in the word 'levanecha.'

"To your sons . . ." literally. Or more loosely, to your children. The mezuzah had been corrected, but Rose had not really been surprised when, on the day of the wedding, Adele had awakened with a high fever and chills. It was a sign, Rose had

felt. For one brief, irrational moment she had wanted to postpone the wedding, to cancel it. But at sunset that evening she
and Herman had walked a medicated, deliriously happy Adele
down the aisle.

Rose was not a superstitious woman, but now she spat onto
the ground to ward off evil spirits just as her mother and grandmother had done in Poland fifty years ago.

Two nights before the wedding Shoshana fainted while
stepping out of the *mikvah*, the ritual bath.

"The water was too hot and she became lightheaded," Adele
told Rose. "That's all it was. Thank God the attendant was right
behind her and caught her. She could have cracked her head on
the tile floor, God forbid."

Rose thanked God, and worried. She worried about the
invitations that had been reprinted three times and finally
mailed with yet another error because time had run out. Over
fifty of them had come back, the stamps apparently having fall-
en off. She worried about the wedding gown, a Vera Wang
made modest with long sleeves and a raised neckline, that had
been lost en route from New York to the Beverly Hills bridal
shop. Little things, things that happened to other brides, incon-
veniences one laughed about later. But they worried Rose. And
now this.

"Check the mezuzahs," Rose advised her daughter.

"We had them all checked a year ago, Ma," Adele said
impatiently. "They say you should check them every three."

Rose insisted. Adele sighed, exasperated, and had Marvin
remove all the scrolls that night. In the morning a rabbi exam-
ined them and returned them several hours later to Adele. All
except one, in which he'd found a defect.

"I guess you were right, Ma. There's a letter missing in *'levanecha,'*" Adele said. "It was in the mezuzah on Shoshana's bed-

room door. Isn't that weird?"

Rose agreed that it was weird. Her hands and lips tingled and she was suddenly very tired.

"But the main thing is, Ma, now we have a new mezuzah up. Do you feel better?"

"Much better," Rose lied.

Against a backdrop of white orchids, roses, and lilies and an airy arrangement of deeply swagged swaths of tulle, the bride sat on a white-satin-covered chair in the middle of a raised platform, reciting psalms from the small white leather-bound book on her lap in between greeting guests. Serene and radiant, no hint of pallor on her face though she was fasting, she accepted kisses and *mazel tovs* and slips of paper bearing names of individuals on whose behalf, while standing under the *chuppah*, she would beseech God: for a mate for someone single, restored health for someone ailing, a child for a woman trying to conceive. According to the sages, Rose knew, God pays special attention to a bride's prayers on her wedding day.

The partitioned ballroom, which had been frigid an hour ago before the first guests arrived, was crowded with people talking and sampling the generous display of hors d'oeuvres. Rose felt stiff and uncomfortably warm in the pewter-colored, beaded lace and satin gown, and her eyes itched, unaccustomed to the eye liner and mascara the young woman had applied. Rose had wanted to wash off the makeup, but Adele had said, "Wait until after the pictures, you'll look white."

Adele, with Rose next to her, sat on a satin-covered chair on the bride's right; on the bride's left was the groom's blond-wigged mother, Eva Landers, a tall, thin-faced woman who Rose hoped would treat Shoshana well when the young couple eventually settled in London. The two mothers had just returned from a smaller reception room where the groom, hold-

ing court surrounded by family and a host of noisily rejoicing
men, was celebrating the signing by witnesses of the *tenayim*,
the agreement between the bride and groom that they would
marry. After the signing, Adele and Eva had broken a plate, at
once commemorating the destruction of the Holy Temples and
symbolizing the binding nature of the *tenayim*, which, like
china, once shattered could never be repaired.

"The plate almost wouldn't break," Adele whispered to
Rose. She dabbed at her forehead with a tissue. "We held it
upside down and slammed it seven, eight times on the chair top
before it finally gave. I thought the *sotton* was holding it together, trying to ruin everything." Satan

"Don't make jokes," Rose said sharply.

"They're coming!" someone announced excitedly, and the
words hummed like electricity through the room.

Two violinists and a harpist had been playing soft background music swallowed by the noise of conversation and forks
clattering against plates. Now Rose could hear the increasingly
loud sound of trumpet, saxophone, and accordion. Her heart
thumped.

Shoshana was beaming, one delicate hand in her mother's,
the other in her mother-in-law's.

They were almost here. Guests hurried to either side of the
platform, making room for the entourage of men and boys,
singing and dancing as they led the way for the black-suited
groom flanked by his bearded, black-hatted father and father-
in-law. When the procession was twenty feet from the platform,
pairs of men joined their raised hands to form a canopy under
which the groom strode and climbed the three steps to his waiting bride.

They gazed at each other for a long moment—he looking
down, she with her chin tilted upward, their faces so rapt in
mutual adoration that Rose's heart swelled and all her heavy
unease slipped off, like a discarded shawl. Sighing her content,

wanting to share it with those dear to her, she clutched Adele's hand and glanced fondly down at Marvin. What was he thinking, Rose wondered, her eyes misting, now that his little girl was about to be married?

Her eyes moved to the groom's father, and the gray-haired man whose arm he was supporting. The grandfather. The old man was staring at Shoshana, his lips half parted. And why not, Rose thought proudly. She was a beautiful girl.

She returned her attention to the groom. Leaning close to Shoshana, he whispered something that made her smile deepen and her eyes glisten. Then, with clumsy fingers, he reached above her head and carefully lifted the top layer of her sheer veil and drew it over her face.

Marvin was next. Placing his hands on his daughter's head, he blessed her and murmured in her ear. Then he kissed her, lips pressed against the veil for a long, tender moment that brought tears to his eyes and to all around him. Stepping backward, he made room for the groom's father, who recited a blessing while keeping a modest distance from his son's bride.

A moment later the father walked down the steps and helped the grandfather slowly ascend the platform. Herman should be here, Rose thought wistfully with more than a little envy. Herman should be blessing his granddaughter, like this old man who was standing awkwardly staring at the bride, his mouth working but saying nothing. Herman would have known what to say.

The grandfather glanced around, first at Adele, then at Rose. That was when Rose saw his eyes, dark pools of deep brown that had stared into hers over fifty years ago, eyes that had haunted her long after she had forgotten the contours of his face and body, the all too brief touch of his unfamiliar, untutored hand.

She stifled a gasp with her knuckles, smearing the lipstick the young woman had applied so carefully, and twisted her head aside. The color drained out of her face.

Levanecha.

"Mom, are you okay?" Adele asked, anxious.

"I'm fine," Rose said, bending her head down, pulling at the neck of the gown she was sure would choke her. "It's a little hot, is all."

Dead, she thought numbly. The cousin had said she'd seen him near death, and for Rose that had been proof enough. She was shivering now beneath the satin and the heavily beaded lace. The buzzing in her ears was making her lightheaded.

"Do you want some water? I'll have someone get you some water."

Rose shook her head. "I'll be all right. Don't worry, I won't *farshter* the wedding." Put a damper on it. "Let them finish, then I'll get water."

Tell the rabbis you saw Yossel die, Rose had convinced the cousin. What's the harm, since he's dead? And Rose, officially widowed, had stood under the *chuppah* with Herman Greenberg. It had been natural at that moment, hadn't it, to think back to her first wedding, to wonder, What if . . . She had quickly banished the notion from her consciousness, but sometimes, when she had least expected it, his face would suddenly appear in front of her eyes. Ghosts, she had thought.

Levanecha.

To your children. Defective, like both mezuzah parchments, rendered invalid by the letters missing from the telling words. Illegitimate, since Rose had still been married to Yossel when she and Herman had conceived Adele. Her poor innocent daughter and her offspring, prohibited forever by Jewish law from marrying another Jew unless he, too, had the same taint . . .

The groom's father was steering the old man's hands toward the bride's veil.

Perhaps she was mistaken, Rose told herself. The cousin had seen him near death. But that was desperation speaking. She couldn't deny the shock and bewilderment she'd read in his eyes. Had he seen past the wrinkles and the gray hair? More likely, he had recognized in Shoshana's heart-shaped face the likeness of the woman he had married. The cupid-bow lips, the deep blue, almond-shaped eyes. The widow's peak.

The old man held his trembling hands in front of Shoshana's face, about to bless her. With an abrupt motion he lifted her veil and stared at her. A startled murmur buzzed through the room—this wasn't done. The groom's father, his face red, gently removed the old man's hands and lowered the veil again, but not before a guttural sound emerged from the grandfather's voice.

Raizel.

Her old name. Rose quaked. Hadn't everyone else heard?

The sound was followed by a low, keening wail. He's going to stop the wedding, she knew, and she was powerless to prevent him. This was her punishment.

"Why doesn't he just say it?" she whispered urgently, unaware that she'd spoken aloud.

"He can't talk well," Adele whispered. "I thought I told you. He has Alzheimer's, and a few weeks ago he suffered a minor stroke. They thought he could manage the *bracha*, but I guess he can't. Poor man." Adele clucked.

Was it God's forgiving hand, Rose wondered dully as she watched the grandfather being led off the platform, or cruel irony that had pulled them all back from the precipice of disaster? She wondered, too, at what moment she had decided not to tell.

☙ ☙ ☙

At dusk, when the last rays of the sun glinted off the glassy surface of the lily ponds, Rose walked down the aisle on the arm of Marvin's nephew to the strains of violins and flute and harp and seated herself in the front row reserved for family. On the other side of the white satin runner sat the grandfather and the teenage boy who had escorted him down the aisle.

Under a *chuppah* adorned with creamy white flowers and ivy trailing down the poles, the groom, wearing a lace-edged white robe called a *kittel*, rocked slowly between his parents and faced the guests, who rose to their feet in a wavelike movement as the bride, her parents on either side, made her entrance.

Moments later Rose watched as Shoshana, one hand in Adele's, the other, behind her, in her mother-in-law's, circled the groom seven times. With one eye on the grandfather, Rose listened as the rabbi performed the ceremony. Was it her imagination, or did the old man start when the groom slipped the plain gold ring on Shoshana's right index finger and recited in Hebrew the *Ha'rei aht* blessing: *Behold, thou art sanctified to me with this ring according to the laws of Moses and Israel.*

Levanecha.

Or maybe it was guilt, Rose thought. Was it fair to the groom and his family to enter, unknowing, into a marriage that would forever sully their lineage and brand their progeny?

Only if someone told . . . And if not, where was the harm? To whom? This was her sin, Rose told herself. Not Adele's, not Shoshana's. Not Shoshana's unborn children's.

Another rabbi read the *ketubah*, the marriage document. Rose didn't understand a word of the Aramaic text but she nodded anyway at each mention of Shoshana's name and the groom's, nodded after each of the seven wedding blessings, recited individually by other rabbis and close family. After each one she whispered a fervent "Amen."

A napkin-wrapped glass was placed beneath the groom's shoe. A moment of hushed expectation, then a sharp, resounding crack. Amid a chorus of *"Mazel tovs!"* the saxophone and trumpet erupted into boisterous sound, and the new couple, hands locked, their faces lit with smiles, made their way through a throng of well-wishers.

Rose looked for the grandfather, but he had disappeared.

She saw him again, when the bride and groom emerged from their brief seclusion, in the room reserved for the post-*chuppah* photos. Most of the seemingly endless shots had been taken, and they were ready for the final one of the newly joined families. Rose felt her stomach churn when the portly photographer positioned her on a chair next to the grandfather.

He gazed at her, his mouth working, the lids of his dark brown eyes blinking rapidly. Dizzy with fear, Rose smiled stupidly at the camera sitting on the tripod, certain that her heart, beating so rapidly she was amazed no one else heard it, would give out.

She would have to tell.

But the moment passed. On the dance floor an hour later, with her granddaughter's hands clasped around her neck, her sweet face pressed against Rose's bosom, Rose knew she had been right to keep silent. She would tell no one, would whisper the truth only to the cinnamon camphor trees. They would keep her secret.

It was someone else's turn to dance with the bride. Slipping out of Shoshana's embrace, Rose moved back into the larger circle of women and found herself standing next to the groom's mother.

"A beautiful *kalleh*, inside and out," Eva Landers said, using the Hebrew for bride. "May they have a life of *mazel* and *bracha*." Luck and blessing. "And may *Hashem* grant them many children."

"Amen," said Rose. The Hebrew words sounded more formal, she thought, pronounced with a crisp British accent.

"You're from Poland, your daughter told me," Eva said. "My father was born there, too. His name was Goronowicz, but he changed it to Goren when he immigrated to England and married my mother, may she rest in peace."

So she was to be allowed not even the pretense of doubt.

Rose felt a belt tightening around her chest. "I'm sorry he's not well."

"Thank you. He's resting in one of the rooms. If he had been feeling better, he would have recited a blessing under the *chuppah*. But as it is . . ." Her voice trailed off into sadness. "I'm afraid this has been too much for him. You saw what happened earlier," she continued, and now the sadness was tinged with embarrassed apology.

Rose nodded.

"He insisted on coming to the wedding, on participating. 'I lived for this day, so now I should stay home?' he told me and my husband."

"Yes," Rose said simply. "Yes."

The woman gazed at Rose with interest. "It's strange, you know. He was certain that your granddaughter, may she live a long life, was his first wife, who died in the war. That's why he was so agitated." Her eyes lingered on Rose, taking in her features—the lips, the nose, the eyes, the gray hair on the high forehead that blossomed from a widow's peak.

The belt was tighter and tighter. In a moment Rose wouldn't be able to breathe. "I told him that was impossible, of course," Eva said. "But it took me quite some time to quiet him." She sighed. "It's the Alzheimer's, and the stroke. It's terribly sad, isn't it, the cruel tricks the mind can play?"

"Terrible," Rose murmured.

She watched her granddaughter. The white satin covered arms, spread wide like angel's wings, embracing the circle of friends and the music: the sweet, lovely face, shining with innocent joy, framed by billowing layers of gauzy veil that trailed behind her, never quite catching up, as she danced in the center of the ballroom, spinning round and round and round.

NANCY PICKARD

✧ ✧ ✧

Nancy Pickard is the author of the Jenny Cain mystery
series and has won the Anthony, Agatha, Shamus,
Macavity, and American Mystery Awards for her novels and short stories. She is two-time Edgar Award
nominee and is a founding member of Sisters in
Crime. She lives in Kansas. Her most recent book is
The Whole Truth.

SPEAK NO EVIL

BY NANCY PICKARD

WE CALLED HIM the Devil because he killed women at spiritual retreats: convents, motherhouses, religious communes. Each victim was slain with an article of her faith: a rosary, in one case; a cross upon a deadly chain; a veil.

I was pulled into the case from an unusual angle when I got a call from an FBI field supervisor in Kansas City.

"Joseph Owen?" he inquired.

When I agreed that was me, he said, "We've got one, Joe."

"When was she killed?" I asked, holding my breath for the answer.

When he said, "Yesterday," I felt both relief and dread, because that was half of the answer I'd been waiting for since June.

"The victim was Lila Susan Pointe," he reported. "P-o-i-n-t-e. Twenty-seven years old. Caucasian. He strangled her with a white silk altar cloth from a chapel on the grounds of a religious retreat called Shekinah: S-h-e-k-i-n-a-h. I don't know what they're all about; it may be a cult. This murder fits the Devil's profile, Joe, except that we've got something nobody else has ever had: an eyewitness."

When I heard that, I pounded my fist on my desk, feeling exultant, like a kid saying, 'yes!' It was the other half of the news I'd been waiting to hear.

"Our witness," he said, "is a woman he attacked but didn't kill because other people almost walked up on him. That's the good news, from which you may infer bad. In addition to taking vows of poverty, obedience, and chastity, our witness added a vow of her own. Care to guess which one?"

When I didn't, he said, "Okay, I'll tell you: Our eyewitness took a five-year vow of silence . . . two years ago." His voice combined frustration with irony. "She won't say a goddamn word to any of us. I hear you're good at getting serial killers to chat, Joe. Would you come out and see if you can get her to talk?"

What he meant was that serial killers were my specialty within the FBI.

More than two dozen of them had spilled their repellent guts to me. But I had never yet had the chance to talk to one of their victims, since up to now, they'd all been dead. For the first time, I had a live one.

I flew to Kansas City that morning.

For three years, the Devil had haunted the Midwest, striking seemingly at random, until a former priest within the FBI came to me with a hesitant theory.

"I've noticed," he said, "that the murders always fall on a saint's day associated with the Virgin Mother, or with other saints named Mary."

I would have laughed, because it was absurd, except that I knew the world of serial killers was like a cold, strange planet where each inhabitant lived according to his own weird logic. No doubt this one had an abusive mother named Mary, or Maria, or some damn thing. It was often that simple and that nuts.

"Has the Devil ever killed in the month of June?" he asked me, and I told him no. "Has he killed in every other month?" he asked me, and I said yes.

"June," he said then, "is the only month in which there is no saint's day for a Mary. July is also an exception because there are two celebrations on the same day, the sixteenth."

It was May when he told me his theory.

He and I waited anxiously through June and, sure enough, no murders were reported. Now, one death and a second attack had been reported for July sixteenth, right on schedule. If the ex-priest was right, I had to make our eyewitness break her vow of silence before July twenty-second, which would be the saint's day of Mary Magdalene.

It was six days away.

Before my flight, I said confidently to my wife, "She'll talk. Under these circumstances, only the devil himself would refuse to cooperate."

By that afternoon, July seventeenth, I was rocking over dirt and gravel in a rental car on a Missouri farm road south of Kansas City. The end of the line turned out to be a parking lot cut into the thick woods and situated in front of a long, low building constructed of redwood planks.

I stretched, working fifteen hundred miles of tension and stiffness out of my muscles. As my nostrils opened to let in more air, I smelled wood smoke. I heard the single human sound of wood being sawed and tasted the dust of a dry summer. Because I was an amateur horticulturist—a hobby I began because I wanted to pull something alive out of the earth, for a change, instead of dead and mutilated bodies—I could identify the trees around me: maples, pin oaks, sycamore, locust, and evergreens, rising to mature heights. Creeping vines filled the spaces between them.

I had a sense of people existing like squirrels, or termites—breathing, smelling, eating, sleeping in trees. In fact, I already had been informed that the members of this community called Shekinah did, indeed, inhabit simple lofts built on stilts among the trees. At the moment, those private cabins were invisible to me; I could see only the headquarters building, which looked like a long, fallen redwood tree. I walked toward it, watching out for poison ivy and snakes, worrying about ticks.

Most signs of the police, sheriff's department, and FBI presence were gone, though very recently they would have been as thick on the ground as leaves. They'd had all the previous day and night and most of this day to gather their evidence, interview people—the ones who would talk and remove the body.

They'd be back, but for now I seemed to be the only investiga-
tive authority on the place. That suited me well, because I
planned to make friends with this woman, our silent witness. It
wouldn't help for her to see me as one more demanding man in
an intrusive gang of pushy cops and agents.

Her name, I'd been told, was Sara.

I planned to come on to Sara quietly, respectfully, slowly.

I had it all figured out, down to the crucial moment when I
would carefully slip my pen and notepad into my hands. Of
course, she would talk to me. How could anyone refuse to talk if
saying something would save a life? I marveled at how clumsy the
cops who preceded me must have been to prolong her silence. I
would put an end to that nonsense. She would talk, for me.

I was taken to a small, plain office occupied by a woman
who appeared to be in her seventies. She was white-haired, lean,
and tanned brown as a pecan. I thought she looked capable and
strong in her commune uniform, which consisted of
forest-green trousers and a matching overskirt.

"I'm Joseph Owen," I told her, flashing my FBI identification.

"How do you do, Joseph Owen?" she said, smiling as easily
as if nobody had been murdered in her little community. "I am
what you might call the director of Shekinah, although my title,
my nom de spirit, you might say, is Grandmother. They call me
the GM when they think I can't hear them." Again she smiled,
and her blue eyes twinkled. "If you think you can stand it, I
invite you to call me Grandmother, too."

"I'll try," I said, and she laughed at the wry tone in my
voice.

I knew her real name; in fact, I knew a fair amount about
her and this commune, because I had taken time in Kansas City
to copy and study the information a local field agent had put
together, and I had all of that, plus copies of the police interviews, in my car. I knew, for instance, that Sara's vow of silence
was total, allowing not even the sign language that is traditional

with Trappist monks. She didn't write notes. She didn't nod, she didn't shake her head. In no way did she communicate.

"What's Shekinah?" I asked the GM, because the files were vague on that.

"It's a bona-fide religion," she replied, rather quickly.

"That's not what I meant," I said carefully. "But if you're suggesting the government can't make her talk because that would violate her religious freedom, of course you're right. However, I hope you won't fool yourself into thinking the government won't try to force her if they have to. They can make her silence a miserable and expensive experience for all of you."

"They?" she asked, making the point that I was one of them. "I'm afraid I have no talent for misery, Mr. Owen. And I will remind you that we already live under a vow of poverty."

I felt something like heartburn rise under my breastbone when she said all that, refuting my every point. I recognized the discomfort as frustration, not indigestion. Looking at her serene and contented face, I suddenly had the feeling it was going to become a familiar sensation in this case.

The GM walked me down a forest path that appeared unoccupied by humans until we looked up. Then we could see the lofts among the trees where members of the community lived alone. There was no indoor plumbing in the lofts, no electricity. Not because of their religious beliefs, she told me, but because it was cheaper that way.

"You want to know what we believe, Mr. Owen? We believe in the Ten Commandments, and that's all."

"Which of them forbids her to speak?" I asked.

The Grandmother stopped suddenly on the path and looked back at me. "That was very astute of you," she said, and I felt like a schoolboy who had guessed right on a test and pleased the teacher. "It is the ninth commandment from which

Sara draws her will to silence."

I had to search my Sunday school memory to come up with it.

"'Thou shalt not bear false witness,' right? But nobody's asking her to lie."

"I'm afraid you do not fully understand the commandments, Mr. Owen, at least not as we do. We believe that personality is an illusion, a spider web of lies spun over the truth. We believe the true essence of every person is already perfect, forgiven, and saved. In regard to the ninth commandment, we believe that to say otherwise of any human being is to bear false witness against him."

"Or her," I suggested.

She smiled. "Those distinctions, too, are illusions."

"No original sin?" I asked.

"Only trite and unoriginal ones," she said gently.

We had arrived at a wooden ladder where a rope hung down.

"Pull this," she instructed me, "and it will ring the bell in her cabin. Come see me afterward if you wish."

I stopped her before she could walk away.

"You haven't said a word about the victim, Grandmother."

She stared off into the trees before she looked up at me again.

"Neither have you, Mr. Owen. The difference between us is that in my belief system, Lila Susan is no more dead than you and I are. It's you and the FBI who say she's dead, and who insist on finding her supposed killer. If you believe—really believe—in immortal life, as we do, you understand that no one can ever really die, and so nobody can possibly kill you."

As she walked calmly away and I pulled on the damn rope, I felt the heartburn rise again.

∞ ∞ ∞

A trapdoor opened in the floor of the loft above me. I climbed the ladder, ten rungs hand over hand, and entered a

Lilliputian chamber. There was a cot with a young woman seated on it, her back propped against the wood wall, her face turned down. There were books stacked against the walls, a basket of what looked like clean underwear under the cot, another basket with eating utensils, a small desk with a straight chair, a neat stack of towels, and a folded green uniform like the one she was wearing. Apart from four tall, ugly green plants in plastic pots, that was all there was in the square little room. Four windows provided cross ventilation; at one of them, the metal tubes of a wind chime clinked in the breeze. I left the trapdoor open and sat beside it, cross-legged in my suit, on her wooden floor.

I felt hot, sweaty, itchy, but she looked cool.

"Sara? My name is Joe—Joseph Owen—and I'm an FBI agent. You must be sick of us by now, and I apologize very much for intruding on your privacy." I paused, carefully feeling my way into her silence. She had glanced up at me long enough for me to see a young, plain face with no makeup. All of the Devil's victims were young, in their twenties or late teens, many of them had brown hair, like hers, and several of them wore their hair pulled back from their face in a long ponytail, as this woman did. After a moment, I started in again. "I'm really sorry about what happened to your friend yesterday, and for what he put you through. We're all glad you survived!"

I let that thought lie between us for a moment while the wind chime played in the window. I was intimate with silence because my own mother had been a profoundly silent woman, except when she exploded in rage at something I—her only child—had done to prick the bubble of her silence. I knew how to wait it out, to coax and manipulate it. Because of my childhood, I hated silence, which was perhaps why I was so adept at getting stubborn people to talk to me.

"Sara, I don't want to frighten you, but the fact is, I'm here to protect you." Her body made an involuntary movement, and I had a feeling I had startled her, which was what I hoped to do in a sly way. I wanted to pull her off of her calm, silent pedestal, and to prod an exclamation out of her, even if it was only an Oh! or a No! If I could break the dam, force one word out of her compressed mouth, her vow would be irreversibly broken, and then she might as well tell me everything. I wanted to go slow, to win her trust, so she'd do what I wished her to do, but there wasn't much time. I said, "If he thinks you can identify him, you're a threat to him, Sara. So I'm going to stick around to protect you."

That was her chance to indicate in some way that she hadn't seen his face, or that she couldn't really identify him, but she didn't do that. She just sat, not moving or speaking. I resisted an urge to shake her until her teeth rattled and words came tumbling out of her mouth. I wanted to tell her she was a spoiled brat, enjoying the luxury of a silence she could end at any time, but that her friend was not so fortunate. Lila Susan Pointe and the other victims were silent, too, but they would never open their mouths and speak to me.

"I'll be around, Sara," I promised her.

I descended from her loft, pulling the trapdoor shut behind me.

The truth was that she probably wasn't in any danger, because he had never killed between saint's days, and never in the same place on another day. The Devil was probably traveling toward his next victim, or even now stalking and studying her. But Sara didn't know that, and now I had an excuse for snaking my way into her life and her trust.

The GM offered me a sleeping bag and a commune uniform when I told her I was Sara's temporary bodyguard. The uniform was even more than I had hoped for; wearing that, I'd soon look as familiar to Sara as any member of her community.

In the GM's office, I said, "What are those ugly plants she grows?"

"They're milkweed, Joseph Owen. I imagine she grows them because they attract monarch butterflies."

Rather stupidly, I asked, "Why does she want to do that?"

The GM smiled. "Who wouldn't? Watch them sometime, Mr. Owen. You'll have the feeling of being in conversation with them. They don't appear to be afraid of us, they hang around as if they want to talk to us, as if they have something really important to tell us."

I tried to keep the cynicism out of my voice. "So she won't talk to people, but she talks to butterflies?"

The GM gently shrugged. "I don't know." She looked meaningfully into my eyes. "Milkweed itself is sensitive to disturbance. You can't jostle them or they'll die, or grow crooked."

"So what are you telling me?" I asked her. "That I shouldn't disturb Sara?"

Instead of answering me, she said, "Are you a reading man?"

"Do you count Clancy?" I asked her. "Koontz, King?"

"Of course." She smiled. "I think people who are readers are more likely to see symbolism where other people just see life."

"So you're saying I'm reading too much into milkweed and butterflies."

"I mean the truth has depth, but no layers."

"What the hell is that supposed to mean?"

The GM smiled at my annoyance. "It means you'll get nowhere by trying to peel the layers off her psyche."

"Jesus Christ!" The profanity exploded from my mouth into the peaceful atmosphere. The entire law enforcement community was seriously annoyed with these people, and I was especially irritated by the sight of the smug old lady standing so serenely in front of me. "There has been a murder. Of one of your own people. And she won't talk, and you talk in goddamn riddles instead of really cooperating. You are selfish, infuriating people."

I was a lot more startled by my outburst than she appeared to be.

"I apologize," I said, and tried to put a rueful, charming smile on my face. "Obviously I am a rude and frustrated man."

She smiled kindly. "Think nothing of it."

I berated myself all the way back down the path into the woods, where I changed clothes behind a tree and spread out my borrowed sleeping bag to sit on while I waited for Sara to make her first descent from the loft. I was tired, and under time pressure, but that was no excuse. I was going to have to get myself under professional control, or I'd blow it and scare her away.

Day after day I followed Sara like her shadow, and every night I slept under her loft, sometimes staring up at the floor of it in utter frustration.

She wouldn't talk; she wouldn't damn talk.

But I talked, chattering like a friendly magpie, sometimes about serial killers in general, sometimes about the Devil in particular, frequently about the heartrending stories of his victims and their families.

And nothing moved her to speak.

On our way to the latrines, with me shuffling behind her in the leaves, I said, "He has already killed a lot of women, Sara. We know his pattern. The next time he will strike is only five days from now."

Her job at the commune was janitorial work, so I grabbed a sponge and scrubbed floors right beside her. While we worked, I said, "I don't know how much you know about serial killers, Sara, but they come in two types: the disorganized kind and the organized kind. Our guy is the latter. He's very organized, very clever, very careful. He scouts out his locations and studies his victims before he makes his attack."

Sitting beside her at the communal dinner table, I whispered, "A place like this, Sara, all he has to do is hide in the woods and watch and wait for his chance."

Going to chapel at sunrise, I said, "We think we know how he gets into some of the places, Sara. He arrives as a repairman, or a deliveryman, which is the only possible way he could worm himself into convents, for instance."

In the evenings, because she didn't object, I climbed her ladder and propped myself on the floor beside a milkweed pot, and I carried on a one-sided conversation with her. "As far as we know, you're the only person who can identify him, Sara. An artist could draw a portrait from your description, but we don't want too much time to go by or you might begin to forget what he looked like. We could broadcast the picture, pass it out to places like this, so they can protect their members. We can find him, Sara, with your description. You can save lives."

Once, I said, "It's you and me and God against the Devil, Sara."

As Monday passed, then Tuesday, Wednesday, Thursday, it became more difficult for me to be gentle and patient with her. I thought she was ridiculous, a fool playing an egotistical, dangerous game with other women's lives.

I asked the GM, "Why silence?"

Her answer was to hand me a cassette tape, which I took out to the parking lot where I could listen to it privately in my rental car.

The voice that emerged from the car's dashboard was light, girlish, and a little breathless, as if she were nervous, or as if she'd been running and had only stopped long enough to drop a few thoughts into a tape recorder:

"This is Sara," the voice on the tape announced self-consciously. It felt strange to finally hear the voice that went with the silent face I'd been studying so closely. The words tumbled out so fast I had to reverse the tape several times to understand them.

"This is Sara. I've said enough in my life. Way too much. Lots of things that hurt people. Things that make me feel awful, just knowing I said them. I'm good at saying all the wrong things. Mean things. Lies. I talk all the time, too. I lie like a rug, I lie like a whole carpet store! I can't stop it, I don't know how to stop lying, except to stop speaking altogether. I drive people crazy with my talking and lies. They can't trust me, they tell me so. Nobody should ever trust anything I ever say! I'm boring, I'm self-centered, I never listen to anybody, and I know that, and the words keep coming, all the same. I'm sick of the sound of my own voice! I'm going to stop talking, because all I ever do when I open my mouth is lie and hurt people. So, I'm going to start listening. I'm not going to say anything, not anything, unless God puts the words in my mouth. Starting now. Right now. This is the last word. Honest."

The next sound on the tape was her giggling, and then she said once more, and dramatically: "Starting . . . now!"

There was nothing more on the tape.

I sat in the car, thinking the amazing thing was that she'd done it, for two years, so far. Amazing.

In the GM's office, I handed back the tape and said, "So what did she lie about that hurt people so much?"

"It wasn't anything big," the GM told me, "nothing like falsely accusing a man of rape or murder, for instance. Just a constant stream of little lies, gossipy, vicious little fabrications that hurt people's feelings more than anything. She was disliked as a consequence. Now she's quietly accepted everywhere she goes in the community."

"Like a house plant," I said dryly. "What does she get out of it?"

"Relief, I think," the GM replied. "She used to steal things, too. Clothing, mostly, which she would wear in front of all of us and claim it was hers. Blatant, outright lies, looking you straight in the face."

"Does she still steal things?"

"No, that stopped soon after she went silent."

"So it's working, her silence?"

"I don't know," the GM admitted. "There's no way for me to know if she has finally learned to tell the truth to herself."

On Saturday, one day before the saint's day for Mary Magdalene, I confronted the GM in her office. "She's lying to herself," I said, "if she thinks she's doing the right thing this time."

"But Mr. Owen, if she talked to you, how would you know she was telling the truth? Have you thought about that? What kind of witness would she make in court, a self-confessed, nearly pathological liar?"

∞ ∞ ∞

"I don't care what she does in a courtroom." Suddenly, I was angry again and yelling at the old woman. "I just want her to tell me enough to stop him! Don't you get it? He's going to kill another woman . . . tomorrow . . . and another and another after that, unless Sara identifies him. When we catch him, we'll gather other evidence, so we won't even need her for a conviction, but right now, she's got to talk. If she doesn't talk by tomorrow morning, she'll have a lot more than lies on her conscience."

The GM smiled patiently at me, as a grandmother might at a toddler having a tantrum, and she merely said, "Well, she might even lie about his appearance, you know."

I felt like strangling both of them.

I didn't sleep that night in my bag under the goddamned loft, because I felt haunted by the ghosts of the other women he'd killed, all of them urging me to do something before other women joined their dreadful sorority.

Sunday, July twenty-second, passed in silence, with me dogging Sara's footsteps as usual, but for once I remained as silent as she. That night the telephone brought word of what I feared most: The Devil had struck on schedule, killing a woman at a Buddhist retreat north of San Francisco.

I stalked on stiff legs to Sara's cabin and climbed the ladder, clumsy in my fury and sorrow.

"Well, you've done it," I told her, my voice as cold as the sound of the metal wind chimes. "You've let him kill another one."

I gave her the details, all of them, sparing her nothing.

If she had a reaction, I couldn't see it in the dark cabin where she sat on her cot, her back turned toward me, her face to the wall.

That night, I raged over the phone to the field supervisor.

"I hate these people," I told him. "They don't give a damn about the victims, and I don't give a damn about them."

The supervisor laughed, but it was a cynical sound of understanding, rather than amusement. "So, Joe . . . no more Mr. Nice Guy?"

"Hide and watch," I advised him.

The next day, methodically, I set about turning the other members of the community against her. I took them aside individually and in little groups under the pretext of interviewing them one more time, and I spoke to them of the suffering of the victims, the heartbreak of the families, and of their own potential for becoming a next victim. I played on their compassion, their fear. I allowed them to get a glimpse of my frustration, of my decent motives, of my anxiety, and of how terrible I felt over my failure to get Sara to talk. By the time I finished with them, I had them looking over their shoulders for fear the Devil was hiding in the woods, watching, waiting, looking them over, winnowing them out, selecting his next victim from among all of them.

One by one, they responded as I hoped they would, in frightened or indignant or sympathetic words. They said, "I'll talk to Sara!" or . . . "Sara has to break her silence!" or . . . "It's not right, what she's doing, it's not holy!" One of them even said to me, "Sara is being selfish and wicked, and I'm going to tell her so."

For the first time, then, I left the commune.

For twenty-four hours I stayed away, luxuriating in a motel while I allowed my poison to do its work.

When I returned, the GM met me at the headquarters door. She said, "What have you done, Joseph Owen?"

Instantly, I felt triumphant.

"Is she talking?" I asked.

"No." But the GM looked worried for the first time since I'd met her. "You'd better see her. She's in her cabin."

I hurried down the path, feeling exultant.

At first, when I stepped inside the cabin, I didn't think she was there.

"Sara?" I called, which was silly, because there was hardly anything left in the cabin except her cot. The milkweed pots were gone. The blankets and sheets had been pulled off the cot and pushed under it. The baskets of underwear and eating utensils were gone. So was the stack of towels, and the books.

Dammit! Had she run away from me?

I felt shocked by rage and disappointment.

But then I saw a movement in the jumble of bedclothes under the cot and I realized Sara was wrapped up in them. She had crawled under her cot and covered herself from toe to head in the sheets and blankets.

I heard a muffled sound, and thought at first it was a bird.

Then I realized she was weeping, unable for once to control the sound of her own voice.

My thought was savage: Good!

But now I could afford to be gentle, now I could play the good cop once again. I knelt down near her and said softly, "Sara? When you're ready to talk to me, I'll be right here. I won't ever leave you, Sara, not until you're ready for me. I'll be here for you when the time comes."

I slept in her cabin that night, instead of underneath it.

There came a point, however, when my own nature silently called, and I had to descend the ladder to find a john. I took the opportunity to make a fast trip to retrieve the sleeping bag from the GM's office. Sara was going to talk that night, I knew it, and if she didn't, I was going to lock the trapdoor if I had to and keep her a prisoner in her cabin until she did what I wanted her to do.

The GM walked in as I was leaving her office with the bedroll.

Once again her face was unlined, her smile pacific.

"Aren't you worried anymore?" I asked her. "You seemed worried earlier."

"Prayer is a marvelous antidote to worry, Mr. Owen."

"You could probably force me to go away," I told her.

"This is Sara's opportunity for growth," was her calm reply.

"If I were Sara," I said, and I actually laughed, "I think I'd shoot you."

"That, too," said the Grandmother, smiling, "would offer enormous spiritual opportunities for her."

But this time, I was determined to have the last word.

"Your other members don't seem quite as convinced as you are that they're immortal. I get the feeling they're afraid to die."

I was astonished to see tears appear in the GM's blue eyes.

"Thank you, Joseph," she said, "for giving all of us a chance to face our own worst fears."

Damn the woman, she left me speechless, as usual.

I brushed past her, but she surprised me again by putting a hand on my arm to stop me. "Mr. Owen, tell me again about the pattern of organized serial killers, will you?"

I did it quickly, because I was in a hurry to resume my vigil over Sara, so she wouldn't try to escape while I was gone.

"They are methodical, careful, clever," I recited. "They study their victims, who are often very similar to each other, so as to know the best time and means of approach and attack. Frequently, they win their victim's trust by coming on as friendly and sincere, or in need of help. Often, once they have their victims, they hold them prisoner for some time, toying with them, before actually killing them."

"I see," the GM said, and her blue eyes looked brightly into mine. "Are you a good listener, Mr. Owen?"

"Of course," I said, curtly. "That's my business."

"Good," was all she said before releasing me.

I hurried back down the path thinking, what the hell was that all about?

The next saint's day on which the Devil would strike would not come until September, so there was a little time for us, but probably not for me. There was no way the higher-ups would let me stay out in the boonies trying to pressure just one witness. I figured I had only a little more time left before they called me back to my other work. But I would make the most of every minute of the time I had with Sara, if I had to tie her to her cot and show her photographs of the Devil's victims to make her finally talk to me.

It was a hot July, and the air was thick with humidity.

I heard a sound in front of me and realized it was Sara's trapdoor opening.

No! I thought, she's not getting out of there, I'm not letting her leave that cabin until she talks!

I ran forward, through the trees, nearing the stilts on which her home was built just as she kicked the ladder away.

Hell! She couldn't defeat me that way, I'd just prop the ladder up again! I slowed my pace, laughing at her for thinking she could keep me away from her.

And then I saw her feet and her legs drop through the hole.

I expected her to drop on down to the ground.

Instead, her legs dangled through the opening; her body knocked against the edges of the hole.

"Sara!"

With a sudden, horrible realization, I comprehended what she had done. I stumbled toward her, yelling her name. Reaching her legs, I embraced them, and lifted them, so that her full weight couldn't fall downward. Above me, through the hole, I saw that she had tied her sheets together, tied one end over the beam in her cabin, and circled the other end around her neck. Then she had jumped through the hole in the floor.

I shouted desperately for help.

Members of the community came running. Two of them got into her cabin through the windows. They untied her and lowered her gently into our waiting arms. We laid her on the ground in the leaves.

"Sara?" I whispered to the still and silent face.

She had tried to hang herself.

Was she still alive?

Had her neck been broken as she fell through the floor?

After a moment, Sara's eyelids quivered and she moaned, the most beautiful sound I had ever heard.

When I was sure she would live, I ran to find the Grandmother.

After that, I simply walked to my rental car and drove away.

My hands trembled on the steering wheel because the Devil was still out there, and I knew him well. I glanced in the rearview mirror and saw a white-faced man. My foot shook on the accelerator as I thought about my reputation for understanding serial killers. Again, I glanced in the mirror. Oh, yes, I knew them as well as I knew myself.

I had studied her and stalked her, imprisoned her, tortured her by my presence and my demands, and I had nearly killed her.

And she was only the latest of my victims.

On my flight home, I mentally reviewed the names of the men who were dead because of my investigations, men who were, in many ways, all alike. They'd been killed upon capture, or by the death penalty. They, too, I had stalked and studied, before snatching them and imprisoning them until they were put to death.

I went home to my wife—but then, many organized types of serial killers are married, or have girlfriends. I was no different.

I was no different.

The Devil was apprehended within the year, but I was gone from law enforcement by then, having quit in order to use my law degree in ways that would not tempt me to become what I hated. Somebody had to catch the killers, but it didn't have to be me.

I do a lot of gardening now.

I'm very familiar with milkweed and monarchs.

Three years after I left Shekinah, I received a letter from the Grandmother.

"Dear Joseph Owen," the letter began, in her own unmistakable style. "I thought you would want to know that Sara has recovered beautifully, with no ill effects. She is talking now, rather like a baby with her first words. Her voice sounds rough from lack of use, and she is shy about what she says and to whom she speaks. I do believe she accomplished what she set out to do: to learn to love the truth, and to speak only that, as best she can. The world is, I believe, a sweeter place as a consequence. Frequently I hear her laugh, a welcome and lovely sound to me.

"She told me she desperately wanted to speak to you when you were here, but that she could feel lies building up inside her mouth, and she was terrified that if she spoke she would lead you in such wrong directions you would never catch your killer, and many other women might die. She remained silent to save their lives. Then she tried to kill herself in order to make sure she could not harm you or any woman by speaking the lies that were tempting her.

"Now Sara dreams of the women whom you speak of as being killed, and they talk to her and tell her they are alive in spirit. I hope this will comfort you, Joseph Owen." I threw away the letter, but not in anger. I've thrown away my scrapbooks, too, the ones I used to keep on the serial killers I helped to stalk, imprison, and kill. Like Sara, I've learned to tell the truth to myself. And so, I no longer allow myself to keep trophies of my victims.

MARGARET FRAZER

∽ ∽ ∽

Margaret (Gail) Frazer is the pseudonymous author of the nationally best-selling Dame Frevisse series of medieval mysteries (in which Bishop Beaufort occasionally figures). She currently lives in Minnesota on ten acres of wood and meadow, with a great many books and not enough bookshelves, but seems to spend most of her time in the 1400s.

VOLO TE HABERE . . .*

BY MARGARET FRAZER

The matter had seemed likely to be a straightforward one. Not pleasant but easily settled. The question was simple: Were the couple married or not? Their parents, on both sides, were determined that they were not, while young Stephen and Catheryn protested the contrary, and when it had become clear to the priests of their parishes that neither side would give ground, it had come to him, as their bishop, to rule on whether irrevocable vows had been made or not.

Hal could have let it go to his episcopal court to be sorted out in due course and for due fees, but Richard Medford, one of the principal officers of Hal's own household council, was betrothed to the said Catheryn's sister and had asked the favor of Hal's judgement, to have the matter sooner settled, because if Catheryn held to this ill-match of hers, her parents had sworn to disinherit her. If they did, then there would be a greater jointure come to her sister when she was married to Medford and, "Better to have it all settled and done before any agreements are sealed that might be hard to change afterward," Medford had said, and Hal could only agree with him, having a keen sense himself of the value of well-made and well-kept agreements.

But then Hal had a keen sense about many things and knew it. It was what had helped make him bishop of Winchester at age twenty-six, a year ago, the Year of God's Grace 1404, and what would surely take him higher before he had done, God and St. John willing.

In the meanwhile, this fine autumn day of piercingly blue

* I WISH TO HAVE YOU . . .

skies and golden sunlight, when he might better have been hawking along the Southampton marshes, found him instead in the high-windowed, high-ceilinged great chamber of his palace of Bishop's Waltham in Hampshire, dressed not for the pleasures of hunting but in a long, sober (never mind that the fur at the neck and cuffs and was Russian sable), black gown to suit the solemnity of the moment. He sat in his massive chair behind the table where such documents as there were in the case were spread, one elbow resting on a chair arm, his chin resting on his hand, as he regarded the grouped people in front of him and thought that Medford had landed him in more trouble than either of them had intended.

All he should have been deciding on was whether Catheryn Dauntsey, next-to-youngest daughter of a well-landed knight, and Stephen Hameden, younger son of an even-better-landed gentry family, had indeed, as they insisted, said words between them that married them to each other. It took very little to be married, nothing more than a man and woman saying between them that they took each other for husband and wife. Despite debate and opinions to the contrary, for centuries both Church and civil law had held that neither witnesses nor the Church's blessing were needed for a valid marriage, though lack of those could bring trouble later on if one or the other of the couple decided they no longer wanted the marriage and it came down to one's word against the other.

That, at least, was not the trouble here. Both Stephen and Catheryn insisted on their marriage. It was their parents on both sides who were adamantine against it. The Dauntseys had political ambitions and had planned to make a marriage for Catheryn far more advantageous to their ends. Hal was high-born enough himself, with ambitions enough of his own, to understand their frustration at being balked by the girl's stubborn choice of someone who could do nothing to bring them toward greater power than they already had. On the other hand, the Hamedens were ambitious not toward power but toward land. Several generations of careful marriages had given them a scattering of manors in northern Hampshire, and in this generation the well-placed marriages of Master Hameden's eldest and second sons had brought more. What was wanted from his third son was a marriage that would bring, if not land directly into the family, then money enough to buy it.

What Hal had expected when he agreed to deal with the families himself was to confront a stubborn couple and angry, possibly grieving parents. Weighty with his office and authority, he would question them all but particularly the couple as to what exactly they had said between them by way of vows, because wording was all in all in these matters. A straightforward "I take you for my wife . . . I take you for my husband" was both legally and sacramentally binding, but Hal had found that far too often people failed to think through what they did and said. Words fell out of their mouths and they went happily along, supposing the words meant what they intended them to mean, without ever considering what the same words might mean to someone else or if looked at in a different way. A man might say, "If I marry any woman, it will be you" and mean it as a jest, while the woman to whom he said it took it as a promise and raised hellfire when he married someone else. And did "I wish to have you" said between a man and woman marry them immediately, or was it only a promise to marry in the future or nothing but a vague comment?

On such uncertainties were lawyers' fortunes made.

But a main point of the Hameden-Dauntsey matter coming before him was to keep it from the lawyers, and he had counted on it being fairly easy for someone not grappled to it by passions to sort out the rights and wrongs. Have the couple repeat what they had said and determine whether the words had been binding or not, or were perhaps open to interpretation. If they were binding, there was nothing he could do: Stephen and Catheryn were wed. If the words were not binding, then the parents were free to take what steps they could. If there was uncertainty, the matter would be somewhat more troublesome, and he would do what he could—without wasting too much of his day—to help sort it out so that at the end he would have either reconciled the couple to their parents' wishes or the parents' to their children's or brought about some sort of compromise and sent them on their way.

He had not expected Juliana Kyrton.

That she was here was Master Hameden's fault—Master Hameden's doing, Hal amended. Fault should not be ascribed to a man trying to save his son from what he saw as grievous error. No matter how much the woman wept and wailed. And most certainly Juliana Kyrton seemed given to both.

There had been no sign of her when Medford ushered Sir William Dauntsey, Master Hameden, and their erring children into his presence. The fathers had been easily placed as what they were: men successful at their places in life, used to wielding a certain degree of power, and both determined to have their own way in this matter. Stephen looked fair to being in his father's image, a straight-backed, well-featured young man bearing himself with a confidence only somewhat marred by a defiance a more experienced man would have hidden. But that slight flaw was something years would take care of, if he had much in the way of wits, which it seemed he did when Hal first questioned them all, formally, as to their names and purpose in being here. Fully aware that he was over-young to be a bishop—but then, neither his age nor his royal relatives were his doing; given his own choice, all he would answer for were his own abilities and they were, he knew, considerable—he had learned, in his last bishopric, to establish at the outset of anything exactly where the power lay—and where it lay, because he kept it there, was in his own hands. At the same time, he was not that much older than Stephen and could remember far too clearly what it was to be a younger son, with limited likelihood of much inheritance and cut off from many hopes because of it. So he had appreciated when Master Hameden began, "Master Edward Hameden of Lower Weston, my lord, and this is my son . . ." that Stephen had stepped forward from his father's side and said in his own clear voice, "Stephen Hameden, my lord," taking responsibility for himself.

And then there was Catheryn. She had come with downcast eyes and quietly folded hands a few paces behind her father like a proper daughter, but also a long pace to the side, removing herself from his shadow, as it were; and when Hal said, after her father had named himself, "And your name, child?"—depending upon his dignity and office to keep "child" from sounding foolish, he being not that much older than she was, either—she had come forward to her father's side, sunk in a deep curtsy, and said, all without raising her eyes, "Catheryn Hameden, if it please you, my lord."

At her choice of name, her father Sir William gave the short, wordless exclamation of a man driven well toward his patience's end and Master Hameden said, "Not this side of hell," but enough under his breath that Hal could choose to ignore him, saying instead to Catheryn in his gravest manner, "That's what we're here to determine—whether you are Catheryn Hameden or still Catheryn Dauntsey."

She had curtsied again and said, "Yes, my lord," but not stepped back behind her father, a subtle but firm defiance that Hal found himself enjoying.

After that, for a few moments, he thought everything was going to go very simply, because when he asked Stephen what he had said to Catheryn, Stephen answered, standing very straight, chin defiantly up, voice clear and carrying, "What I said to her was, 'I take you for my wife.'"

No chance of mistake or question there, and fairly sure of what he would hear from Catheryn, Hal had asked her what she had said to Stephen. Then, for the first time since entering the chamber, she had looked up, directly into Hal's eyes, and answered with the simple calm of complete certainty, "I said to him, 'I take you for my husband.' And then we kissed, my lord."

Kiss or no kiss, there was no possible question of their vows' validity. In the eyes of the Church and of law, of God and men, they were man and wife; but for the dignity of it, Hal had paused before saying so, and into the pause Master Hameden had said, "What they said or didn't say makes no odds. Here's someone else needs to be heard, my lord."

He raised his voice as he said it, obviously to a man of his who had been waiting, as one of Sir William's was, in attendance just inside the chamber door, and the man was clearly expecting this moment because he immediately moved to open the door to a woman in the outer chamber who, equally clearly, had been waiting for the same moment and entered on a rush that carried her the length of the chamber, past the Dauntseys and Hamedens, to fall to her knees in front of Hal. Tears on her cheeks, clasped hands raised prayerfully to him, she cried out, "Justice, my lord! And pity for a widow, now a wife denied!"

Juliana Kyrton.

What Hal had managed to sort out since then, once he had ordered her to her feet and Master Hameden had taken over telling her tale, was that his son could not by any means be wed to Catheryn no matter what words they had said if, as Stephen and Catheryn both claimed, they had said them last Midsummer-time. . . .

Hal had interrupted to ask if that was what they did indeed claim. They said it was—Stephen with a wary look at his father—and Juliana had burst out, clasped hands pressed to her breast in a passion of certainty, "Then they can't be married because he was my husband before ever he was hers! He pledged himself to me at Twelfth Night, a full six months ere Midsummer."

"I never did!" Stephen cried out, outraged. "I never would."

"You did! How can you say you didn't? We'd kissed under the mistletoe and you said—"

"You said," Stephen broke in, "that we could more than kiss if we were wed."

"And you said you'd have me for your wife and I said I'd have you for my husband!"

"I did not," Stephen said flatly, "and you'll never bring me to say I did. Nor," he added on the sudden, "did I ever bed with you."

"Why deny it before you're accused of it if you never did it?" Sir William put in with a kind of triumph.

Hal thought that if ever he himself had been confronted with Juliana Kyrton, he would have begun denying everything she could possibly bring against him, too, and to forestall whatever Juliana and Stephen were going to say, because both their mouths were open toward answering Sir William, he said quickly, "Enough. This renders the whole matter more difficult of decision, no longer something that can be settled here and now."

Both fathers made to protest even before their children did, but Hal forestalled them with a raised hand and said to their enforced silence, "Tomorrow at nine of the clock be here again to continue."

To that the men perforce bowed acceptance and Catheryn and Juliana curtsyed and only Hal likely saw the desperate look that passed between Catheryn and Stephen then, as her father took her hard by the wrist and his father's hand came down on his shoulder, and for no good reason except he could too well imagine what trouble they would both be given tonight, left to their fathers, Hal added, "But for the sake of peace all around and because I may want to question them myself apart, I will that these two," he nodded haughtily at Stephen and Catheryn, "remain under my roof for the night—"

"Kept well apart from each other!" Sir William said sharply.

Hal fixed him with a cold eye of surprise at being interrupted but deigned to answer, "Of course apart. They—"

"Oh, then let me stay too!" Juliana cried, rushing toward Hal again and falling to her knees, clasped hands raised, more tears starting. "Please, don't send me from him anymore!"

Hal had not grown up as the son of a royal duke—even if a bastard son—to be used to being interrupted and was positively unused to it as a bishop. Twice in the same minute was more than enough and he snapped, "Stand up and stand back. Master Hameden has made provision, I trust, for your lodging, since he saw to your coming here?"

Making a pretty, graceful helplessness of tangling in her long skirts while rising to her feet, Juliana said on a sob, "Yes. At the Mitre on the Salisbury road. But it's—"

"An honorable and cleanly place," Hal said. He made a point of knowing how well run and the prices charged at inns in his episcopal towns. People were enforced to come to his courts and of necessity stay in his towns and he was willing fair profit be made from that but not unfair nor undue advantages taken. Most especially of him. Juliana was not staying under any of his roofs tonight, ample though Waltham Palace was.

And Juliana must have read his determination because she gave up her plea, but instead turned to fling herself at Stephen, wrapping her arms around his neck and trying to catch his mouth with hers, pressing the full length of her body against him. Stephen in return wrenched backward and his head aside to avoid her kiss, taking hold of her wrists and prying her loose from him while she sobbingly begged him to remember what they were to each other and his father came to draw her off, saying, "Not yet, not yet," and Sir William said, "You see," at Catheryn, who ignored him.

But finally they were gone, sorted out among servants to see Catheryn and Stephen to rooms here, their fathers and Juliana, sobbing softly to the last, to the outer gateway; and with the chamber momentarily cleared, Hal turned to Medford and asked with all the querulous offense he had managed to subdue while she was here, "Who is that woman? And how does she come into it?"

One of Medford's virtues was a wide-ranging knowledge of

whom needed to be known in the diocese and he answered, "Mistress Juliana Kyrton of Southampton. She was married young. . . ."

"Very young . . ." Hal said. She was no older than Catheryn Dauntsey, surely.

"Very young," Medford agreed, "to a husband far her elder. He died a year ago with no children, and his considerable wealth has gone to a nephew of his and Juliana." And one thing widowhood and wealth did was make a woman independent to follow her own ways. "Now she's minded, so the word runs, to make up for her years of an elderly marriage with a young, fresh one and leave Southampton merchant life behind by rising into the gentry."

Ambitions that would be fulfilled at a single stroke by marrying Stephen Hameden, while equally fulfilling his family's ambition toward wealth. Hal as bishop of Winchester and therefore lord of many acres and much income had a deep-seated appreciation of money and could well have wondered—if he had not just spent a quarter hour in Juliana Kyrton's company—at Stephen's choice of trouble over a wealth so pleasantly accompanied by a young and well-formed woman. But at the same time he could equally wonder why Juliana, who with her wealth could surely marry higher than a third son of an only moderately important family, was so set on Stephen. It argued she had a real affection for him, and the affections of as silly minded a woman as Juliana were usually neither reasonable nor to be reasoned with. Trying to determine what had actually passed between her and Stephen Hameden was not going to be an easy thing and Hal was most assuredly not looking forward with any pleasure to the morning.

But by morning Juliana Kyrton was dead.

∞ ∞ ∞

"In her room at the inn," Medford reported to Hal across the table in the great council chamber where Hal had been several hours at work on greater matters of his diocese before this was brought to him. "Throttled in her bed."

Hal crossed himself. "God have pity." To be dead so young and brutally was bad enough, but to go unshriven as she must have done was worse. "Was she otherwise . . . interfered with?"

"The innkeeper's wife says not."

"You've talked directly to this innkeeper's wife?"

"I went to her as soon as word was brought me."

"Who brought it?"

"Someone Sir William sent as soon as he heard."

"How did he come to hear? Is he at the same inn?"

"No. He's at the Crossed Keys. But word of something like this spreads like plague."

"What of Master Hameden? He sent no word? Where's he staying?"

"I met his man coming to me on my way to the Mitre. He stayed the night there, too."

"But was behind Sir William in getting word to us."

"He was probably too taken up with what had happened."

Very probably. The death of the woman you depended on to save your son from a marriage you did not want for him and bind him into one that you did was bound to distract.

But Hal was not distracted, only mightily annoyed to have all this suddenly in his hands. Not that it was. It was the crowner's problem, to investigate and determine, if he could, the murderer and call in the sheriff if need be. But he nonetheless heard himself asking, "The innkeeper's wife. What did she have to say about last night?"

"That Mistress Kyrton went directly to her room when she returned from here yesterday and never came out."

"To supper?"

"It was taken to her room."

"Visitors?"

"None that anyone saw."

"Not even Master Hameden?"

"Not that anyone saw, and there were people in the inn's main room all night and he would have had to pass through there to go to her. He had a room on the ground floor, Mistress Kyrton on the first. The last that was seen between them was when they parted at the foot of the stairs after returning from here."

"Peacefully, not quarreling?"

"As peacefully as might be, given Mistress Kyrton was still weeping. Weeping and assuring Master Hameden she knew what she knew and would go on saying so."

"The innkeeper's wife heard that?"

"She did."

"What else did she have to say? Anything more about the murder? Or were you able to see the body for yourself?"

"I both questioned the woman and saw it." And looked less than happy that he had but went on steadily. "Mistress Kyrton was lying on her back, straight out under blankets and sheet. That's the way she was found, the innkeeper's wife said. All that had been done, because she was plainly throttled to death, was the bedcoverings stripped back to be sure there was nothing else . . . done to her. Then she was covered again."

"No sign she struggled?"

"The bedclothes were kicked loose and somewhat tangled at the bedfoot, probably by her death throes, but aside from that, no, no sign she was able to do anything except die. My guess would be the man came on her sleeping, knelt on the bed astride her, pinning her arms under the coverings and her body to the bed, choked off any outcry before it happened and went on choking her until she was dead."

Hal looked down, trying to blot out the ugly picture, belatedly bethought him of something else and looked up to ask, "What of her waiting woman? Or women?" Because surely Mistress Kyrton had traveled attended by at least one woman who, in the common way of things, would have shared her bedchamber, sleeping on a pallet on the floor or, if fortunate, on a truckle bed pulled from beneath her mistress's.

If possible, Medford went more grim. "She was there, dead on a pallet across the room. The murderer probably killed her first, with a hard blow with something blunt to her head. Probably with a dagger's pommel. Her skull was crushed in a considerable way."

So he had been armed—but any man would be—but chosen the more surely silent ways of skull-cracking and throttling. Cold about his killing then. Or not, Hal amended. With throttling he would have felt Mistress Kyrton's dying more directly than almost any other way. He would have felt her body heave and try to twist under his, felt the frantic struggle for life in her throat as he choked it out of her, felt her go slack as she lost the fight and her body's utter stillness, like none other in the world, when she was fully dead.

It had been a very personal killing.

And angrily Hal asked, "How did he enter the room?"

"We assume by the window."

"It wasn't shuttered and latched?"

"There are freshly slivered places on the shutters' edge that could have been made by a knife blade slid in to lift the latch."

"And the window was an easy climb from the yard probably."

"I wouldn't call it difficult, no. If nothing else, there are things enough that could be dragged over to stand on to make it easy."

"Was something dragged over?"

"I'd say an empty barrel across the yard, waiting to go back to the alemaster, could have been. But it's an innyard with all manner of things going on, and there's been no rain of late to make mud to take any clear marks of what might have been done."

"And no one heard or saw or suspected anything."

"Nothing."

A chance killing? A murderer looking for someone to kill and she and her maid happened to be his choice? Hal couldn't make it seem so and asked, "Who knew which was Mistress Kyrton's room?"

Medford shook his head. "How hard would it be to find out? Anyone downstairs when she passed through could have seen where she went above stairs if they'd wanted to. Or asked a servant, in which case whoever was asked will remember it now and say something. Why the interest, my lord?"

Why indeed? Report that she was dead, with perhaps a few details, should have been enough and the rest left to the coroner, with some degree of thankfulness that the question of marriage was finished.

Why was he seeking to know so much more?

Because he did not like what was in his mind and knew it would be as quickly in other people's minds too. Who had more reason to want Juliana Kyrton dead than Stephen Hameden? Except for Catheryn Dauntsey, perhaps, but Hal did not see how she would have had the strength for those two deaths, let alone been able to pass through the town in some black hour of the night and manage her way into an upper room. And how would she have learned which room? The first two of those Stephen could possibly have done, and there were ways he could have learned which was Juliana's room. She could have sent him a message begging her to see him, for one. It would have been like her. Or he could have sent a servant of his to follow her and see which room was hers. Though that was something Catheryn could have done too.

Questions would have to be asked those ways, though a loyal servant would lie for his master about any message or errand, and if Stephen denied a message, it would be his word against whoever said they had brought it to him.

Hal realized he was staring at the tabletop in front of him without seeing it and had not answered Medford's question about his interest, and so looked up to him and said slowly, "Because the coroner is either going to be satisfied with saying it was a chance murderer and no hope of finding him, or he is going to look for the man most likely to have done it and see Stephen Hameden."

"You think he did it?"

Slowly Hal shook his head, not denying he might have, only uncertain. "I don't know. He maybe had best reason and could have made the chance, but there could well be things we don't know. I would like to know them before anything is done that can't be undone." Facing squarely, to himself but not aloud to Medford, that he would not like to learn that Stephen was a murderer.

But if Stephen was, it would be worse not to learn it. For Catheryn Dauntsey's sake, if no one else's.

Dearly wishing he had chosen to go hawking yesterday instead of involving himself in this, Hal told Medford what questions he wanted asked next, gave word he would delay seeing the Dauntseys and Hamedens, and sent strict orders among the servants that in no manner whatsoever were Catheryn and Stephen to have any access to each other or their fathers to them until he said otherwise.

With all that settled, he turned back to what ordinarily needed doing in his day—seeing officials from his various properties and businesses, going over accounts, dictating letters and answers to letters—deliberately putting the matter aside until Medford returned to him with answers just ere dinner.

Unfortunately nothing Medford brought him looked to be of much use. The Mitre was an inn and people came and went, as one of the ostlers there had pointed out to Medford's questions. "If you tried keeping heed of all of them you'd wear out your wits," the man had said. "When it's time, I go to bed." And took no interest in what went on after that, he apparently had not added but might as well have.

No one had seen Master Hameden anywhere but in the inn's main guest hall or his room. But then what reason would he have had for having his witness against his son's marriage dead? Nor had anything more useful come out at the Crossed Keys concerning Sir William. He had spent the evening playing draughts with another guest, then gone to his room and not been seen until morning. And of course both men's servants swore their master had been nowhere else than his room through the night.

It would have been more helpful if they had been poorer men and of necessity spent the night sleeping in the inn's main room with their fellows, who tended to notice if folk went stepping over them or moving about in the night. But then, if they had been poorer men, they would not have been on Hal's hands at all, and with a sense that he was no further forward in the matter, he went to dine with his usual state at the high table in the great hall.

Household officers and guests sat the length of the hall below him, along the lower tables, and today included Catheryn Dauntsey and Stephen Hameden. He noted without giving sign that he did that they were kept well apart from one another, never within speaking distance, though he saw looks pass between them; but if a cat could look a king, as the saying went, two sworn lovers could look at one another, even in a bishop's hall.

It was an hour later, at the end of Hal's after-dinner time spent walking in the garden, that Medford brought him word that Juliana Kyrton's husband had arrived, in search of his wife.

For a long moment Hal stood silently regarding a carefully kept lily in a Spanish painted pot with an extreme disfavor directed neither at the lily nor the pot but at this new turn in the matter, before he said, "Have them all—Dauntseys, Hamedens, and this man—summoned to the council chamber."

It was useful to have one's word be law, Hal thought not much later, regarding them all across his council table, but he wished he did not have to use it this way. Sir William and Master Hameden stood side by side, still united in their purpose, with Catheryn on her father's other side, Stephen on his father's, and Raulyn Fyncham, the alleged husband, to one side of them all.

If the man's claim on Juliana Kyrton was true, Hal had to admit that, judging by him and Stephen Hameden, she had had an eye for fine-made men, but Hal could not help eyeing him with much the same disfavor he had turned on the lily because what this whole business did not need was a complication and Raulyn Fynchem was, first and foremost, a complication.

He was also acquainted with Sir William, it seemed. Brought in last, he cast a curious glance at Master Hameden but exchanged a nod of greeting with Sir William; and Hal, making introductions, ended them with, "You know each other, Sir William, Master Fyncham?"

"He's nephew to Sir John d'Arundel," Sir William said. "I've met him at his uncle's."

And Sir John moved in royal circles, making him important to Sir William, who, so Hal knew from Medford, would not have minded doing the same, but Hal kept that thought from showing on his face. Not showing thoughts on one's face was a useful skill for both a royal bastard and a bishop, he had found over the years, and now said blandly, "Master Fyncham, you know what passed here yesterday? The cause why these people are all here and why Mistress Kyrton was?"

Fyncham made him a respectful bow. "Yes, my lord. I've been fully told."

"And to that you add your claim of marriage to Mistress Kyrton?"

"Yes, my lord. We pledged ourselves to one another this Eastertide last past."

Why, Hal wondered, were people so ungoverned in their ways? On his part, even in the warmest times between him and the one woman for whom he had ever had deep desire, he had never been fool enough to vow himself to anything with her. Nor had she asked it of him, both of them knowing, accepting, that when it came time for him to take his vows to the priest-hood, everything would end between them, and it had, except for their daughter for whom he made steady provision, because for him a vow was a sacred thing, not lightly made and, once made, not to be denied, because it was made not merely between men but to God, and as God was eternal, so must a vow be. And yet people threw vows around as if they were breadcrumbs, to judge by the stories they told on themselves.

But aloud all he said was, "Why was this marriage unknown, as seemingly it was?"

"It was simply a thing between us, no one else's matter," Raulyn said. "We didn't keep it secret but it went untalked of, I suppose, because the while since then we've lived out of the way together at Hurston Manor she owned by way of her first husband, not far out of Andover. Any number of the servants there will say so, an it please you, my lord."

"And she never made mention of any vow already made to Master Stephen here?" Hal asked.

Fyncham took a deep breath before saying unwillingly, "She told me of him, my lord, before ever we wed. She said that they had sported together—" He broke off, made a bow to Catheryn with, "I'm sorry, my lady, but so she said." And to Hal again, "She said she had teased him with promise to marry him but it was only words, never vows. She said he was too much a boy and his father would likely disinherit him if ever he wed other than he was told to."

"Then why was she here, making claim otherwise?" Hal asked.

"We quarreled of late." Fyncham paused, gathered himself, and went on, subdued and regretting. "It happens, no matter the love there is. It was our first falling out and would have passed but Juliana rode her feelings higher than most do. At the worst of our arguing, she declared she didn't want me for her husband after all, said she wanted a better and knew who he would be and how to have him. I was that angry, God forgive me, that I told her he was welcome to her and she slammed away into her room. I never thought it would go farther than her staying there until she was quieter and had thought better of it all and we could make up, but next I knew, she was gone and I've been on the trail of her ever since." He swallowed as if the words had been coming painfully and finished, "She was ever stronger of heart than head."

Letting go by Fyncham's comment on his wife—if his wife or anyone's she had been—Hal looked to Master Hameden. "She must have come to you then."

"Aye." Master Hameden sounded faintly puzzled. "Four days ago, just ere we were to set out here. She never said anything about being with this man, though. Just asked to talk to me private, and when she'd told me about what had passed between her and Stephen, I thought best to keep it quiet until we were here." To take his son by surprise with it, hoping for the best, Hal supposed. "So I sent her on ahead with her woman and two of my men, bade her find somewhere to stay in Bishop's Waltham, and sent one of my men to fetch her here on our heels when we were set to meet with you."

"You might have said what you had in hand, instead of shaming my daughter in front of everyone," Sir William said hotly.

"It had to come before my lord bishop anyway, so why not this way?" Master Hameden returned. "Better she be shamed than my son made a fool of. And a poor fool at that, because I meant what I said when I swore he'd have no acre or penny of mine if he keeps his wrong-headed way."

"He'll have none from me, that's sure," Sir William returned. "Nor would Catheryn either if this had come to them being truly wed. That still gave you no right to shame her, for everyone to see."

Hal had taken good note of Catheryn yesterday while Juliana carried on with tears and claims, and he had not thought she looked shamed but cold-eyed with disgust and disbelief, except in that moment when Juliana had flung herself against Stephen and tried to have a kiss from him, and then, rather than shame, Catheryn's look should have been enough to drop her rival where she stood. Now, standing more apart than anyone from the arguing, farthest of everyone from her embattled lover, she had made no move or sound all this while but Hal had seen, without showing he did, how anger and stubbornness were darkening in her face as the arguing went on.

But Master Hameden was saying at her father, "What difference, man? The end is that you have your daughter back and I have my son."

"Except it's a lie there was any vow between Juliana and me!" Stephen declared angrily in the same moment that Catheryn, at last whipped from her silence, flared at her father, "You never will!"

So much for thinking Raulyn Fyncham's tale would sway her against Stephen.

"Catheryn," Sir William said with far-strained patience, "you can see what sort he is, throwing promises around to women as it suits him."

"What I see is you believing what you want to. Give me leave, in return to believe what I know is true."

"I give you no leave of any kind!" Sir William turned angrily to Fyncham. "A year ago there was talk you had interest in marrying my daughter. If you want her now, she's yours!"

"Sir . . ." Fyncham began as Catheryn cried out, "No!" and Stephen with a furious step toward Sir William said, "She's mine!"

"Whatever words you said between you at Midsummer," Sir William shot back, "count for nothing since you were already wed to someone else!"

"I wasn't!" and "He wasn't!" came from Stephen and Catheryn together.

"Don't be a fool, boy!" Master Hameden shouted. "You're in the clear of any woman now. You can start over and use your head this time!"

Hal rose to his feet, as angry as any of them but hiding it behind an ice-edged order to "Be silent!" Silence absolute fell through the room, and looking back at all their startled stares, he saw they were seeing not the Duke of Lancaster's bastard or a man too young for his office but all the episcopal authority he embodied, exactly what he meant them to see, and he sat again, because that was part of his authority, too—that he could sit while they had to stand—and after a judicious moment more, said evenly, as if no anger had happened at all, "Nothing is settled because nothing is proven. At best, all we're certain of so far is that Juliana Kyrton was an unsteady creature whose word in any matter has to be taken as less than sure. That, and that someone was willing to kill her."

"That she was killed had to have been chance," Sir William put in. "Some madman. Or your son," he added to Master Hameden.

Master Hameden turned wattle-red, but before he or anyone else could say anything, Hal said, "Enough of that." But then thought better of stopping them, because when people talked, they said things that most of the time could as easily have gone unsaid, things that all too often would have been better left unsaid, and sometimes in their talking they said what very surely they should not say at all. So here and now it might be better to keep people talking until someone said something else they should not, and in a deliberately bland voice, Hal offered, "After all, Stephen was here for the night."

"Under guard?" Sir William shot back.

"Of course not," Hal answered, still blandly, judging Sir William was someone who would go bulling forward unless openly opposed.

And Sir William did, seeing a way to be rid of this trouble over his daughter once and for all, giving a hard nod toward Stephen and saying, "Then he could have come and gone at his pleasure and anyone can see why his pleasure would be to kill this woman. Who better?"

"It was a chance killing!" Master Hameden declared again.

"Chance!" Fyncham scorned. "Not likely. He didn't know of me, that there was anyone who would be able to discount her claim to him. For all he knew, she'd make her claim hold good. He had every reason to want her dead."

"But not the chance," Stephen said. "I never left here last night."

"So you say," Fyncham returned.

"Come to that," Master Hameden said back at him, "we have only your word for what passed between you and her. Maybe there were no vows there at all, eh? Just your wish to get your hands on her money as supposedly her husband."

"Hah!" Fyncham was bold about that. "Unlike some, she and I had the wit to have a witness to our vows!"

"A witness?" Hal said, suddenly impatient. "You have a witness and haven't said so, man?"

"There's hardly been chance," Fyncham defended. "I failed to overtake Juliana before she reached her death here because once I'd followed her as far as Master Hameden's manor and heard where he and his son were gone and why, I guessed what was toward and turned back to fetch the man and bring him with me. I thought it would save time." Over that, Fyncham was bitter. "Instead it made me too late. I came as soon as might be but it wasn't soon enough."

Hal was not interested in his regrets. "Where is he, this witness?"

"In the outer chamber here, please you, my lord. Waiting."

Hal made a small gesture and one of his own servants standing near the outer door moved immediately, going out and shortly coming back in with a man who, judging by his clothes, was of commoner sort than the others and plainly torn between being pleased and almost unbearably unnerved to be there. Hat off and being twisted between his hands, he made his way the room's length to lout a bow to Hal and wait, eyes lowered, and to reassure rather than frighten him further, Hal said mild-voiced, "Your name and place, fellow?"

"He's John Gybys of Hurston, my lord," Fyncham answered.

Hal flashed him a silencing look but said in the same mild voice, "I'd hear it from him. Fellow, your name and place? And you may look at me."

The man did, a shy, quick glance up, down, up again, holding long enough to say to Hal instead of to the floor, "John Gybys, an it please you, my lord. Of Hurston. Like he said."

"Thank you, John Gybys of Hurston. And thank you for being here." And because suddenly it seemed the best thought, he said then to everyone else, "I'll talk with him alone. Draw off," adding as Sir William and Master Hameden headed toward each other, "Apart from each other. There and there. And there, Master Fyncham," he added as the man moved as if to go with Sir William and Catheryn to the corner toward which Hal had pointed them.

They went as he had bid them, and behind all their backs Hal looked to Medford with a slight movement of his head that Medford answered with a nod of his own and strolled away after Sir William, to make talk with him before moving on to Master Hameden and then to Raulyn Fyncham, to keep them reasonably satisfied until Hal was ready for them again.

Left alone with John Gybys, who was distinctly unhappy at it, Hal said, still carefully mild, "So, you witnessed the vows between Master Fyncham and Mistress Kyrton, did you?"

"Aye, my lord."

"Do you remember what they said? The exact words?"

"Nay, my lord." The answer clearly worried him. "I fear I don't."

It would have made it all too easy if he had, Hal thought resignedly and tried instead, "Did it seem to you they were firmly wed by the words, whatever they were?"

John Gybys cheered up noticeably. "Oh, aye, my lord. I mind I thought at the time, 'There, that's done, they're wed, certain enough.'"

Hal let the man see he was pleased with that while thinking behind his smile that whatever else he got from John Gybys, it was not going to be lies. The man did not seem likely able to make any up for himself nor have any that Fyncham might have tried to teach him stick in his simple head, especially when confronted with a bishop wanting to know the truth.

But neither would it be well to startle or frighten him, and still careful, Hal asked, "How did you come to be their witness?"

"I'm a servant there. In Mistress Kyrton's household, my lord. She's really dead then, is she?"

"She is. You're a groom or such like?"

"Oh, nay. Just there, doing things that needed doing. You know."

"And what were you doing when they asked you to be their witness?"

"Nothing. Waiting. It was late one night. Master Fyncham had been there a week or something like and that night they were sitting up late over wine, talking and . . . suchlike, by the fire. I was told off to be there if they needed aught while everyone else went to be bed, and I was that tired I nearly was sleeping where I stood by the door when Master Fyncham called me over, laughing like, and said I was to hear what they said to each other. Mistress Kyrton was laughing, too, and said they were going to be married so listen close and I did and they said the words I don't remember only they sounded proper marrying words when I heard them. Then they said I could go off to bed because they were. Going off to bed, you see. And that was all. My lord."

"When was this? What day or near to?"

John Gybys squinted with thought. "Thursday in Hocktide last past it would have been, and it please you, my lord."

Just after Easter, as Fyncham had said.

"And they were together ever since then?"

"Oh, aye." John Gybys sounded sure of that but there was a darkness under the words that made Hal ask, "Happily?"

John Gybys wryed his mouth. "For maybe a month it went on happy enough, I'd say. After that, none so happy."

Hal raised his eyebrows questioningly, correctly guessing the man would need no more than that to keep going now he was more at ease, and eagerly John Gybys went on. "Quarreled they did. Go at it for days at a time. There'd be yelling, then her weeping and him sullen and sharp-tongued at everybody. Then they'd make up in bed, as the saying goes, and be all lovey until the next time they'd go at it again."

Hal considered asking over what they quarreled but doubted it mattered, and instead asked, "You were at Hurston when Master Fyncham came for you—when was it? Yesterday?"

"The day before, my lord. Aye, at Hurston."

"And he told you why he needed you and you came away with him."

"Aye, my lord."

"In great haste."

John Gybys blinked. "None so great, my lord. We just came, like."

Yes, Hal thought; they would have had to "just came," because great haste from Hurston near Andover to here should have brought them in sooner than today's afternoon, and he asked, "Where did you spend last night, then, John Gybys?"

"In some place called Owslebury, my lord. This side of Winchester."

"What time did you reach there?"

"Oh, maybe midafternoon, say. Shadows were lengthening but not thickening."

"Early to be stopping." When another hour's ride or so

would have had them in Bishop's Waltham.

"Early like," John Gybys agreed, "but Master Fyncham said it would do, said tomorrow—that's today—would be soon enough to be here."

As easy as that, was it? Hal thought, and with a small gesture bade John Gybys stand aside and with another brought everyone back to stand in front of him again.

When they were, he looked to Medford and said, pointing at Raulyn Fyncham, "Take him prisoner, and when the coroner finally arrives, give him over to him, for murder of his wife."

As Medford, with a sign for two of Hal's waiting servants to join him, moved behind Fyncham, the man gasped out, "What? I . . . What? *Why?*"

"You kept lying," Hal said coldly. "And they weren't even good lies. First, you said Master Hameden would disinherit Stephen if he married Juliana, when in truth he would have been pleased to have her money in the family. Next, you said the quarrel that sent her to the Hamedens was the first you'd had. Given what I had seen of her, I doubted Juliana ever went for long without making some manner of upset in her life, simply for the pleasure it gave her, and indeed John Gybys has told me you and she quarreled often. Finally, you said you came after her in all haste but you didn't. Not if you were at Hurston the day before yesterday and reached here only this afternoon. Besides that, you stopped early yesterday, long before you had to, and stayed over the night at Owlesbury. Or your man did. You didn't. You left him there and went somewhere else, on your own."

Fyncham turned on John Gybys, furious. "I told you to say nothing about that!"

John Gybys stammered, confused, "I-I didn't."

"He didn't," Hal agreed. "But now you have, thank you. You came on to here and probably had no trouble worth mentioning in finding out which inn your wife was at. There are only two and I doubt she kept her plight to herself. All you need have done was spend time in the taproom, either place, drinking and listening, and there would have been mention, if not more, about the weeping woman and how she was carrying on. I wonder if anyone at the Mitre will recognize you if they're asked?"

Fyncham tried, openly desperate. "All you have for certain is that I wasn't with him." He pointed at John Gybys. "If you come to it, *he* could have done it as well as me!"

"Why?" Hal asked, interested in the answer.

Fyncham had to cast quickly to come up with answer to that but after bare hesitation said, "Simply because. Maybe he thought I wanted it. Maybe . . . maybe . . ."

"Maybe he was seen through the evening at whatever inn you stayed at, but I'll warrant you never were. If someone is sent to ask questions there, my guess is that is what they'll be told."

"Then *him*." Fyncham pointed at Stephen. "Why isn't anyone wondering about him? Why pick only on me?"

"Because so far I haven't caught him out in a brace and a half of lies, the way I have you. And he had no reason to kill Juliana. Or none so great, let be as many, as you did. First, you were probably unbearably tired of her. She wasn't a woman that wore well, I suspect. But to leave her would be to leave her money, too, while as her widower you would be quit only of her, not of her money. Besides, there was hope that Stephen Hameden would be named for her murderer, and with him removed, you could try again for Catheryn, who, in the upset over the treachery of Stephen's supposed vow to Juliana and her murder, might well look on you more favorably than she did. Or her father, seeing her reputation likely ruined by all this, would have been more willing than last year to give her over to you. At worst, you would have been rid of a wife you were tired of and be left with her wealth. At best, you would have not only Juliana's wealth but another wife and the dowry that came with her. You gambled large, Raulyn Fyncham, but you gambled stupidly and made it worse with stupid lies. Medford, remove him."

It was with satisfaction that after Fyncham had been taken away Hal ruled, to the great displeasure of their fathers, that Stephen and Catheryn's vows had been sufficient and they were indeed truly, irrevocably wed. He then, with equal satisfaction, sent their fathers out and kept Stephen and Catheryn with him, to ask across the table at them standing side by side, at last, hands entwined, "Are you pleased to have your own way? Despite the trouble that's come of it? Despite your fathers have both disowned you?"

They looked at one another, the kind of searching look Hal remembered there had been between his love and him when he had told her he would take his final priestly vows a week from then. A look that read into each other's souls and answered not everything but enough. And very quietly, with great certainty, Catheryn said, "There was nothing else we could do. We love each other."

Yes. And for them that had been sufficient against all the rest. Just as for Hal his need for the priesthood and all that might come with it had been sufficient for him. And without knowing he was going to until the words were there, he heard himself saying, "You will nonetheless need more than love to live on. I have a manor in Berkshire in need of a bailiff. If you would be interested, Master Stephen . . ."

DIANNE DAY

⚬⧓⚬ ⚬⧓⚬ ⚬⧓⚬

Dianne Day has been writing full time since 1993 and now lives on Point Pinos near Monterey, California. She is best known for her historical mystery series featuring Fremont Jones, with six published so far in both hardcover and paperback beginning with *The Strange Files of Freemont Jones*. At present Dianne is at work on an historical thriller not part of her mystery series. She welcomes visitors to her website, http://www.dianne-day.com, and email to dianneday@aol.com, as well as regular mail to P.O. Box 704, Pacific Grove CA 93950.

THE LABYRINTHINE WAY

BY DIANNE DAY

"What is that?" he asked. "I know that thing, that shape! I'm sure I do, but I can't put a name to it. Tell me where I've seen it before."

I remembered him. It was clear he didn't remember me. But then I'd changed a lot in twenty-something years—and when I'm professionally dressed people tend to see the outfit, not the woman.

He hadn't changed, not that much. He was still handsomer than average, with that lazy, amused look in his eyes. I didn't doubt for a moment there would be a hard, flinty meanness beneath the amusement if I gazed into those eyes long and deep enough.

I cocked my head, raised one eyebrow, and glanced up without saying anything. He was the intruder here. Perhaps he'd just go away if I were rude or even simply cold to him, but I wasn't much good at either rude or cold, so probably not. I wondered how persistent he'd be. Wondered what I was going to do. It was a long time since I'd last thought of what he did to me but now it was all coming back—far, far too vividly.

"It's making me nuts that I can't think what you call it," he said, smiling down at me, nodding at the paper beneath my hand. His slightly crooked front tooth had been fixed. I wondered when he'd had that done. Perhaps he'd wanted to be perfect, or at least to look perfect. Or perhaps somebody had bashed his face in, for good reason, and he'd had to get that tooth replaced. Too bad. In

a way the crooked tooth in the midst of all that facial perfection had lent him a kind of rakish charm that was
missing now.

"C'mon," he wheedled, "what is that thing?"

"It's a sketch for a labyrinth," I said, lifting my chin as
I felt a surge of energy. Whether it came from God or the
Devil I didn't know, but I said a quick little silent prayer
to the God I know best, who happens to be female, that
this energy was beneficent. "For the cathedral," I added.

"Ah," he said.

His eyes swept over me, no longer so lazy, giving to
my clerical collar that extra degree of attention most men
will reserve for a hint of nipple. Nipples do not show
beneath a black rabat, or indeed beneath a rabat of any
color, though I doubt whoever invented the garment had
that particular sort of concealment in mind at the time.

"May I?" He gestured toward the empty chair on the
other side of the little round table where I'd thought I was
having coffee and contemplation alone, away from my
office and the telephones with people with problems on
the other ends of the line. This coffee shop, not one of
the cathedral's several small chapels, was my refuge and
my thinking place.

So once again, as long ago, this man was the invader.
Yet this time we were in a public place—I could send him
away.

I felt my moment of choice hang in the balance, like a
skip in the beating of my heart.

Then I shrugged and smiled, which he took for an
invitation, as I'd known he would. He slid into the empty
chair, and back into my life, this man who once had bru-
talized me and taken away my innocence. No matter that
then we'd both been not much more than children. He
was evil then and he was evil now, I could feel it.

I wondered if our unlikely meeting here had been fated. This city was half a continent away from the little town where we both grew up, one of those small towns where you didn't dare tell—not then and probably not now either. Certain degrees of unpleasantness are not allowed in little towns; children sense these things. There are people who take advantage of such an atmosphere, even as children.

I wondered how many others he'd hurt in the years since, and how badly. Wondered if he'd slipped up and actually killed anyone in the process of the kind of humiliation that was his specialty. I expected he would have refined his tormenting skills by now. Had he ever been caught? Was he, even now, evading capture?

"You work at the cathedral?" he asked, interrupting my thoughts.

"Yes."

I was thinking I had skills of my own, very different from his and perhaps even more highly refined. I could be dangerous too in my own way—in fact I'd had a conversation with my spiritual director recently on this very subject, how my particular skills could be dangerous to both myself and others. We'd agreed, my spiritual director and I, that I must be careful how I used them.

"I never met a woman priest before," he said, folding his hands under his chin.

"Then I suppose it's about time."

He grinned in a way that was supposed to be rakish but chilled me. He said, "Tell me about your labyrinth."

So I told him: How the pattern beneath my hand was identical to a labyrinth that had been made at Grace Cathedral in San Francisco a few years ago, and how Grace had duplicated their labyrinth from the medieval

Gothic cathedral at Chartres.

"In France," he said, nodding wisely. His shirt collar was ever-so-slightly frayed. His jacket was a good tweed but not new, and somehow I didn't think he was being studiously shabby, like a college professor. I wished I could see his shoes, but I couldn't, and I hadn't noticed them before he sat down.

"In France," I repeated, looking directly into his eyes for the first time. The meanness was there all right, but far at the back of his eyeballs, and the space in between that and his interested outward expression was filled entirely with guile.

"So what's the big spiritual deal about having one of these things," he said, "and why do I remember it? I've never been to Chartres, or to San Francisco either."

Where have you been, I wondered, and how long have you been here in my city? But what I asked was: "Have you ever heard of the collective unconscious?"

"Doesn't ring a bell."

I talked of symbols, of universal meaning, of shapes engraved so deep in our psyches that we need no words to sense or to explain their import. I talked of the true meaning of the word *religion*, which is to bind again, and I explained how universal symbology has been woven into our religions since time began.

I charmed him, intentionally. I bought him coffee, and another cup for myself, when he made no move to do so himself. As if on impulse I added two cookies on a plate, claiming sudden hunger I didn't have. He had such hunger that his face was full of it, and as we ate and drank I continued to charm him. I leaned across the table, closer and closer, gazing all the while into his eyes, my skills at work.

"You're much too beautiful to be a priest," he said.

I smiled, feeling feral.

He was hungry for more than cookies, and he thought I was prey. He was wrong.

The early twilight of autumn was coming on as we left the coffee shop. I asked if he would like to see the place in the cathedral where we were building the labyrinth. He said that he would. Avidly, he said so.

In Europe in the Middle Ages the cathedrals were constructed over periods of perhaps a hundred or even two hundred years. Our cathedral had been under construction for only seventy-five, but it had all the quirks and oddities of any place constructed by many hands over many years—easy to lose oneself, to become confused in such a place, especially in that deceptive hour that is neither night nor day.

The cathedral was vast: The nave soared up into arched vaults, its space echoed even of its own silence, and was full of shadows. The chapels in the apses were darker still, some of them closed for the night behind barred gates, like prison cells. I led my guest, my old acquaintance, my violator, down a long side corridor beneath the ribs of flying buttresses. Along the way I withdrew a penlight from the pocket of my jacket; because there were so many dark places in the cathedral, even in broad daylight, I always carried a light.

I switched on the narrow beam and said, "We're going down a flight of stairs now."

"Down stairs," he repeated. I heard a note of satisfaction in his voice. The darkness and the isolation would feel to him like a natural habitat.

"Watch the light," I said.

He echoed, "Watch the light."

And we went down into the dark.

The space to which I led him would have been, in a

medieval cathedral, the crypt. In ours it was a simple empty space within walls of stone. Americans have sanitary laws about burials being confined to cemeteries, so there were no dead bodies here. Nevertheless it was, like any proper crypt, directly beneath the altar. A sacred space, but the right place for the labyrinth? I wasn't sure; that was one of the things I'd been mulling over in the coffee shop before he came. I held up my penlight and in its surrounding glow I saw his eyes follow as I moved the light from side to side.

"To walk the labyrinth is to make a journey," I said, "into the heart of things."

"Heart," he said.

"As in heart's desire," I said, testing him.

"Desire," he repeated. He went on, his next word revealing he was not yet sufficiently under: "I desire you."

I knew I was on very dangerous ground. If I were unable to deepen the hypnosis I'd induced in him at the coffee shop, then my body was likely in danger from this man—yet the real danger was not to my body but to my soul—for which I must assume responsibility myself. The action I intended to take against him was not entirely without malice; I could not claim spiritual purity in what I wanted to do. I was placing my soul at risk.

But if I succeeded, I might bring an evil man to justice. At the very least I would right the old wrong he had done to me.

"Women fill you with strong feeling, I know," I said, slowly moving my point of light from side to side, at the same time murmuring *sub voce*: Watch the light. In my normal tone I went on without missing a beat. "I understand. But that feeling is not desire. You know it's something else."

He nodded. His eyes glistened, fastened to the light.

His lips were moist, salivating slightly.

"In the center of the labyrinth, the answers can be found. All the answers. That's what you want, isn't it? You want to know what that feeling really is, and why you do the things you do."

But now he shook his head, and I trembled; the light in my hand trembled too. Perhaps with my interpretation I'd gone too far; ill-advised interpretations are a particular failing of mine.

"I want to smash it," he said, without defining it. "Find and smash!"

In spite of the violence inherent in his words, he uttered them without inflection. He was stating a fact, telling the truth. My interpretation had been a little off, that was all. He'd just demonstrated that people under hypnosis will often, contrary to popular belief, hold to their own opinions.

He was not only under, he had gone deep. I suppressed a sigh of relief and steadied my hand, directing the beam of light at the floor where I'd drawn a chalk outline of the labyrinth. I had walked it once. No one else had seen it yet but me, and now him.

"Look, there is the pattern. You recognize it. You know this."

Suddenly I remembered how superstitious he'd been in years past, how as a teenager the others had teased him for it. I said, "You remember that old saying, 'Step on a crack, you break your mother's back'? Well, this is probably where it came from. When you walk the labyrinth, you have to keep your feet inside the lines."

"Uh-huh."

"You will walk this labyrinth." I moved my light slowly across the pattern on the stone floor. The white chalk seemed to glow.

"Yeah."

"You will walk inside the lines, very carefully, all the way to the center."

"Yeah."

"When you get to the center you will stand very still, close your eyes, and wait for me. While you are walking you will hear nothing, you will see nothing except the pattern of the labyrinth on the floor."

"Yeah."

"And when you reach the center you will stand and wait until you hear my voice."

"Yeah."

"Do you understand? If you do, say 'Yes, I understand.'"

"Yes, I understand."

"Then take my hand and I'll start you on the path."

He took my hand and I tugged him a bit to the right and a step forward, so that his feet were lined up with the opening into the labyrinth's sacred path. I'd wondered about his shoes before and now I saw what I'd thought I might see: the shoes were good leather in a classic style, but scuffed, edging toward shabbiness.

"Now walk!" I said.

And he walked.

I left the penlight standing on its end upon the stone floor, where it shed a surprising amount of light, like a candle.

From my office I called the police. "I have someone here I think you may be looking for," I said.

A serial rapist had been terrorizing our city for eight months.

When the two officers arrived and went with me back to the crypt, we found him standing in the center of the labyrinth. He was red-faced, seething with rage, but he did not open his eyes or utter a word.

Like the root-word *religio*, I had bound him with the power of the labyrinth, which is the ancient power of The Mother.

I called him by his childhood name and then he opened his eyes, roaring.

G. MIKI HAYDEN

❧ ❧ ❧

G. Miki Hayden, a long-time journalist, has published mystery and science fiction stories in numerous national magazines. Miki's novel about Japan's domination of the Pacific, *Pacific Empire* was on the *New York Times* recommended reading list. Miki writes regular columns and interviews for the mystery press, including *Murderous Intent Mystery Magazine*, *BlueMurder.com*, *Futures*, and *The Third Degree*.

THE SHAMAN'S SONG

BY G. MIKI HAYDEN

Coyote Man hadn't been one of those who in 1863 had surrendered to Kit Carson and his soldiers. He had fled into canyon country, where a band of renegades had survived on what game they could kill and wild vegetation. Only later did he follow the others to Fort Sumner where many of their number had given themselves up.

Coyote Man was a farmer, as were most of his people. The Dine (or Navajos as they were known to the white man) had been raising sheep, goats, cattle, and horses for centuries. They also grew corn, which was a sacred crop. But in addition to the observance of his daily chores, Coyote Man served as an *hitali*—or what some tribes called a shaman. He carried out several of the intricate rituals needed to keep the Dine well and in harmony with the Holy People.

It was through his function as a shaman that Coyote Man had once earned the major portion of his modest livelihood. The ceremonials were of the greatest importance to the Dine, and they must pay their priest his due. But after the wars and the treaty, the Dine had returned to their country between the Four Sacred Mountains with little in the way of material wealth. So these days, many went without the healer's rites and those who hired Coyote Man to perform the chantways gave him less in compensation than they would have in more prosperous times.

Riches were not Coyote Man's object. Marriage, however, was, and a man needed some money to attract a wife—especially a wife as fine as Yellow Flower Girl. Coyote Man was now riding to her family *hogan* beyond Huerfano Peak in pursuit of his courtship.

The *hitali* was young, and his eyesight was good. In the distance as he rode, he spotted three men on horses, trotting along toward the nearby Blanco trading post—or so he presumed. The only thing that surprised him about their presence here was that the men he saw were not Indian; they were white. Coyote Man could tell that simply by the way they sat on their mounts.

He was likely to run into them, Coyote Man realized, and that wasn't an entirely agreeable prospect. He didn't know who they were or what they were up to and he certainly had good reason to mistrust the whites. On the other hand, Coyote Man was on Dine territory, or what was left of it. This was their land, according to the treaty with General Sherman, and he would not run from confrontation.

As he got closer to the strangers, he could see that they were not soldiers, as he had feared. They were simply ragtag cowboys cutting through Navajo country. Coyote Man had no intention of crossing their path directly, but they would ride within a short distance of him.

"Look, an Indian," the shaman heard one say in the language he had learned while in captivity.

"Never mind," said the man on the broken-down mare. "There's only one."

"Where there's one, there's bound to be a whole nest of them," the third white said.

Coyote Man halted his pony, Kintahgoo. He didn't care to ride on, turning his back to the strange travelers. He sat still for a while and watched them go.

His stopping thus, for their part, made them obviously ill at ease, with two of the three twisting in the saddle to see what the red man was up to as they continued on. The shaman waited until the cowboys were out of sight, then headed toward the family *hogan* of Yellow Flower Girl.

Coyote Man sat with Yellow Flower Girl's maternal uncle in the place of honor on the west side of the *hogan*, facing the doorway. The women were on the north side, whispering. Although Coyote Man's thoughts were to the north, he paid careful attention to Chee Bonito. The men had not yet concluded arrangements for the marriage.

Surely Chee Bonito favored Coyote Man as a husband for his niece due to the suitor's status as an *hitali*. On the other hand, Yellow Flower Girl was a great prize and there were men from clans better preferred for a wedding with the Yucca-Blossom-Patch woman than the Bitter-Water Coyote Man—men better placed materially as well.

It was this last issue, in fact, that seemed to weigh heavily with Chee Bonito. The uncle pointedly listed a number of items needed by the family, while Coyote Man nodded sagely, as if to say the purchase of the required blankets, metal cooking pots, and sheep-shearing knife could hardly be considered much of a problem.

Coyote Man had three pennies to his name, tucked into his well-worn boots. The items mentioned would surely cost as much as seven dollars.

In agreeing to the price, Coyote Man hesitantly noted that a late-spring wedding would be auspicious, and Yellow Flower Girl's uncle joked that with so few of their people left, it was best for the young ones to get on with life and the making of babies. Chee Bonito slapped Coyote Man jovially on the knee and the shaman rotated his head slightly to see if Yellow Flower Girl was listening.

But just as the shaman turned to look, he heard the sound of horse hooves pounding against the too-dry earth. He swiveled his head back to see Chee Bonito's son, Brown Pony, riding furiously toward the three-forked-poles *hogan*. The young man simply had too much energy, in Coyote Man's opinion.

Within moments, Brown Pony had settled his horse and was inside preparing to sit with the men, despite his father's frown of discouragement. Brown Pony stooped, still out of breath from his fast-paced ride.

"There was a robbery at the trading post," the young man exclaimed at once, not pausing to express the proper greetings of respect to the shaman and his parent. "The white clerk was killed and about two hundred dollars was taken. They don't know who did it yet."

Coyote Man recalled the three cowboys he had crossed paths with on his way here. "Huerfano trading post? Or Blanco?" he asked Brown Pony.

"Blanco," replied the younger man.

Coyote Man carefully considered the situation. It was certainly likely that the men he had seen had taken the money from the store and killed the clerk. Perhaps he ought to ride to Blanco and shed some light on the occurrence. The owner of the store, a man named Steven Hill, was not a bad sort for a white. Not that Coyote Man thought all whites evil. He had known one or two decent ones at Bosque Redondo.

He would go and have a talk with Hill. If the cowboys had been seen by others, that would be good. It was best if Hill did not think this to be the Dines' doing.

ೲ ೲ ೲ

There was a small group of Indians gathered outside the Blanco trading post, gossiping. Coyote Man didn't pause to join this band. He had his position as *hitali* to uphold. Then too, he wasn't a man given much to idling. He walked directly into the small log structure.

The dead clerk was still stretched out on the wooden floor and Hill and Indian Agent Dennis Riordan stood talking softly a few feet away.

Coyote Man grimaced and quickly averted his eyes from the corpse. He had the typical Dine revulsion toward death. Someone should reverse the dead man's boots—put the left boot on the right foot and vice versa. That was the way the Dine did it, to keep the man's ghost from finding its way into the fourth world again. Someone should also break a hole in the north trading post wall to remove the body.

Coyote Man wasn't about to take those tasks upon himself. Let the white men do it; they weren't afraid of being haunted by the dead man's evil spirit.

Coyote Man's eyes unconsciously roamed over the displayed merchandise. Some beautiful blankets there. And cooking pots.

Hill became aware that the Indian was standing nearby. "Can't help you now, son. Don't you see we're busy?"

The shaman had a sudden inspiration. "I'm a finder of lost objects," he answered in English. "I can find your money for you." It was true, in fact, that he had the gift of knowing things, as had his grandfather, Hosteen Yazzie Nez. Coyote Man could divine the cause of an illness or the whereabouts of lost objects—and if those objects had been stolen, he was usually able to name the thief.

The Navajo had Hill's attention. "How could you find my money?" demanded the merchant. He stared at Coyote Man as if he suspected the shaman himself of stealing the cash.

"I'm a medicine man," explained the Indian.

Hill relaxed visibly and smiled. "Oh well," the trading post owner responded. "I won't be needing any of that."

But Riordan had seen Coyote Man locate a fellow farmer's lost sheep in an inaccessible canyon. While the white might have thought the recovery of the animal good luck or educated guesswork, he must have figured the shaman's art was worth a try. "Sometimes they find things, these fellas," he said to the storekeeper.

"All right," Hill returned, after a pause. "It might be good for doing business with you people."

"It'll cost you five dollars to hold the ceremony," Coyote Man slowly replied. The figure seemed to him outrageous, but it would go pretty far toward netting himself Yellow Flower Girl as a wife.

"Five dollars!" exclaimed the merchant in amazement. "First I have two hundred stolen from me, now I have to give you money as well."

Coyote Man couldn't imagine why he'd asked for so much, but there was no backing down. He nodded confidently. "And two more dollars when I get your property back."

Coyote Man was a hand-trembler. That was his means of obtaining information. He would fall into a state and the Gila Monster would enter him and cause his hand to tremble, revealing the origins of a disease or the place where missing possessions had been stashed. The *hitali* was certain of his abilities because they never failed him—or rarely.

He was glad to walk outside the store on this occasion in order to get away from the white cadaver inside. Hill had covered his clerk's body with a tarp, but there was no two ways around it—the whites hadn't any idea how to deal with the dead.

Coyote Man went to the well to rinse his hands. He had to cleanse himself before he could receive knowledge from the Gila Monster.

As the *hitali* washed and prepared with prayer for the ritual, he heard the thunder of many horses approaching at once. The disturbance annoyed him. There were five silver dollars stuffed into his boot and he was ready to begin his divination.

Grey Wolf, Laguna Boy, and Silverworker arrived. With them rode the three vagrant whites Coyote Man had come across earlier in the day. Grey Wolf held a rifle on them.

At first this distressed Coyote Man. Since the thieves had been caught by the other Dine, Hill might demand the return of the money paid for the divining. But then the shaman decided the appearance of the whites could be a good thing. If the strangers had the money with them, which likely they did, it would be that much easier to locate it.

Hill and Riordan appeared outside the door as the newcomers dismounted. Grey Wolf tried to convey to the Indian Agent in Navajo what was happening, but he failed to communicate his message adequately.

Coyote Man came over to his "client" to translate. "Grey Wolf says these are the men who stole your money. He and the others found them riding south on the path to Nageez."

"We're no thieves," protested the first of the white men vehemently. "We've only come down this way from Colorado trying to find work."

"Oh, hell, Major, these people will never believe us," broke in the second cowboy in disgust.

"Major?" inquired Riordan with curiosity.

The white stranger who had denied the charge against them drew himself up to his full dignity. "Major David Stanson and my men. We fought at Champion Hill, Big Black River, and Vicksburg for the Confederacy under General Pemberton. After the war, we came out west, just trying to keep body and soul together."

Grey Wolf displayed a six-shooter to Riordan, indicating it had been found in the possession of the white major. The Indian sniffed at the barrel to show the gun had recently been fired.

"What have you been shooting at, Major?" Riordan asked the ex-soldier coolly.

"Rabbits," said Stanson, as if he knew his story wouldn't be accepted. "Me and my men have been going hungry."

Hill grabbed at Stanson's saddlebag and looked inside while Coyote Man waited, barely breathing. He supposed the money would be discovered in there and his fee for the divining would be lost—along with his chances at winning Yellow Flower Girl.

But Hill withdrew to examine the saddlebags of the other cowboys, evidently finding nothing of particular interest in any of the possible hiding places.

Coyote Man sighed audibly and Hill glanced around at him. "All right, go ahead with your magic," the trader said.

The shaman explained in Navajo to those assembled that he was going to perform a divination. The Indians muttered among themselves for one or two moments. It disturbed them that the *hitali* would conduct a sacred ceremony for a white man, but when Coyote Man began to sing to ask the Gila Monster to guide him in his quest, quiet descended.

As soon as Coyote Man started his chant, his right arm and hand began to tremble violently. He observed the three white men from between narrowed eyes and they seemed nervous. He was on the right track. The five dollars at least would remain in his possession. He let the Gila Monster take over his mind and was barely aware that Grey Wolf and Laguna Boy were making for their horses. Then Gila Monster whispered to Coyote Man that the white cowboys were not the thieves. The two Dine had killed Hill's clerk and had taken the money belonging to the trading post owner.

Gila Monster must be correct as usual. Why else would the Navajo men leave the divination before it was over? They were afraid of discovery by the shaman. Coyote Man's arm raised up and pointed at the two fleeing Indians.

The Dine, who a moment before had been observing the ritual, jumped up to take their fellow Navajos into custody, wrestling the two uncovered murderers to the ground.

"Those are the guilty ones," Coyote Man pronounced in English.

"I'm not so sure," responded the shopkeeper dubiously.

Neither the whites nor the Indians had the two hundred dollars on them and Grey Wolf and Laguna Boy denied their guilt as passionately as the former Confederate soldiers had. But the Dine who were present knew that the deed had been done by those of their own kind. The Gila Monster had named them as the evildoers. And Coyote Man, for his part, was pleased with a job well done. All he had to do now was find Hill's money.

Although the Navajos had abandoned all interest in the three white wanderers, Hill and Riordan were intent on keeping the ex-soldiers within sight. There was still some doubt in their minds as to who the actual murderers were.

"We weren't running," insisted Grey Wolf in his native tongue. "I had to go home and water the sheep." His fellow Indians broke out into derisive laughter.

Coyote Man asked the obviously innocent Silverworker how he'd gotten involved.

"I met them on the road near here and they told me they were after the men who'd killed the trading post clerk."

Coyote Man nodded wisely. The only thing that puzzled him was why Gila Monster had not revealed the location of the stolen cash. Putting his hands on the money would assure the shaman of an early marriage to Yellow Flower Girl and enhance his reputation as a diviner. But perhaps Gila Monster did not wish Coyote Man to enjoy such success. Was there anything he had failed to do?

"Why are you helping us and putting the blame on your own people?" the white major abruptly asked Coyote Man.

"Because they're the ones who robbed the store," Coyote Man answered. What did the major mean by that question?

The white culture was so strange, Coyote Man mused. The

whites had even left the clerk's body lying in the store. The Dine shuddered to think of it and tried to place his mind back on the topic of the money. Still, he wondered if any of his people would ever set foot in that store again. They would probably shift all their business to the Huerfano trading post. That was where Coyote Man was going to buy the blankets and pots for Yellow Flower Girl's family.

Presently a bold idea came to him. The shaman drew himself up to Grey Wolf and Laguna Boy. "You left something inside when you did your job earlier today," he told the two with a blaze in his eyes.

The about to be convicted killers glanced at one another in some fear.

"You shot something and left it behind. It's still there." Coyote Man referred to the dead clerk as plainly as he dared without inviting the ghost to haunt him as well. "I want to know where the money is. If you don't tell me, you both will spend the night inside that store." No Navajo could stand such a thing.

He started to drag the smaller of the pair, Laguna Boy, by the shoulder into the trading post where the body lay.

Laguna Boy screamed in terror at the top of his lungs.

"Where's the money?" demanded the *hitali*. He shook the man as he questioned him.

"Buried. In a hole not far from here," the thief cried out. "Don't make me go in there. Don't put me in there with his ghost."

Laguna Boy preferred to be hanged than haunted.

∞ ∞ ∞

Coyote Man had three cents to his name. But the *hogan* of his wife's family boasted several beautiful blankets and large metal pots—along with a brand-new sheep-shearing knife. Hill's money had been found where Laguna Boy had said, assuring Coyote Man of his entire fee.

As was traditional, the shaman had moved in with Yellow Flower Woman and her relatives. Now that it was summer though, they would all travel to better grazing land and live in a more or less impromptu summer shelter.

In the fall perhaps Coyote Man would begin to build a *hogan* nearby for himself and his wife. He would need dollars for some of the materials, and to pay an *hitali* for a Blessingway ceremonial.

But money was sometimes easy for Coyote Man to obtain.

THOMAS KREITZBERG

⚬⚬ ⚬⚬ ⚬⚬

Thomas Kreitzberg is an award-winning writer whose short stories and doggerel have appeared in a variety of print and on-line magazines, including *Murderous Intent Mystery Magazine*, *Red Herring Mystery Magazine*, and *TheCase.Com*. His stories feature a Catholic PI who once left a stakeout early to go Mass. He also constructs mystery logic puzzles and has published non-fiction articles on such topics as the detective stories of G. K. Chesterton and writing and selling mystery poetry. He is a member of the Short Mystery Fiction Society and the Private Eye Writers of America. Tom lives with his wife and children in Maryland.

THE CHARITY OF A SAINT

BY TOM KREITZBERG

"I know what brought you to Domedale."

The young man to whom this comment was addressed stopped midstride, looked over his shoulder at the car he had just stepped from, then gave a puzzled smile to the old man who had spoken. "Do you, now?" the young man, whose name was Marvin Quinn, asked in a soft Irish accent.

The old man, who might have been leaning against the churchyard wall all his life, nodded. "Aye. It's St. Alice, ain't it?"

The Irishman broke into a broad grin. "Do I carry my piety so openly?"

"No, no." The old man shook his head gravely. "But it's St. Alice who's bringing all the strangers to town these days. Hope to make your fortune?"

Quinn eyed him steadily for a moment. "Perhaps I do. I have to take a look round the church first, but I'll be looking for a pub later, to spend the little fortune I have now."

Now it was the local man's turn to grin. "The Brewers Arms is the best spot for that," he said, pointing a thumb up the street.

"Then we may run into each other there." With a nod, Quinn walked up the steps of St. Dunstan's Church, Domedale, which lay in the southern folds of the Malvern Hills in Worcestershire.

The old man was right; St. Alice was the reason Marvin Quinn had come to Domedale. An old friend who lived in Great Malvern had called Quinn that morning to repeat a marvelous tale: A local farmer named Henry Lance claimed to have had a vision in which the saint, who was buried in the village church, told him where to find hidden treasure on his property. Whatever else may be true, Quinn's friend assured him, the fortune in old silver and jewelry Lance showed to his astonished neighbors was no dream. "I spoke to a fellow here who saw the loot yesterday. He says it looks to be all genuine Elizabethan work, a lot of silverware and a few necklaces and such. Worth perhaps two thousand pounds."

"And how does this saint figure into all this?"

"The story the fellow is telling is that he stopped by her tomb to pray for some financial assistance, and that night she appeared to him in a dream and told him about the silver."

"But Anglicans don't do that sort of thing!" Quinn insisted.

"I expect they shall after this," his friend replied with a laugh.

A journalist-at-large for a small weekly paper, Quinn decided this was a story he wanted to look into. Once his friend offered a place to stay and an automobile to borrow, Quinn had rushed to the train station without even contacting his editor. His plan was to send a telegram to the office from Great Malvern, then use the afternoon to begin his investigation. By which time, of course, it would be too late for his editor to say no.

It was, then, midafternoon when he entered St. Dunstan's, a cross-shaped church dating from the Early English period. St. Alice's resting place was easy to spot: a carved granite slab set into the back wall in the northwest corner of the church. Quinn knew it was hers before he was close enough to read the inscription, because on the floor beneath it was a small carpet of flowers. He walked over to the plainly carved marker, which read:

HERE LIES
SAINT ALICE OF LEWES
TRANSLATED TO DOMEDALE AD 1327
RESTORED 1874
"THEY HAVE WASHED THEIR ROBES,
AND MADE THEM WHITE IN THE BLOOD OF THE LAMB.
THEREFORE ARE THEY BEFORE THE THRONE OF GOD,
AND SERVE HIM DAY AND NIGHT IN HIS TEMPLE."

Quinn stood before the simple shrine and bowed his head for a moment. Then he began the socially vulgar but journalistically valuable task of counting the flowers on the floor. There were nine bundles, of from two to five flowers each, a detail he was jotting down in a small notebook when the door of the church opened, washing the interior in bright sunlight.

A middle-aged man entered briskly, but stopped at the sight of Quinn. Not till the door closed and Quinn blinked once or twice could he make out the newcomer's black cassock and the frown with which he was regarding the flowers at the journalist's feet.

"This must be your church," Quinn said quietly.

The clergyman, slightly shorter and heavier than Quinn, eyed him cautiously. "Yes. I'm Donald Rorty, the vicar here. May I help you?"

Quinn showed his broad grin. "The flowers aren't mine, you know. I'm merely a journalist, here looking into St. Alice's recent miracle."

"I see." The vicar appeared pained by this answer. "I suppose the newspapers must find sensation where they can, but I'm afraid you won't find much to our little story beyond the bare bones—so to speak."

"Perhaps not, but the readers of *G.K.'s Weekly* are sometimes satisfied with just the occasional bone to chew on." Rorty's face brightened slightly, and Quinn laughed. "I know, not exactly the *Illustrated London News*, but we do have a few loyal subscribers."

"Shall we talk in the vestry?"

Walking with the vicar through the nave, Quinn complimented him on the church's fine stained-glass windows, which portrayed a number of somber-looking apostles. "Yes," Rorty said, "they were one of the first changes my predecessor, Hollis Richardson, made when he came to Domedale. About the same time," he went on, glancing over his shoulder, "the shrine of St. Alice was restored."

Rorty turned to the left in front of the main altar, heading for a small door in the north wall. Through the door was the vestry, in a state of organized clutter Quinn found inviting. Half a dozen vestments of different colors hung in an open wardrobe, and two battered chairs were pushed against a table piled high with organ music and handwritten sheets of what were probably sermon notes. Rorty pulled both chairs away from the table and sat in one.

"St. Alice of Lewes," he said once Quinn had settled himself in the other chair, "is a person about whom I can learn nothing for certain. Obviously, she died before 1327, when her relics were translated here. From where, no one seems to know. Why, no one seems to know. It is possible that she was a Benedictine abbess of the ninth century, of whom one or two passing references exist. Whatever reason someone had for bringing the remains here, they don't seem to have played much of a role in the life of the church. I can find no records of any pilgrimages to, or even of any lone pilgrims in, Domedale. There's no indication that the locals even celebrated her feast day, or the day of her relics' translation, beyond a few candles and hymns on All Saints Day.

"In 1536, when King Henry was beginning to move against the monasteries, the Benedictines in Great Malvern, who controlled St. Dunstan's, sold it to a sympathetic cleric from Worcester. He moved here, quietly dismantled the shrine, and gave the remains to the Wilsons, the most prominent recusant family in the area. The church and village rode out the rest of that tumultuous century without incident."

"Everyone kept their heads down," Quinn said, "so everyone kept his head on."

"Quite," Rorty agreed with a smile. "Moving ahead some three hundred forty years, a man named Porter approached my predecessor and requested that the shrine of St. Alice be rebuilt. It seems Porter had married into the Wilson family and discovered in his wife's dowry both the bones of St. Alice and their story. Naturally, Mr. Richardson had never heard of her before."

"Naturally," Quinn echoed, his pencil scratching steadily on his notebook.

"When he uncovered the historical records, such as they were, Mr. Richardson allowed Porter to build the memorial you have just seen. What the shrine looked like prior to 1536, no one has any idea."

Quinn looked over his notes. "So Alice of Lewes is an unknown saint, whose relics rested here for two hundred years, disappeared, then showed up centuries later only to sit out there without fanfare for the past fifty years."

Rorty shrugged. "That is, generally speaking, as much as I know about her. And I know as much as anyone about her, I think." He smiled modestly. "I've made the history of the area something of a hobby, building on a collection of material Mr. Richardson was kind enough to bequeath me. I was his curate for some years before he retired."

Quinn was about to ask a question when Rorty sat up quickly. "Speaking of my collection, I've just remembered that Anne Lance, the wife of the man behind all this, borrowed a book from me several weeks ago. She has a brother with some, ah, peculiar ideas regarding Cromwell, and he was interested in a book on the Civil War I happen to own. I wonder . . ." Rorty fell into silent thought.

"Surely," Quinn said, "the location of the treasure isn't mentioned in the book. The story I heard placed the silver-work solidly in Elizabethan times."

Rorty laughed. "Oh, no, I wasn't thinking of that. I was wondering whether you would do me a favor. I assume you are planning on interviewing Henry Lance? Then could I impose upon you to pick up the book while you are there? I would write you a letter of introduction, to ensure he will talk with you. And when you drop off the book we can discuss your impressions of this affair, after you've heard it from the horse's mouth. I'm most interested in how the press will view it."

"And what are your impressions of this affair, Mr. Rorty? I assume you've already discussed it with the horse?"

"Oh, yes, certainly." Rorty studied the young journalist for several seconds. "Henry's concern right now is to find out how much the treasure is worth and whether he will ever need to work again. My concern is that my parishioners keep their heads about what Henry may or may not have experienced, and what they might expect could happen to them. The flowers out there . . ." He nodded toward the door. "Don't think I object to simple piety, but I don't want people treating St. Alice's tomb like some sort of conjurer's hat."

"Do you have an opinion about what really did happen to Henry Lance?" Quinn asked, turning to a fresh page in his notebook. "For the record?"

"For the record, the Lord moves in mysterious ways, and there seems little question that Harry Lance has been blessed by Providence."

"And St. Alice?"

Rorty spread his hands and smiled. "She's been a perfect lady for as long as she's been a guest in our church."

⚮ ⚮ ⚮

Quinn stood in the street in front of his borrowed car and blinked in the late afternoon sun. He looked south, in the direction of the Lance farm. He looked north, in the direction of the Brewers Arms. "Interviewing," he said aloud after a moment's thought, "is thirsty work," and he strolled toward the pub whose sign he could see about two hundred yards away.

As he walked, Quinn wondered what sort of man Henry Lance would prove to be. Rorty had given him directions to Lance's farm, and even written a brief letter of introduction, but meeting him could keep. Quinn had an idea that Lance's story was the least interesting part of the whole business. What mattered was how the rest of Domedale reacted.

Inside the Brewers Arms were only a handful of customers, including the old fellow who had recommended the pub to Quinn. He stood watching the door, with an empty glass on the bar next to him. When Quinn entered, he called out, "Hallo. Had a nice chat with St. Alice?"

"Yes, but I had to do all the talking, and now I've got the devil of a thirst. What are you drinking?"

"Bitter, thanks." The man shot a triumphant glance toward the bartender, who shrugged and said to Quinn, "Pierce here has to cast his net fairly wide to drag in someone who'll still buy him the first round."

"My pleasure," Quinn replied. "I work for the only publisher in the business who considers beer an allowable business expense."

Pierce cocked his head to one side. "So will all of London descend on Domedale once they've read your piece?"

Quinn laughed. "Not *all* of London. Some Londoners read only the *Times*. But Domedale doesn't seem to have gone mad for heavenly rewards just yet."

"Ah, no," Pierce said with a wave. "Most of us have more sense than that. But I have seen more strangers about that church the past three days than the rest of the year combined."

The talk stopped as the glasses arrived. When Quinn had paid and taken a healthy sip, he said, "You say most locals don't put much stock in Henry Lance's story?"

Pierce set his glass down half finished. "Something made Henry go out and knock down that well. But I'd sooner thought it'd be the devil than God."

"Mr. Lance isn't strikingly devout?"

The bartender, regarding himself as a welcome third in the conversation, said, "Henry's a good enough sort, but he's not what you'd call a saint. The Lord's name is often on his lips, you know, but he's not quoting Scripture."

Pierce laughed. "It makes me wonder whether the wrong

fellow didn't have the dream, and Henry lucked into someone else's fortune."

"Who's the right fellow to have had the dream?" Quinn asked.

"Me, of course!" Pierce answered with a cackle. "Then I'd be the one gone down to London first class."

"Oh, is Henry Lance in London?"

"Aye. Having someone look over the stock, tell him what it'll fetch."

The bartender nodded. "He's been telling the whole town, 'Wednesday we go to Sotheby's.' Like he was going to the king's for dinner."

Quinn took another sip of beer. "So what does the village think of the whole affair?"

"Everyone's got his opinion," Pierce replied. "I heard the vicar talking it over with Dr. Drake. Now there's a pair. The doctor calls himself an atheist, and he and the vicar can't help but go at it with each other. The one was saying how it must just be coincidence, or maybe Lance didn't want anyone to know the real reason he knocked down the well, so he made up a story about a dream. The other was saying hold on now, there's more to life than meets the eye and dreams can tell people things they don't already know."

"But what reason," Quinn said with a frown, "could any man have for waking up one morning, picking up a sledgehammer, and knocking a hole in a well that's stood on his property for four hundred years?"

All three men shook their heads and fell silent. Quinn wondered—and, he thought, the others were wondering too—whether he would have done it if he had been the one to have the dream.

∽ ∽ ∽

The next morning, Quinn drove to Domedale once more, this time a mile past the church to Henry Lance's small farm. The farm buildings—a barn, a chicken house, and one or two sheds, with a small cottage nearer the road—looked slightly shabby, though no worse than those on neighboring farms. Behind the barn, a crop of green plants Quinn couldn't identify was growing under the gray morning sky.

It was after nine o'clock when Quinn knocked at the cottage, Rorty's letter of introduction in hand. Whatever he had expected to see on the other side of the door, it wasn't a portly middle-aged man in a morning coat.

"Ah, Mr. Henry Lance?" Quinn recovered himself quickly.

The big man laughed. "I don't know I'd recognize my own self in the mirror. The wife said it was too fancy for the likes of me, but I just couldn't resist. What do you think?"

Henry Lance stepped back to let Quinn feast on the sight of his new coat. The journalist nodded approvingly. "It sits well on you, Mr. Lance. A present to yourself?"

"Yes, yes. Not that the wife didn't get something for her own self. That's what we've come to, a trip down to London to buy ourselves fancy gifts. If anyone tells you money doesn't change you, lad", Lance set a hand on Quinn's shoulder, "don't believe him."

Quinn joined in his laugh, and was drawn into the cottage for a cup of tea before he could introduce himself. Mrs. Lance called from the kitchen to say the tea wouldn't be a minute, and Lance, who had on well-worn trousers and work boots below his new coat, waved Quinn into a seat with a beaming smile.

"Well, Mr. Lance, let me first congratulate you on your good fortune," Quinn began with a relaxed air, "and let me next commiserate with you on your bad fortune to have admitted a member of the press into your house. I'm afraid I can't be removed with a crowbar until you've told me your full story."

As Quinn expected, Lance looked quite pleased. "Well now, there's not really much to tell," he said modestly.

"Not much to tell?" Quinn cried. "From what I've heard, this could be the most remarkable story to come out of these hills since the water cured Prince Edward's bunions."

Lance grew red from the effort to stop smiling. "I don't know about that, but it is the most remarkable story that's ever happened to me.

"You see," he continued, leaning back in his chair, "the wife and I have been having a rough go of it these last years. If it doesn't rain too much, it rains too little, and the plow broke last spring at planting time, and one of the cows . . . well, I won't go into all that, but we were hard put up, that's for certain."

Quinn nodded sympathetically.

"Well, this is what happened. My wife's brother, who comes to visit often, married a Roman Catholic girl, and he's gone over himself, sort of. At least, he's always going on about what the Catholics got right and we got wrong, and I wouldn't be surprised if he carries beads in his pocket."

"I see."

"So one day, a month or so back, Reggie is visiting—that's my brother-in-law—and he says, 'You're having all this trouble'—he meant with the farm, like I was saying—'and here you've got your own saint to yourself up in the church.'

"'What do you mean?' I say.

"'St. Alice is lying in the church, nothing but time on her hands,' he says. 'You should ask her for a little help.'

"'What,' I say, 'can she milk a cow?'

"And Reggie laughs and goes on about something a bishop said to an archbishop back in Noah's time, and we sort of let the matter drop."

Anne Lance entered at that moment, pushing the swinging door from the kitchen into Mr. Lance's chair. Quinn knew immediately what the wife had bought for her own self; the tea set must have cost them more than all the furniture in the room.

After getting the men settled with tea and cake, and warning her husband to keep his cuffs out of the tea, Mrs. Lance returned to the kitchen.

"So," Lance continued after taking a loud sip of scalding hot tea, "I sort of forgot about Reggie for a few weeks, until this past Sunday, when we went to church. It was one of those beautiful afternoons, you know, with the sun and the clouds that put you in mind to wash up for Evensong."

"I know what you mean."

"And afterward, as we were leaving, I noticed old Alice's marker, and I remembered what Reggie had said. And I sort of nodded toward her and might have something like, 'Well, old girl, how's about it?' Nothing much more than that, you see."

"Sure."

"I mean, we don't really go in for waving incense in front of old bones and whatnot, but what could that have hurt?"

"Exactly."

"And what," Lance asked, laying a finger against his cheek, "do you suppose happened that very night?"

Quinn leaned forward, slipping his notebook out of his pocket. "That was when you had your dream?"

"I don't know it was a dream, exactly," Lance said with a frown. "More like a vision, maybe. Anyway, there I am in bed, sound asleep, when suddenly I see myself, and there I am digging a hole. Only I don't know why I'm digging a hole, and then I get the idea that I need to dig a well.

"So I decide that what I'm digging is a well, and then I hear a voice say, 'Knock down the well, and all manner will be well.'"

"And you believe the voice belonged to St. Alice?"

"Who else?"

"Well . . ." Quinn shrugged. "What did the voice sound like?"

"A woman, of course."

"Young? Old? Educated?"

Lance frowned. "Dunno. Maybe," he finished with a nod and a wink, "it was ageless and pure. What do you think?"

"Hmm." Quinn studied his notebook. "What happened after the voice said, 'Knock down the well'?"

"I woke up, and at that very moment it was morning. I told the wife, 'I'm going to knock down the old well today.'

"I should explain that we've got two wells here, only one, the old well, hasn't really been used for I don't know how long. A hundred years at least, I'd say. It sort of sticks up in the middle of a field, not convenient to any of the buildings, and my family have been saying we'd knock it down some day for the last hundred years."

Lance chuckled. "I don't know which surprised the wife more, seeing all that silver or seeing me finally knock down the well."

After draining his teacup, Lance led Quinn out to the old well, which sat half-ruined in the middle of a hayfield about fifty yards beyond the barn. Quinn noted the ground-level cavity where the old wooden box had been concealed, and agreed with the farmer each time he marveled at his good fortune and the goodness of Providence.

Back in the cottage, Quinn probed Anne Lance for her opinions regarding her husband's vision, but she just shook her head and repeated, "Whatever Henry says, he's got all the proof of in that chest."

Shortly before noon, Quinn was sitting by the window in the Plume of Feathers, a plate of cheese and a pint of ale on the table before him. He had already inquired into the opinions of the barmaid and three of her customers regarding St. Alice and the treasure box. The barmaid believed Lance's story, as did one customer, although something in his manner toward the pretty young woman told Quinn that he was prepared to believe anything she believed. Another customer thought Lance had made up the story to make himself as grand as the treasure he'd found, while the third simply said it was bad luck to talk about such things.

While eating his lunch, Quinn paged through the history book he had picked up for the vicar from Henry Lance. Lance had looked surprised when Quinn finally produced the letter Rorty had written, but, after a brief search, he discovered the book under some papers on a small desk in the corner of the sitting room and handed it over.

The English Civil War was a topic that had never interested Quinn, and he reached the end of the volume before he reached the end of his drink. He was just closing the book when something about the binding caught his eye. The back inside cover was partly torn along the bound edge, forming a small pocket in which, it appeared, something had been tucked. Frowning, Quinn dug at it with his fingernail, and then with a pocketknife. Using his blade, he managed to remove a yellowed piece of paper.

Unfolded, the paper was about five inches long and three across. It looked like an old sheet of writing paper, with one edge unevenly torn as though it had been ripped out of a journal. There was writing on one side, in faded ink and a scratchy hand.

Quinn peered closely at the paper, making out the words: *grandfather's old tale of a silver box in a field near Domedale but if he ever knew which well concealed it he's forgotten.*

The journalist read this fragment through twice, set the paper gently on the table, and leaned back with a thoughtful expression.

At that moment, the door to the pub opened and a robust man rushed in, hailing the barmaid by name and including Quinn in his more general nods and greetings. He looked to be about thirty, though his hair was already thinning, and he peered at everything through round-lensed glasses as if he were looking through binoculars. The barmaid replied with an enthusiastic, "Hello, Dr. Drake!" but Quinn had already deduced, from the black bag the man swung casually at his side, that this was the village doctor whom Pierce had mentioned the day before.

A minute later, Quinn was at the bar with his empty glass, ordering a fresh pint and nodding to the doctor, who sat next to him. Drake made a favorable comment about Irish stout,

Quinn replied with a compliment regarding English cider, and the two spoke for some minutes about the medicinal properties of Scotch whisky. When the doctor's lunch was set before him, Quinn invited him to join him at his table.

"So the superstitions of rustics still interest the sophisticated London crowd, eh?" Dr. Drake asked between bites of his stew.

"I write for sophisticated rustics," Quinn explained with a smile. "I may live in London, but I write for *G. K.'s Weekly*."

"Oh, the Distributist crowd? Three acres and a cow, and that sort of thing?"

"Yes, and you can see how the prospects of everyone finding ten thousand pounds buried on their own three acres would do wonders for our circulation."

Drake laughed. "Though if everyone found ten thousand pounds on their land, ten thousand pounds would be worth only be a handful of acorns."

"But a handful of acorns can grow to become a forest."

"It's visionary talk like that that will keep you Distributists from making nothing but a little noise."

"Speaking of visionary talk," Quinn said casually, "is it your opinion that Mr. Lance's story is nothing more than rustic superstition?"

A smile flashed across Drake's mouth. "Before I answer, let me make clear that I have not been consulted in a professional capacity by anyone involved in this matter. So the best I can give you is my personal, not professional, opinion."

Quinn bowed his head, and Drake continued.

"I don't know how well read you are in the science of psychology, but there is a lot of very exciting work going on. The subconscious turns out to be a fascinating place, and we are only beginning to understand how it functions."

"Subconscious?" Quinn asked with a frown.

"Yes. So you ask me whether this business is rustic superstition. The simple answer is, of course! People are interpreting events within a framework of ancient beliefs. And I don't mean simply Christian beliefs. Much of what Christians believe—which may, if you like, be distinguished from what Christianity teaches—is really of ancient pagan origins. Well, I suppose I don't have to tell you about the paganism at the root of so much of religion in Ireland."

"I've always found that to be one of its charms."

"You could put it that way, I suppose," Drake said with a shrug. "But just because we have a culture that believes dreams foretell the future doesn't make it false, or even unscientific, to say that dreams recall the past."

"Are you suggesting that Henry Lance had some sort of, oh, atavistic memory of the silverware being hidden in the well?"

"Not at all. Although", Drake took another mouthful of stew while considering his words, "although I can't rule it out in some sense. Lance is not the reincarnation of whomever hid the treasure, of course, but it's within the realm of scientific possibility that knowledge of it has somehow been imprinted on him or his progenitors, and it finally emerged into his conscious brain as a result of an event he wrongly believes to be a religious vision."

Quinn scratched his chin. "How very odd. Oh, not you!" he added quickly, holding up a placating hand toward the doctor. "What you're saying isn't so very odd. What I meant is that I am in an odd spot, being faced with a thought I had never prepared for."

He stood up before Drake could decide whether to feel insulted or complimented. "Excuse me, Doctor, but I must send off a telegram before my editor runs my obituary. Thank you for your company. It has been a very enlightening conversation for me."

 os os os

When Quinn called at the vicarage later that afternoon, he was sent directly to the study, although Mr. Rorty did not arrive for nearly half an hour. When the vicar came bustling in, apologizing for keeping his guest waiting, Quinn was reading a small devotional book he had taken from one of Rorty's many bookshelves. Quinn rose and placed it on the vicar's desk, next to the history book Lance had given him.

"Ah, I see you've run my errand," Rorty said. "My thanks for picking it up for me."

"No trouble at all, Mr. Rorty."

"Please, sit." Rorty picked up the book and sat in a chair next to Quinn's. "And if I may ask, what do you think of Domedale's mystic?"

"I think Mr. Lance would make an excellent mystic," Quinn replied. "He has both feet planted firmly on the ground, as any good mystic must."

"You say he *would* make an excellent mystic. Does this mean you don't think he is one?"

"I do no thinking myself, Mr. Rorty. My job is to find out what others are thinking."

"I suppose what I am asking," Rorty said dryly, "is what sort of article you expect to write for your newspaper."

"One in which all the truly interesting features are missing." Quinn pressed his fingertips together. "At this point, I can only conclude the obvious. Mr. Henry Lance reported a dream or vision. He also reported the discovery of a very valuable treasure box. But while Sotheby's is verifying his treasure as we speak, no one can verify his dream." He shrugged. "Fraud, coincidence, the subconscious, a miracle. Which choice in the matter people make says more about them than about Henry Lance and St. Alice of Lewes."

"I see," Rorty said, fanning the pages of the book absentmindedly. He glanced down, stopped what he was doing and said, "Hallo, what's this?"

"What's what?"

"There's some sort of incision," Rorty murmured as he looked at the inside back cover of the book. "But . . ."

Both men were silent for several seconds. When the silence was broken, it was Quinn who spoke.

"You're wondering where the paper is. You went to a lot of trouble for me to find it, and now you can't find it yourself."

"What do you mean?" Rorty asked in a tight voice. "If you found something in my book—"

"Oh, I've returned it. I'm no thief." Quinn tapped the devotional book he had set on Rorty's desk. "I put the sheet back where it belongs. You did rip an end leaf out of this book yesterday afternoon, didn't you?"

"What do you mean?" Rorty asked again.

Quinn shook his head. "You're not very good at this sort of thing, you know. I told you I'm a journalist. I spend more time than any honest man could stand talking with scheming liars. A strictly average liar would bluster his way through this interview without giving a hint to a third party that anything was wrong. You look guilty enough to hang."

Rorty's eyes narrowed. "I think you ought to leave now."

"The mechanics are all of a common or garden variety," Quinn continued. "Everyone in the village knew the Lances were in London yesterday, and that note couldn't have taken you very long to write. You must know enough about antiquarian writing to fool a casual observer like me, at least long enough for your purposes. You probably had the note tucked safely inside the book before dark, although we both know they couldn't get back by train and car much before eleven."

He wagged his index finger in the air. "But I'm assuming that you didn't think of this until you met me, and decided in the vestry to plant something in the book. It is possible you had been waiting for a gullible journalist to come around and retrieve it for you, though I would hope you could come up with a better plan if you had more than a minute or two to devise it.

"Whichever the case, you next made sure I would get the book. A man less insistent on letters of introduction than

Henry Lance can't be imagined, so your purpose in writing one can only have been to impose on my good nature to run your errand for you. A chancy thing, to depend on the good nature of the press, but it worked.

"Then you have left me alone in a room for half an hour with, as it might seem to you, nothing to do but paw through the book I'd brought you, with luck finding the note myself. Alas, an unsupervised journalist doesn't scruple at rummaging through a vicar's office. I spent the time searching books of the same size and color as the paper to see if I could find a match." Again he tapped the book on the desk. "The tear matches perfectly."

"What makes you think I wrote the note?" There was a defiant note in Rorty's voice, but Quinn laughed at the question.

"Oh, come now. The paper came from your book, you knew where it was hidden, and," Quinn reached into his pocket, "I have here what I'm certain are quill shavings I found in your dustbin. Yes, I apologize for my scurrilous behavior, but I've grown used to rooting through others' garbage. I am certain these shavings came from the goose feather, or possibly a duck feather, you used to forge the note. If you can give me another reason you'd have quill shavings in your dustbin, I'll withdraw the charges."

Rorty said nothing, and Quinn took a deep breath. "But if you mean what made me take the trouble to search your garbage and your bookshelves, what made me suspect you in the first place, it was a conversation I had with Dr. Drake at lunch. I'd heard about a discussion you had with him regarding Lance's vision, but I heard it exactly backward. I didn't realize until I'd spoken with Dr. Drake that it must have been he who argued for there being more to life than meets the eye, while you insisted it was at best coincidence."

"Coincidence!" Rorty snorted.

"But the puzzle that remains is why? Why go to all this trouble to convince me that Lance got the idea of hidden treasure from a purely natural source? Who would think otherwise simply because he spoke of visions?"

Rorty laughed sharply. "You don't know very much about human nature, do you? You don't know how readily people throw away their common sense whenever a charlatan comes along and promises them an easy way. Especially when life is so hard. Have you considered how expensive hope can be, when it's borrowed against in return for an empty promise?"

He leaned toward Quinn, speaking rapidly. "What was it you said? Fraud, coincidence, subconscious, miracle? You've met Henry and Anne Lance, and you can still suggest it could be a miracle? What sort of god do you worship? One that showers riches on some witless farmer in thanks for a kind word to a pile of bones that have been dead for a thousand years? That can let something like the War happen, then turn around and make some fool rich because he said please? Is that what you think Christianity is about?"

"The doctrine of grace—" Quinn began with a wry smile, but Rorty shouted him down.

"The doctrine of grace be damned! I'm not talking about a theological castle built on clouds. I'm faced, every day, with what people have, and can expect to have, and have a right to have, right here, in this life. I won't let them believe in some capricious fairy godmother who just might solve all their problems with a magical treasure chest. I can't have them hoping for something there's no hope for in this life." In a voice gone suddenly dull, he added, "False hopes are for the next life."

Quinn stared at Rorty for a long moment before saying, in the same flat tone, "Mother of God, what has it come to when the village atheist is the parish priest?"

Then he rose and left the room.

RHYS BOWEN

∞ ∞ ∞

Rhys Bowen is the creator of the Constable Evans mystery series, set in the mountains of Snowdonia, North Wales. She is British by birth, and childhood summers spent in a little village in Wales were the inspiration for her setting and eccentric characters. After working for the BBC, Rhys decided to write what she likes to read. Now on its fourth book, the Constable Evans series has won critical acclaim and devoted fans. The second book, *Evan Help Us*, was nominated for a Barry Award, for best novel of 1998.

THE SEAL OF
THE CONFESSIONAL

BY RHYS BOWEN

It had been a slow afternoon for confessions. Not that there were anything but slow afternoons these days—unless national disasters threatened. Nobody believed in hell anymore, thus seeing no need to confess sins. Not more than a hundred souls showed up at Sunday masses either, very different from the good old days when he had been a young priest and churches were packed.

Father Mike Costello shifted uncomfortably on the hard seat. There was no sound except for the sigh of the wind through the church tower and the new watch his parishioners had given him for his twenty-fifth anniversary, ticking the seconds away. It was too dark to see in the narrow confessional. He wondered how late it was. At least half past three, anyway. Surely nobody else would come now. All of the old faithfuls had already been: Miss Connor, who never had any sins to confess but managed to invent some misdemeanor or other, Mrs. Heathley and young Liam, who was serving at Mass in the morning and wanted to get in father's good books by showing up at confession. He was too holy by half, that one. And rubbed it in too. He'd probably wind up as pope! Father Mike smiled to himself. Not like himself in some back-of-beyond parish on the West Coast of Ireland. But then he'd never had much ambition. And now he was past the age when any kind of promotion was likely and he didn't care anymore. All he wanted was time for his garden, a good book, a good fire and his pipe.

He wondered if he could slip away early today. Nobody would ever know and his garden was calling to him. He had

had a shipment from the seed company this morning and exciting packets of runner beans, peas, and marrows were waiting to be planted. Moreover, it had been a bright, brisk spring day when he had entered the little box an hour earlier. In this part of the world bright days were to be treasured and made the most of. He had already turned the soil and it lay there, moist and rich as plum cake, waiting for his new seeds.

This year he'd been extravagant and ordered some flowers too. He'd got sweet peas and phlox seeds and lily of the valley bulbs waiting to be planted. He had always loved lily of the valley since he was a small boy. Fairy bells—that's what his grandmother used to call them. And only fairies were allowed to touch them too, she'd told him . . . He sat up with a start. He hoped Mrs. O'Hare hadn't discovered them on his desk and thought they were onions! A very interfering woman—Mrs. O'Hare. He didn't know why he put up with her, except that it was hard to find anyone willing to take care of an elderly priest for very low wages these days. Then he remembered that she'd muttered something about popping down to the shop for some milk to make a custard, which should mean she'd be out for the whole afternoon. There was nothing Mrs. O'Hare loved to do more than gossip—apart from rearranging his desk so that he couldn't find anything.

Father Mike had half decided to take a peek outside and then beat a well-timed retreat. He had risen from the seat when he heard the sound of approaching footsteps—heavy, even, measured. Definitely not one of the women of the parish with their light tapping heels or soft, reverend creeping. He put his eye to the convenient crack in the door and gasped when he saw a large dark shadow right in front of him. It was almost as if the person knew Father Mike was peeking and was staring back. But after a second or two the shadow moved away. Father Mike heard the door to the penitent's side of the box open and a wheeze of exertion as someone sank to the kneeler.

Father Mike slid back the grille and gave the customary blessing to the shadow behind the grille.

"Bless me, Father, for I have sinned." The voice was male. Soft like many of the locals, but that might just be in deference to the current surroundings. "It's been . . . years since my last confession and during that time—"

A long silence.

"Father?"

"Yes, my son?"

"Father, it's still true about the seal of the confessional, isn't it? I mean, anything I tell you here—"

"Anything you tell me here is between you and me and God. It goes no further."

"Oh, thank you, Father. You don't know what a relief that is. It's been preying on my mind for so long."

"Go ahead, my son. There's nothing you can say that will shock me or surprise God, you know."

Another long pause. The new watch ticked loudly. Outside Father Mike thought he could hear the waves crashing on the distant shore. He was about to give the man another encouraging prompt when he blurted out, "Father, you remember Maggie MacMahon?"

Father Mike didn't for a moment. Then a picture formed in his head—two long blond plaits, dancing out behind a little girl as she skipped out of church and her mother called after her not to go dancing about like some heathen after she'd just received the blessed sacrament.

"The little girl?" he asked. "The one who used to come here for the summers and who"—he tried to form the words—"who was murdered?"

"That's the one." Long pause. "It was me, Father. I did it." Father Mike fought to control his voice. "Are you telling me that you killed that little girl?"

"And the others."

Father Mike remembered all too clearly now. It had been at least ten years ago now. Three little girls, each of them holiday visitors, had disappeared, one after the other. Their bodies had been discovered, months later, buried in similar shallow graves. And the police had never got close to finding the killer. It was a wild stretch of coast with few people even in the summer. Nobody had seen anything. And little girls are easy to spirit away. . . .

"Three little girls," he said heavily. "You're telling me that you killed the three of them?"

"Yes, Father. I didn't mean to. At least, not the first time. She cried out, you see, and I put my hand over her mouth to keep her quiet. I've got big hands, Father. It took a moment to realize she wasn't breathing anymore."

Father Mike felt sick. He tried to fight down the anger that was rising. The voice behind the grille sounded so soft, so gentle, so reasonable. He must have looked like a gentle, reasonable man to get little girls to go with him, Father Mike thought.

"I didn't want to harm her, Father. I swear that. She came into my shop to buy sweets. I run—I used to run the newsagents by the car park at St. Finan's Bay. She came in with her mum one day. She stood there in the doorway with the sun shining on that golden hair like a halo. I thought she looked like a little angel. Next time she came in alone. I took her out the back to show her my rabbits. I just wanted to touch that hair—to stroke it but she got scared and said she'd tell her mum. I grabbed her. She started screaming. And . . . I put my hand over her mouth." Father Mike heard a big, heavy sigh. "After that I didn't know what to do. I knew they'd be coming looking for her. I stuffed her into one of the rabbit hutches and covered her with straw. Then that night, I took her up to the hills and buried her."

"And the others?" Father Mike asked. He tried to sound detached and professional. "Were they accidents too?"

"I was just turning them into angels," the voice said, still calm and reasonable.

"Turning them into angels?" Too loud again. He swallowed hard.

"Just like it was with Maggie. I carried her in my arms and all that lovely hair was soft against my cheek. It suddenly occurred to me—she looked like a little angel and now she really was a little angel. I'd helped her become one. She'd have no chance to grow up and sin and get ugly and old. She'd be young and lovely forever, up there with God. So when I saw the other little girls, I thought . . ." He left the words hanging. "That can't be so bad, can it, Father? More like a good thing, really."

Not so bad? He wanted to yell. You left three grieving families. You snuffed out three little candles of hope. But he mastered himself and said in a measured voice, "You know very well what the commandment says, don't you?"

No answer.

"Don't you?"

"Thou shalt not kill." Yes, I know. That's why I came here, Father. I don't want to go to hell. I want peace of mind, Father."

"For me to give you absolution, I have to be sure that you've truly repented of these sins. Have you truly repented?"

"Oh, yes, Father. I was sorry instantly."

"And yet you repeated the offense, didn't you?"

"A madness must have been on me, Father. It's been ten years now and I haven't touched a little child since. I want peace."

Father Mike adjusted his position on the hard bench. Do your job, he commanded himself. You are not the judge here.

"Very well, make an act of contrition."

"I've forgotten the words, Father."

Father Mike spoke it, line by line, and the voice repeated.

"And with God's help I will not sin again," he concluded.

Father Mike lifted his hand and traced the sign of the cross in the air as he spoke the words of absolution. His hand felt as heavy as lead.

"I'm glad you finally decided to come forward and make a clean breast of things," he said. "It must feel better now to have that off your chest before you go and turn yourself in."

"Oh, no, Father." The voice sounded shocked. "I'm not turning myself in. Whatever gave you that idea? I couldn't. They'd send me to prison, wouldn't they? And I know what they do to child molesters in prison. I couldn't take it. But don't worry—I'm going away. Far, far away from this place. I leave for America in the morning."

"America?"

"That's right. I've got a cousin in Chicago. I can stay with her until I get settled. It's what I need. A new start in a new place where nobody knows me."

Father Mike swallowed hard again. "And what's to say the madness won't come on you again, my son?"

"I told you, Father. It's been ten years. I've fought against the temptation that long. I can keep fighting against it "

"Do you not think you need professional help?"

"I've had professional help, Father. I came to you."

"I was thinking more of counseling, therapy, guidance with your problem."

"I don't have a problem anymore, Father, I told you. I moved away from the beach. I shut myself away with my books. I'm sure I'll be able to resist it in America."

Father Mike got to his feet. "I sincerely hope so."

He came out of the box at the same time as the man. He recognized him right away. Those bright blue eyes and that chubby innocent face with its wisps of white hair around it. He had been at Maggie's funeral, standing alone by the big yew tree in the churchyard. Then he had taken the man for a kindly uncle, alone and devastated in his grief.

The man held out his hand. "Thanks again, Father. This

means a lot to me."

Father Mike shook the proffered hand. The man turned to walk away. On impulse Father Mike called after him: "Look, would you like a cup of tea before you go? I was just about to have one myself."

The cherubic face broke into a big smile. "I don't mind if I do."

"This way." Father Mike led him out of the church door, down the path beside the yew hedge and into the rectory garden.

"Going to do some planting, are you, Father?" the man commented. "I'm a bit of a gardener myself."

"Are you now?" Father Mike's eyes lit up. "I just got a shipment of seeds and bulbs today. I was hoping to get started this afternoon, while the weather is fine."

"Don't let me stop you then, Father. I'll be on my way."

"Oh, no. I was going to have a cup of tea anyway. Hearing confessions always gives me a powerful thirst."

He opened the front door and ushered the man into the cool, slate-tiled entry hall. "Mrs. O'Hare?" He called. "I've a gentleman for tea." He waited, then shook his head. "Dammit, where is the woman. Never here when she's needed. Oh, well, why don't you go on into the parlor and I'll make the tea myself. I might be useless, but I can boil water."

He opened the door on his right. It was a comfortable room with a lived-in look. The walls were lined with books. Long windows looked out on the distant ocean. The sofas were covered in worn chinz. Newspapers were piled on the table next to a vase of snowdops. There was a big fire in the fireplace.

"I'll be back in a jiffy," Father Mike said. "Make yourself at home."

Once inside the kitchen he stood with his heart hammering, resting his bulk against the familiar firmness of the door. "There's no other way," he said to himself. "You know what you've got to do. Now do it."

He glanced across at the telephone on the wall. Then he took down a small saucepan, rummaged around, filled it with water, and set it to boil. While he waited he poured himself a cup of tea from the pot which always sat ready on the hob by the fire. Then he set a tray with milk and sugar and waited for the water to boil. His hand was trembling as he carefully poured boiling water onto the tea bag in the cup.

The man had chosen the armchair by the fire. Father Mike's armchair.

"Here we are," he said, attempting a smile as he put down the tray. "Help yourself to milk and sugar."

"Thanks. I will." The man took a spoonful of sugar and a generous amount of milk. Then he drained the cup in a several large swallows. "Ah, that hit the spot," he said. He rose to his feet. "Now I must be going, if you don't mind. I've got a lot to do before I catch the flight in the morning."

Father Mike followed him to the front door and opened it. "I wish you a good journey, my son," he said. "Godspeed."

He watched the man walk down the path to the road, then down the road until he vanished behind the hedge.

He was just clearing up the kitchen when the door opened behind him. He felt his heart almost leap out of his chest.

"What on earth are you doing, Father?" came Mrs. O'Hare's accusing voice.

"Just making a cup of tea, woman. Keep your hair on."

"But there's a full pot on the hob. I told you I'd made a full pot before I left. And what on earth were you doing using the saucepan when we've got a perfectly good kettle?"

"What is this, the Spanish Inquisition over again?" Father Mike demanded. "I had a guest for tea and he told me he couldn't take his tea strong, so I made him a fresh cup with a tea bag. And you know very well I'm not good at picking up that wretched kettle without burning myself. Now, if you don't mind" he gathered up the seed packets from the kitchen table "I've got planting to do. I've been looking forward to it all day."

"Make sure you get those horrid bulbs planted," she called after him. "You're lucky I didn't mix them up with the onions, lying right there on the kitchen table. I knew a family down at Cahersiveen—the mother put lily of the valley bulbs in the soup by mistake. Killed the lot of them, just from drinking the juice.

"Don't worry, I'll plant them," Father Mike called after him. He intended to plant them right away. He didn't think they'd grow though. Cooking killed most things.

He wasn't really surprised to hear that a man had collapsed and died on the four o'clock bus to Kenmare. The doctors decided it was a heart attack. Poor man. And just when he was all set to go to America too. The excitement must have been too much for him.

The next day Father Mike went to see Father Connelly at St. Brendan's and asked him to hear his confession. He knelt on the penitent's kneeler in the narrow dark box and tried to decide if he felt real remorse . . .

The grille opened.

Father Mike crossed himself.

"Bless me, Father, for I have sinned," he said.

John Lutz

⚮ ⚮ ⚮

John Lutz is the author of more than thirty novels and
two hundred short stories, as well as many articles and
book reviews. He is a past president of Mystery Writers
of America and Private Eye Writers of America, and his
work ranges from political thrillers to psychological
suspense. Lutz's novel *SWF Seeks Same* was made into
the hit movie *Single White Female*, and he co-authored
the screenplay for the movie *The Ex*, adapted from his
novel of the same title. He is the recipient of the Edgar
Award, the Shamus Award, the PWA Life Achievement
Award, and the Trophy 813 Award for best mystery
short story collection translated into the French language. His latest books are *Final Seconds*, co-authored
with David August, and a collection of short stories,
Until You Are Dead.

DILEMMA

BY JOHN LUTZ

The streets teemed with thousands of people watching the parade as it left the square built by Spanish conquerors, wound through the financial district, then proceeded down the Paseo de Flores, which was the city's downtown shopping area. Despite the fact that it was only one o'clock in the afternoon, many in the crowd seemed to have drunk too much as they jostled each other and lunged reaching for the shell necklaces and carved trinkets tossed from the costumed people riding on the floats. Standing near the ornate entrance of Jurado's Department Store, Police Corporal Alana Martinez, newly graduated from the Law Enforcement Academy, found herself watching the All Feast's Day Parade with the rest of the crowd, and from time to time had to remind herself that she was on duty.

And duty was what interested Alana most, even on this day of celebration before the beginning of Lent. The city's police force, like much of the rest of the government, was corrupt. It was new officers like Alana who had vowed to return integrity to the department, to regain the trust of the citizens. A new country was gradually but surely being born, one in which the directions of right and wrong were clearly marked, and those roads followed.

She knew it was because of her newness as a policewoman that she'd been assigned to this wealthy stretch of the parade route where there would be a minimum of trouble. Most of the crowd here was from the nearby luxury neighborhood of Jacaranda or the luxury condominiums that lined the downtown oceanfront. So Alana found herself almost as much spectator as police officer. There was no real need for crowd control among the rich, who had little reason to riot or steal.

Ten minutes ago Lieutenant Ordaz had contacted Alana on her

walkie-talkie and asked if everything was in order, then began flirting with her.

She had curtly reported that everything was fine, then cut him off. Alana was an attractive woman in her twenties who enjoyed good times, but not when she was working. She took her job far too seriously to flirt.

She was looking at a beautiful white cocktail dress on a mannequin in the department store show window when in the glass's reflection she noticed a man in dark clothing roaming the edges of the crowd. He was acting suspiciously, and not many people dressed in black in this climate.

When Alana turned around she noticed the white collar and was relieved to see the man was a priest, and one she recognized but didn't know personally. The young and handsome Father Miguel of St. Andrew's parish.

He was a medium-height, slender man whose direct and compassionate dark eyes had caused many a female parishioner to muse on what a waste it was for him to have chosen the church rather than marriage.

Alana was about to turn back to admiring the dress when she saw something extraordinary. So quickly and deftly that it wouldn't have been noticeable to anyone not looking directly at it, Father Miguel simultaneously bumped into, apologized to, and picked the pocket of a hefty man trying to see through the crowd to the parade.

It had all been so smooth and practiced that Alana thought her eyes might have played a trick on her. Surely she had not seen what she thought she had seen!

But St. Andrew's parish was in the *barrio* where the parade would eventually be passing through narrow streets. Why wasn't its priest there, where he would be watching it among people he knew and administered to in his church?

Father Miguel strolled a few meters down the block, and Alana surreptitiously followed and watched.

There! Again!

Father Miguel bumped into another prosperous-looking man and with incredible speed and nimbleness removed the man's wallet and slipped it beneath his priest's black shirt.

Had the pickpocket been anyone other than a priest, Alana would have stormed him, handcuffed him, and only then would have called for assistance. But this was a priest, and a good one. It was Father Miguel who'd talked a teenage friend of Alana's brother out of joining a gang of juveniles who terrorized the *barrio*. It was Father Miguel who had defied the wrong kind of police and given the last rites to a young robber shot outside a bank; Father Miguel who had talked some of the city's high-priced restaurants into donating their almost-spoiled food to the poor rather than throwing it away. And often the poorest and most desperate of families were given generous financial help by his church. Alana now better understood how that last was possible.

However ill-gotten the gains, this priest had done good work. There were those in the *barrio* who considered him almost a saint.

Wouldn't the arrest of such a man cause the community more harm than good? Harm to the *barrio* where Alana herself had grown up and left only after graduating from the university and joining the department? And perhaps there was a reason for what the priest was doing. Maybe he was ill, a kleptomaniac who couldn't help himself. If that was the case, wouldn't it be better for all concerned if he found help rather than a prison cell?

Alana—newly created Police Corporal Martinez—could not bring herself to arrest this priest. Instead of doing what she knew was her duty, she was paralyzed by doubt. Street crime and government corruption she was prepared to fight with all her soul and with a clear sense of duty, but this was different. This required consideration. The choice between right and wrong, integrity and corruption, was proving to be not so simple.

She turned and walked in the opposite direction, away from the priest.

∞ ∞ ∞

That night she slept fitfully, waking every few hours to lie quietly in the dark with her mind working furiously. Her duty as a policewoman was clear, but to perform it would undoubtedly result in taking food from the mouths of the poor. For Alana, there seemed to be no guiltless course of action. It wasn't until morning that she thought of a compromise, a way out of her dilemma.

Her shift didn't start until four o'clock that afternoon, so after breakfast she put on a modest blue dress, beige pumps that matched her purse, and walked the five blocks to St. Andrew's Cathedral.

It was one of the city's oldest churches, constructed by the Spanish to resemble the great cathedrals in Europe. Its stones were darkened by age, its flying buttresses and soaring spires impervious to time and change.

Much of its interior was the same as it had been hundreds of years before, and it was dimly lit despite the arched stained-glass windows lining its south wall. It took a few seconds for Alana's eyes to adjust to the faint light.

Father Miguel had recently finished mass and was still wearing his vestments. As he noticed Alana and walked up the center aisle toward her in all his pristine finery, what she'd seen yesterday seemed all the more incredible.

He smiled at her, obviously not recognizing her. "Are you one of my parishioners? If not, you're still welcome."

"I live nearby," Alana said nervously. This would be more difficult than she'd imagined, but it would free her of her burden. She remained determined.

Father Miguel watched her, waiting for her to say more.

"I'm here because I have doubts," she stammered.

His smile widened. "Then you've come to the right place. I'll help you if I can. Or if you'd rather simply sit and contemplate, or pray . . ."

Alana shook her head.

"What is it that you doubt?" Father Miguel asked.

"Myself. I'm a policewoman, Father, and I see so much corruption."

"It depresses you?"

"Of course, but I expected that."

"Ah! You fear that you might become a part of it."

"Yes. I have a decision to make. Because I am a police officer and am sworn to fight that corruption."

"I'm afraid your work will be difficult, Alana, even if worthwhile. This is a country in which ninety percent of the wealth is controlled by five percent of the people. Every aspect of government is corrupt, and those who suffer the most are the poorest.

"Here in the *barrio* those who speak against the government mysteriously disappear. Youth gangs steal for food and fight among themselves, until one day their members also join the disappeared. Mothers steal only to feed their children. They are not evil people, Alana. They are forced by the system to do evil things."

She realized that he'd called her by name. So he had finally recognized her. Or knew more than he pretended. "Everything you say is true, Father, but don't we all bear responsibility for our actions? Isn't that what the law is about? What the church is about?"

"The laws of man are made by man, the church's laws by God."

"But how can I and others like myself change the system if we're forced to become a part of it?"

"That's an ancient question, Alana. I don't have a convenient answer." Father Miguel motioned with his arm and began walking slowly, leading her toward the alter and confessional booths, deeper into the church.

"We all must look into ourselves," he said, "confront our own conflicts, and not expect perfection. We are nothing more nor less than human." At the front of the church, beneath the giant crucifix, they paused. "Have you any ideas on how to solve your own personal dilemma?"

Alana had, and perhaps it was a coward's way, but it was the best she could do. She would make her dilemma Father Miguel's.

Wasn't that why he was here, to bear the burdens of our sins?

Then why not his own sins? Alana had done nothing wrong— it was he who had stolen. Let the dilemma, the burden, be his.

"I'd like to confess, Father."

He looked searchingly at her, then nodded and turned. She watched the sweep of his vestments as he went through an oak door behind the alter.

After waiting a few minutes, Alana entered the first of the confessionals.

She had been there before. As a child when she'd stolen money from her mother's purse, and later as a teenager after her first sexual experience. Both long before Father Miguel had arrived at St. Andrew's. Now she laid her own purse on the small shelf near the latticework that separated her from the priest. It was dim in the confessional, and she couldn't make out his features on the other side of the tightly woven wood lattice.

Only his voice and absolution could penetrate.

Alana began: "Forgive me, Father, for I have sinned. I failed in my duty. Yesterday while I was helping to monitor the crowd watching the parade, I saw someone commit a crime and didn't take action or report it."

"Why didn't you?" There wasn't yet anything in his voice to indicate he thought she might be talking about him.

"I couldn't bring myself to act. It seemed wrong for me to arrest this man, though I knew it was my duty."

Father Miguel was silent for a long time, and when he spoke his voice was now slightly different. "What sort of crime was it?"

"I saw a man, a pickpocket, steal the wallets of two men watching the parade."

"Were they prosperous men, among the city's richest and most powerful? Men who had work, jobs to go to?"

"I'm sure they were, but I'm sworn to protect and serve them."

"As am I. Alana, why didn't you arrest this pickpocket? What stopped you from performing your duty?"

She had to force the words from her throat, and they felt jagged. "The pickpocket was a priest, Father."

"Perhaps he was merely wearing priest's clothing. As a disguise."

"No, he was a priest. I recognized him." She was sure she could hear Father Miguel's labored breathing on the other side of the ancient latticework. The confessional became stifling and seemed to close in on her. She was perspiring and wiped her forehead so the salt of her sweat wouldn't sting her eyes.

"What do you intend to do, Alana?"

"I decided to make it the priest's dilemma rather than mine. His decision. To me that seems fair."

"But that is impossible. The matter is between you and God."

Alana didn't answer. She was already throwing open the confessional door.

". . . impossible, Alana. Alana?"

She bolted and ran up the center aisle, then through the old marble vestibule of the cathedral.

It wasn't until she was outside in the square, in the bright sunlight, and could see the glass towers of the new financial district buildings glittering imposing and somehow reassuring in the distance, that she stopped running and walked.

What she had done in a church! And to a priest! She was still shaking.

But she had accomplished what she'd set out to do. The dilemma was no longer hers; it was now the priest's. She was sure he would either turn himself in or stop stealing. The choice was his alone, as was the burden.

Either way, the thievery would stop.

Her duty was done.

Near the Fountain of the Saints, which had been dry for years, Alana sat down on a low stone wall and dabbed at her moist eyes with a tissue.

Only when she put the tissue back in her purse did she realize that her wallet was missing.

Alana bowed her head and began to sob.

Joyce Christmas

Joyce Christmas is the author of the Lady Margaret Priam and Betty Trenka mystery series (Fawcett Gold Medal). Her short stories have appeared in *Ellery Queen's Mystery Magazine* and in numerous anthologies such as *Malice Domestic V*; *Murder, They Wrote*; *More Murder, They Wrote*; and *Women of Mystery*. Her short story "Takeout" was nominated for a McCavity Award.

THE CHOSEN

BY JOYCE CHRISTMAS

"Remember me telling you about Rose Costello?" My husband barely managed to tear his eyes away from the Sunday *New York Times* sports page and its ruminations on the early days of the baseball season, the closing days of the professional basketball and hockey seasons. When he finally met my eye, he had that blank expression that meant he didn't want to know what I was talking about, but after all these years, he couldn't fool me. He just let me talk on, repeating things he'd heard before.

"She was my best friend back in Bayleyville when I was a kid." And how that happened was beyond my Yankee mother's control. Rosie was Irish, and Catholic, of course. "At least your little friend isn't Polish," my mother once said, suggesting that there were degrees of being Catholic. From the point of view of her rock-solid Congregationalism, in the midst of a heavily Slavic small town in Connecticut at the edge of the Litchfield Hills, perhaps there were.

Well, it just happened. Rosie's family and mine were neighbors, living around the corner from each other. We played together when we were little, and, in fact, my mother and Mrs. Costello were quite friendly as small-town neighbors often are. I guess I probably noticed early on that my mother did assume a certain aura of superiority when in Mrs. Costello's presence. My mother, I realized years later, believed she was what passed for upper class in a basically working-class town.

Rosie and I went to the same public schools, but had there been a Catholic parochial school in the town, Rosie's mother would certainly have sent her there to be educated by the nuns. Alas, Bayleyville was too small to attract teaching sisters and brothers for a Catholic school, so she and I went to Hill Street Elementary, and on to Bayleyville High. There was a Catholic girls' high school a few towns away, but the Costellos could never figure out how Rosie could be transported there and back on a daily basis. Our part of Connecticut didn't have much public transport, and Rosie's father's job at Bayley Manufacturing didn't allow him the time to drive her there.

Still, Mary Costello saw to it that Rose fulfilled all her obligations to her religion, studying her catechism and attending Mass faithfully. Rosie's mother prayed constantly that her youngest daughter would find a religious vocation like her aunt, Sister Angela, a formidable nun who visited the Costellos occasionally. Sister Angela's severe black and white habit frightened me, and although Mrs. Costello deplored the new trend for sisters to wear civilian dress, Sister Angela appeared to be firmly attached to her traditional habit. She treated me kindly enough, as though charitably taking into account my near-pagan upbringing. Now and then, I would attend a special service at Saint Agnes Church with Rosie to mark some holy day. Sister Angela approved, presumably thinking it was a step toward capturing an errant soul for her faith. I was quite taken with the flickering candles in front of the saints' shrines and the scent of incense and the dark, quiet corners where the faithful knelt and prayed, but I knew that it was not for me, even as I admired Rose's dedication to her beliefs. Mother, of course, disapproved.

"I remember her," Charlie my husband said finally. Then he went back to his paper, but said from behind it, "You told me about her almost the day we met. And when we went up to Bayleyville for your father's burial, we stopped at her family's house but no one was home. You showed me the place where she supposedly had a vision. I always think of her as the hallucinator."

"Charlie … " The warning in my voice was clear. "I always think of her—of it—as a great mystery."

He lowered his paper. "Sorry, Julia. You know how God stuff makes me uncomfortable."

"It was more than that, you know." I tried not to be irritated. "It was much more." But I knew that Charlie wouldn't want to discuss what happened so long ago in the turbulent sixties filled with war and protests, and one small miracle that uncovered a great evil.

More than thirty years later, I could still see that spring afternoon, and the garden and the house once again. It was almost as if I was dreaming, but I knew I was sitting in the living room of my Manhattan apartment, only half awake on a warmish spring Sunday afternoon. At the same time, I was back in Bayleyville, Connecticut, on another warm spring day. I could smell the new grass, and hear the chirps of sparrows and robins in the trees. I could feel the sun as Rosie and I stumbled along the rough hillside path from the high school at the end of a school day in Bayleyville, in the middle of May. Rose Costello and I had taken the back way home from Bayleyville High where we were both freshmen, instead of going the long way around along Main Street and stopping at the soda fountain in Mercer's Pharmacy where the kids liked to gather after school. Rose seldom had time to stop at Mercer's. She had a lot of responsibilities at home after school, helping to fix supper for her big family, and giving her mother some respite by minding the little kids.

I was pretending to diet, as usual, and was trying to avoid ice cream sodas, but I knew Rose liked the chance to run into Donny Bayley, the senior boy she had a crush on. I thought he was kind of cute, but he was distantly related to me, so I never allowed my heart to beat faster at the sight of him chatting up the girls at Mercer's. Although Donny seemed to like Rose, I kept telling her it was hopeless to expect that the son of Harry

Bayley would fall for her, pretty though she was.

That day, we left the big redbrick school by the back door, walked across the pebbly playing field, squeezed through the gap torn out of the chain-link fence, then made our way down the steep, crooked path through untamed weeds and scraggly trees struggling to grow on the hillside. At the bottom of the hill, we found ourselves in the remnants of the garden that had been the glory of the old Bayley mansion.

The house still stood then, but it's gone now, replaced by the new Town Hall. Back then, it had been empty for years, with boarded-up windows except for the row of French doors on the ground floor looking out onto the garden behind the house. The glass doors were covered on the inside with ratty white curtains that hadn't been removed when the family abandoned the place. When I asked why nobody lived there anymore, my mother said that old Mrs. Harriet Bayley had taken sick after one grandson had been killed in the early days of the Vietnam War, and had just closed up the Colonial-style house and moved to Florida, never to return.

"She died a few years ago, and none of the other Bayleys left in town wanted to take on the burden of such a big place," my mother said. "I know I wouldn't." Then she'd drawn herself up proudly as if to remind me that she certainly could manage any house, and we could hold our heads up too, even though the Bayleys of Bayleyville were merely her second cousins. According to my mother, Old Harriet had disapproved of my mother's marriage to a man from out of town who wasn't on a par with the Bayleys, whose history went back to the Revolutionary War and included the founding of the town itself and the Bayley Manufacturing Company on which almost everyone in town still depended for a livelihood. "She stopped speaking to me—us," Mother said. "Her loss, if you ask me." Nevertheless, I fantasized that the mansion might have been ours, instead of crumbling away to dust.

The white paint of the old house was flaking and dingy, some of the black shutters dangled from their fastenings, and a drainpipe at the far end had fallen down and lay across a thick stand of irises like a great white club. Still, to our fourteen-year-old eyes, the house was a palace, three stories high, with a spacious sunporch on the side and a still-elegant front facade facing East Main Street but shielded by a stand of maple trees and mountain laurel bushes. There was a lustrous fanlight over the front door that I wished we had on our own simple but rambling Victorian house just up the street.

Naturally, both my mother and Rose's warned us about hanging around the old house. "Trespassing," my law-abiding mother called it. I wanted to argue that since we were a part of the family, I had a perfect right to be there, but I knew I wouldn't win. Mary Costello feared we'd encounter wicked men who would ravish us and destroy our girlish purity, especially Rose's, since she was marked down by Mary for a religious life. In fact, both mothers had been rightly insistent during the school year that was just ending about not going off to any secluded places.

Mary Jane Phillips, a girl in one of the upperclasses at school, had disappeared the past fall just as school opened, and had never been seen again dead or alive. It caused a great sensation in the town. Rosie's big brother Declan had been her classmate, and had even been among the many boys, and workers, at Bayley Manufacturing who had been questioned by the police about the disappearance. Declan had told Rosie that Mary Jane was wild and starstruck, and had probably run off to New York or Hollywood, and would show up in town someday, rich and famous. We were taken with that romantic plotline, since we didn't have many young runaways. Most of the young people were drained away when they were a bit older and could see that Bayleyville held few opportunities.

Then Declan had departed via the draft and been sent to fight in Vietnam. Mary Jane was gradually forgotten except for the residual fears of our parents. Rose and I continued to enjoy the guilty pleasure of visiting the grounds of the mansion.

Rose and I, together and separately, loved to walk around the old garden in all seasons, picking late-blooming asters in the fall, gathering fat cigar-shaped pinecones for Christmas decorations, making angels in the snow, spying out the first crocuses and violets in the spring. When we were little, before we got to be grown-up high school girls, we used to play out our fantasy games here, pretending to be captive princesses, royal ladies waiting for their shining knights, or fairy tale heroines like Rapunzel and Snow White and Sleeping Beauty. Rosie was especially good at making up stories and acting them out.

I often wondered if Rosie mentioned our adventures to Father John when she went to confession. According to my confused understanding, walking around a derelict garden shouldn't rank very high on the list of sins. Rose talked about an array of sins that I didn't understand, certainly not things our pastor ever mentioned as sins, and he would have. Reverend Smith was firmly against evil, and spoke fervently about avoiding it during his Sunday sermons. I was convinced that Catholics operated under a different definition of sin.

The garden hadn't fared much better than the house, but the plants refused to die, even as weeds choked the beds that Harriet Bayley's gardener had attended to carefully.

The grass was almost knee-high in places and the ornamental bushes had run wild, but now, in mid-May, the old irises, at least those that had escaped the crush of the drainpipe, stood like little purple- and yellow-capped soldiers, while a rambling rosebush that hadn't felt the snip of pruning shears in years erupted in a tangle of pink blossoms and glossy green leaves along the stone wall at the back of the garden. There were a few brownish, dead daffodil blossoms in clumps along the flagstone path from the French doors to the garden, and a few other perennials had the courage to bloom each spring through the years.

At the far end of the garden stood a couple of tall evergreens with branches that drooped to the ground—I knew later that they were Norwegian spruce. They made a cavern of shade, and in their midst a slender dogwood with outspread branches covered with white blossoms stood like a ghost, half in the sun and half in the evergreens' shade.

"I have to get home," Rosie said. "I can't wait for you." I had begged a little time to pick some pretty yellow flowers that grew along the mossy edge of an ornamental pool placed right there in the garden. The fountain in the middle was a cluster of stone cupids and dolphins. It had never worked in my lifetime, but I liked to imagine a spray of water shooting into the air, capturing rainbows.

"I really got to hurry. Ma needs me," Rose said. "Brian is sick again, and I have to stay with him while she goes to see Father John. Pa won't do it, he's worried sick himself about the factory maybe closing and Declan fighting in Vietnam." She looked so sad and anxious that I touched her soft cheek, then saw a tear on one of her thick, dark lashes. Rose was exotically pretty, while I knew that I was just a sturdy, plain schoolgirl.

"Don't worry," I said. "Your mother will pray for everybody."

Rosie nodded. "Even you, Julia," she said solemnly.

Rose's devout mother always had an appointment with a priest or a nun, or had to say special prayers to a saint, or attend a church service, and her children followed her lead. Sometimes I felt smug in my Congregationalist freedom from all those religious obligations that Rose had to attend to. I had only one younger brother who looked after himself, my mother didn't expect me to cook and sew, and my father wasn't a factory worker dependent on the continuing existence of Bayleyville's one manufacturing plant. He was an executive at a company in the next town, but the rumors of the pending sale of Bayley Manufacturing and the possible closing of the plant had reached even my uncaring ears, and it worried me. What would that mean to Rose and her family?

"Then I have to get supper because Ma has to do some sewing for Mrs. Bayley, even if she doesn't pay much," Rose said. This was the other Mrs. Bayley, the daughter-in-law of Harriet who had lived in the mansion and decamped. "Ma says we need the money because of Brian, and Pa's job going." Rosie looked at me accusingly, as if by virtue of being marginally related to the Bayleys of Bayleyville, it was my fault that her mother wasn't paid more, that her father might not have a job. Well, I couldn't be blamed for what Harry Bayley's wife paid Mrs. Costello. Actually, Harry and his wife should by rights be living in the boarded-up old mansion but they lived in another big white house in a better part of town and this one just sat here on East Main Street and fell apart bit by bit.

Donny Bayley, Rose's modest passion, was Harry's youngest son, and while he never acknowledged his tenuous relationship with me, he did acknowledge Rose occasionally, and Rosie managed to put herself in his way as often as she could, along with all the other girls who hung around Donny like the honeybees that sucked the sweetness from the flowers in the old garden.

I was going to tease Rosie about seeing her talking to Donny just that morning in the hall before homeroom, but then I took a closer look at her. She seemed sad and nervous. Her thick mop of black hair hung lifelessly to her shoulders, and her blue eyes lacked their usual sparkle. I wished I could cheer her up, so I just said, "What did Donny have to say?"

She wouldn't look at me. "Nothing. Just some stuff about wanting to show me a surprise. He said it wasn't far. . . ."

"No! Your mother would kill you if you went anywhere with him."

"I like him so much, Julia." She sighed. "But I know it would be wrong." Rose was so good and patient. I probably would have gone with him if he'd asked me, cousin or not.

"Wouldn't it be fun to live in a house like this?" I said brightly, to change the subject, repeating a sentiment I'd spoken often. "I don't know why the Bayleys bother to keep it."

Rose didn't seem to be listening to me. She was trailing around, looking at the patches of new flowers that had bloomed in the few days since we'd last been here.

"You said you had to get home," I said crossly. I eyed a lush patch of grass near the evergreens where I could lie down on my stomach and read *Katherine* by Anya Seton for a while and revel in the luscious romance of John of Gaunt and his ladylove in long-ago days. I practically knew the book by heart.

"I'm going," Rosie said faintly. But she was walking in the wrong direction, toward the evergreens' shade, a few steps ahead of me. "I just want . . . want to say a prayer for Brian. And Pa."

She stepped out of the sunlight into the deep shade under the spruces and fell to her knees. Well, I was accustomed to Rosie's spontaneous prayers. I reserved mine for Sunday services at our big white church on Main Street, but I understood that Rosie's was the Catholic way.

I saw her make the sign of the cross and take the rosary she always carried from her pocket. Her back was to me. She faced toward the dogwood tree, which glowed with an ethereal light from the ray of sun that evaded the heavy evergreen branches and found the ground. The dogwood stretched out its delicate white flower-laden branches like welcoming arms. I was patient, and accustomed to Rosie's moments of religious fever, so I stopped to pick a few pink rosebuds for my mother while I had the chance. Then I walked over to Rosie.

When I got close I was alarmed by how she looked. She was still kneeling, and her mouth was moving, but I heard nothing. Probably a silent prayer, but her eyes were fixed on the distant dogwood tree and she didn't blink once. Then I got scared. Her face was so pale against her black hair, like the color of the wax that dripped from the tall white candles Mother liked to light for special dinners. She seemed to be frozen in that spot.

"Rosie? Come on, you've got to get home. You said so."

No answer, but the scent from the roses I'd picked was suddenly so strong that I felt faint. A smile appeared on her face. It transformed her familiar pretty looks into something more beautiful than I'd ever seen. She was like an angel almost, or what I imagined an angel might look like. She was scarcely breathing.

"Rosie, are you all right?" Brian suffered from seizures, and I wondered if the same thing was happening to my friend. "Rosie!" I was pretty close to shouting, but still she didn't move. I went to her and touched her hand. It was cold, almost like marble, not at all like skin.

She didn't look at me, but whispered, "Do you see her?"

I looked around, but there was no one there, nothing was there except the dogwood tree, the empty shell of the house, and weed-choked flowerbeds.

"Julia, she's smiling at you. She wants you to kneel." She tugged at my skirt, but I wasn't going to do any such thing. If Rosie was playing one of our games, I wanted to know the part I was supposed to take. We always settled on the story beforehand. Now Rosie was nodding and smiling as if she were in pleasant conversation with someone.

"You're scaring me, Rose Costello. Get up at once." Rosie was always so malleable that I tended to get bossy with her.

Finally she looked at me, and she seemed as beautiful as any princess in my old book of fairy tales I'd put away as being too childish for a high school freshman. "It's all right," she said. "You don't have to kneel. She understands that you're different." Then she looked back at the spot she'd been staring at and waved. After a moment, she stood up, and dusted the grass from her knees.

"Who is 'she' anyhow? Are you nuts?" I didn't like this at all.

"Didn't you see her?" Rosie asked.

"What's there to see except an old dogwood tree and dead pinecones on the ground? What did you see?"

"It was . . . it was somebody, a lady dressed in a long white dress with a blue scarf around her shoulders. She spoke to me."

I shuddered. "It was probably the ghost of some old Bayley. Let's go. I don't like ghosts. They could be bad."

"She wasn't a ghost," Rose said serenely. "And not bad. She was beautiful and it made me feel good, just to look at her. I'd have been frightened if she was something bad, but I wasn't afraid at all."

"You saw an old dogwood tree that you just thought was a beautiful lady, like the ones we used to pretend to be when we were kids. You imagined it." I wanted to stamp my foot in my impatience. Then I said cautiously, "You haven't been trying any of that marijuana or LSD stuff the big kids are getting in trouble about." Even little Bayleyville wasn't isolated from the trends of the sixties.

"It wasn't my imagination," Rose said firmly. "And I don't have anything to do with drugs. She was there." Then she looked at me and frowned. "But promise not to tell anyone, not Ma, not your mother, about what I saw."

"I won't tell," I said. "I'll promise because you didn't see anything. I don't want people thinking I'm crazy too." I turned my back on her, so I was looking at the house with its French doors and raggedy curtains. Suddenly I felt a tight clutch of fear in my stomach. I could see someone standing inside the house, holding the thin drape aside a bit as he looked out at us. At least, I think it was a "he," wearing a white shirt and dark trousers, but the glass was so streaked and dirty, I couldn't be sure.

"Rosie, there's someone in the house. Act natural like there's nothing wrong."

"I don't see anybody," she said, and then I didn't either, but I knew someone had been there. Suddenly our mothers' warnings didn't seem so foolish.

"We've got to run. Now. Fast." I ran, avoiding the pool and the fountain, finding the flagstone path around the corner of the house, out onto the rutted driveway and then to the street. I could hear Rosie running behind me. I stopped on the pavement that ran along the street in front of the Bayley house to catch my breath and still my frantically beating heart.

"Didn't you see him?" I asked Rosie when she caught up with me. I knew that no one ought to be in the house, and I knew it meant something bad.

Rosie shook her head. "I might have seen the curtains move, but I'm not sure I saw anything like a person."

"Maybe it was the lady you thought you saw in the garden."

Rosie got very still. Her breathing was even, and color had come back to her cheeks, almost too much color. I wondered if she had a sudden fever. "No," she said firmly. "It couldn't have been the lady. She doesn't play tricks. You probably saw some kid who broke into the house. Pa says the Bayleys ought to have a watchman, to keep the vandals away."

"And strange ladies out of the garden," I said carelessly. Rosie's face changed at my words, and she seemed to be seeing her lady all over again.

"Don't joke about her, Julia," she said seriously. "She was so beautiful. She had a crown like stars, and I felt that she was protecting me."

Now I was certain Rose was pretending a fairy tale. "Oh, stop it. Beautiful ladies don't hang out in gardens full of weeds. They don't come to hick towns like Bayleyville, for heaven's sake. Admit it. You imagined it. But the guy in the house was real."

Rosie shrugged. "You saw someone in the house, and I saw the lady. Neither of us saw what the other did. Maybe they were both real. What's the difference?"

"He was real, and it sure scared me," I said, and felt another chill of fear.

"I wasn't scared at all when I saw the lady. She looked so kind and loving." She hesitated. "I think she came from heaven. Promise again you won't tell Ma or your mother, Julia."

"*You* didn't see anything," I said in my bossy voice, "but *I* did, and I'm not telling about that either. My mother would never let me take this shortcut from school again if she thought there was some criminal hiding out in the Bayley house." Rosie looked at me pleadingly, so I relented. "Anyhow, I already promised. What were you and this lady of yours talking about anyhow? I saw your mouth moving . . ."

Talk of ladies from heaven made me uncomfortable, but I had to admit that Rose was so good and saintly that maybe heaven did look kindly upon her, but the heaven I imagined didn't include visitors to Bayleyville.

"She said that I should pray and that she'd pray for me, and that everything would be okay, and evil would be found out and overcome."

"Is she coming back? I'd like to get a look at her."

Rosie nodded, very faintly. "She said I should come here in one week, but she didn't say she'd be here. And I'm not sure you'd be able to see her. You didn't see her today."

I was determined to be there next week, even if I was convinced that Rose's imagination had been working overtime, but as we walked along East Main Street toward home, I pondered the meaning of ladies from heaven, and tried to think who it might be. At Sunday school, we'd talked about Jesus and God the Father, but not much about heavenly ladies.

Then, unexpectedly, the light dawned, and I understood who Rose was talking about. Mary, Jesus' mother, was the only heavenly lady I could think of, and then I remembered the pictures of the Virgin Mary in Rose's home, and the statues I'd seen when I'd gone with Rose to her church painted white and blue with a crown of stars.

I had a sudden startling glimpse into the meaning of Rose's experience, and the comprehension of what it meant to have a heavenly creature walk among us flooded through me. I gulped and caught my breath, so shaken was I by my feeble understanding of the mystery.

I was completely overwhelmed. My little Protestant soul had been shaken to its depths by the awareness that just for a moment, a door had been opened between our world and another, and something miraculous had occurred. Rose held the key, and I had been more like the driver of the getaway car, or more correctly, the innocent bystander, but I somehow knew that I would never be the same.

"Did she tell you who she was?" I asked.

Rose smiled. "Not exactly. But I know."

I thought I knew too. And thirty years later, almost to the day, I still retained some of the wonder I had felt that afternoon. Charlie was frowning at me, fidgeting, and not willing to talk about the old days. Like Rose's experience, and my own revelation, it was personal, inexplicable.

"I never said it had anything to do with God or visions or anything like that, Charlie, even if other people did."

That seemed to satisfy him. He returned to his newspaper.

What happened to Rose, though, wasn't so simply finished. She moped around her house, worrying her mother, and in the end, I didn't tell, but Rose did, causing a flurry of concern. Father John was firm in his conviction that Rose was suffering from teenaged delusions arising from concern about her brother's health and her father's precarious employment status.

"Don't you worry about the girl," he told Mary. "She's been praying for a miracle for the family, and, well, sometimes girls of her age imagine things."

Of course, that wasn't the end of it. Word got about town

about Rose's vision, and some of the devout and just curious started gathering at the old Bayley mansion, much to the distress of the remaining Bayleys in town. My mother was appalled to think I'd been taken in by some Papist visionary business, but I said as little as possible.

Sister Angela decided to step in to talk sense into Rose, and it wasn't only Rose who had to face the sister. I too was summoned to an audience in the dim "best" parlor of the Costello home. She sat us down on the hard sofa and fixed us with a stern eye. Mary Costello hovered in the background, wringing her hands at her daughter's unseemly behavior.

"Rose, I understand you have been making up tales of a heavenly visitor," Sister Angela said seriously. "It is sinful to tell lies."

"No, Sister Angela, it wasn't a lie. Julia will tell you. . . ."

Sister Angela looked at me as though no spiritual truth could issue from the lips of a Protestant child. "What do you have to say, Julia?"

"I didn't see anything, Sister, but something did happen to Rose, really. She was . . . different. I remember that the roses I'd picked smelled so strongly I got dizzy, and Rose's skin was like cold, cold marble." By now, I truly believed that Rose had seen a visitor from heaven.

"Hmm. That proves nothing."

"Please believe me, Aunt Angela. I saw her, I really did. But I don't know where she came from. I never said who she was."

"But you imagine she was the Blessed Virgin, isn't that right? Now listen closely, Rose. Our Lady does not condescend to visit schoolgirls in an abandoned garden."

Rose's silence suggested stubbornness, and this did not please Sister Angela.

"'Blessed are the pure in heart for they shall see God,'" Sister Angela said softly. "Have you been pure in heart, Rose?"

"Oh, yes. I mean, I try to be."

I spoke up with some trepidation. "I believe Rose, Sister. I don't know who she saw, but she saw something. I believe that someone was there, even if I didn't see her."

"'Blessed are they that have not seen, and yet have believed.'" Sister was really speaking to herself, not us.

"I did see something, though," I said. "There was someone in the old Bayley house while we were in the garden. A man."

Sister Angela looked at me and then at Rose's mother. "And you, Rose, you plan to visit the garden again next week?"

"She asked me to come," Rose said.

So we went together, Rose and me, Mary Costello and Sister Angela, who made it clear that she was there merely to protect her niece and not to confirm the holy nature of the lady. It was another beautiful spring afternoon, and a gaggle of the curious and devout from the town straggled behind us. Rose knelt facing the dogwood tree whose whiteness was beginning to fade. I don't know that the lady appeared to her that day, but Rose believed to the end that her beautiful lady had come from heaven to summon her home and to save her from terrible evil.

She was changed forever after, refusing to play with me at fantasy games, attending ever more closely to her religious obligations and her responsibilities at home. She was almost too good for me, and gradually, we drifted apart. She didn't hang about Donny Bayley any longer, and eventually, to her mother's delight and relief, she chose to become a nun in one of the contemplative orders, retiring to a life of silence and prayer.

I never heard from her again, but when she died in her thirties, my mother wrote me to say that my little visionary friend had passed away. As for me through all the years since, as I journeyed through a conventional life—college, a job or two, marriage to Charlie the up-and-coming lawyer, a couple of kids, and now a comfortable life here on the Upper West Side of Manhattan—I had never forgotten that day and what came later.

All of the unwanted activity on the Bayley property led the family to reconsider the old house that had almost been forgotten by them. The family decided to renovate the place with an eye to moving in. That was when the body of poor Mary Jane Phillips was discovered, hidden away in a closet on the second floor.

Harry Bayley probably wished they had never bothered to reopen the place, because the state police quickly drew a net around Donny Bayley, ultimately proving that he had a key to the old house, and used the family mansion as a place to bring adoring girls for romantic trysts. One such meeting had gone awry, and he'd killed Mary Jane. Rose might well have been the next, but for her vision and its outcome. I don't know how Rose understood the events, but I was convinced that a greater power had had a hand in the outcome.

Some days I found the time to slip into St. Patrick's Cathedral on Fifth Avenue to light a candle in memory of Rose, wherever she might be today. In spite of my one moment of cosmic revelation, I never became a praying person or even much of a believer in any faith. I felt it was hypocritical to ask favors of a deity I wasn't on close terms with, but I did pray that Rose had truly been chosen.

"I'll never forget Rose," I told Charlie.

"You should. It's not healthy to keep brooding about so-called miracles. Miracles don't happen in this day and age."

I had to smile at that. Apparitions of heavenly creatures and the like were remote from the bustling streets of Manhattan, but I knew that miracles did happen to some people. Evil is overcome, and even if you don't see, you can believe, and be blessed.

GEORGE CHESBRO

❧ ❧ ❧

George Chesbro, creator of the Mongo, Veil and Chant mystery series, is the author of 23 novels and upwards of 100 short stories and articles, and a past Executive Vice President of Mystery Writers of America. The first ten Mongo novels were recently reissued in trade paperback.

MODEL TOWN

BY GEORGE CHESBRO

"Should I call you Father?"

"No. My name is Brendan Furie."

Father Gary Walsh smiled shyly, shifted in the chair behind the small desk in his small, bare office, then ran his hand back through his thick brown hair, which he wore in a blow-dried pompadour that made him look even younger than his twenty-four years. "Word's gotten around since you've been in town. I heard you used to be a priest, but you were excommunicated. Now you're a private investigator working on some special assignment."

"I think your story is far more interesting, Father Walsh. That's what we're here to talk about."

The young curate flushed. "Of course. I didn't mean to pry." He abruptly rose and stuck out a pink, pudgy hand, continued: "Call me Father Gary. Everybody does."

"Pleased to meet you, Father Gary. I appreciate your cooperation. You seem nervous. There's no need."

"I'm not nervous," the other man said quickly, dropping rather than sitting back down in his chair.

"Okay. That's good."

"I'm just kind of puzzled that Father Reilly would allow you to interview me—I mean, he made it plain that I should answer all your questions."

"Father Reilly was the first person I interviewed a week ago. I've also interviewed twenty-four of your parishioners who have seen the weeping Madonna, or had other miraculous experiences."

"There are a lot more than twenty-four."

"It's a sufficient number for the statistical sample I need. Since all of the unusual occurrences that have happened in Craiggville in the past three months began with you, I figured I'd end with you. Why are you puzzled?"

Again the curate shifted in his chair, fidgeted with his Roman collar. "It was Father Reilly, on the orders of the bishop, who told me to stop talking to the press. The bishop himself turned down an offer by one of those psychic researchers to come in and try to prove that the incidents were either really miracles or a hoax."

"It's not my task to prove or debunk anything, Father Gary. I do field research for a group that's studying human behavior in response to extraordinary events like the things that have happened here. I make no judgments on the events themselves, which is probably why your bishop and senior pastor agreed to cooperate. You shouldn't take their previous actions personally. You have to understand that, from the Church's point of view, the question of miracles puts them in a no-win situation. If the Church officially declares some incident to be a miracle and it turns out to be fake, the Church looks ridiculous; if they declare something a hoax, it discourages the faithful who may have come back to the Church because of what they perceive to be miracles. Usually the Church takes no position, which is the case here. I'm allowed to interview the people who believe, but I can make no pronouncement on the belief itself."

"They've already discouraged and driven away the faithful," Gary Walsh said, a trace of bitterness creeping into his high-pitched voice. "In the first few weeks after the miracles first began there were thousands of people flocking to Craiggville every weekend. There wasn't enough room for everybody at each Mass, and we had to install loudspeakers on the front lawn and in the parking lot. One weekend we had more than ten thousand people come here, and there were traffic jams on every road and highway in all directions. That was when the bishop ordered the publicity blackout. Now we're just about back to where we were before—a dying town with only maybe a quarter of the pews filled for

Sunday Mass. When God shows us a sign, you'd think the Church would want the whole world to know."

Brendan studied the other man—who seemed to be having trouble meeting his gaze—for a few moments, then said in a flat tone, "You do seem to be taking it personally. In the last two centuries the Church has officially recognized only a dozen weeping Madonnas and visions of Mary. New Jersey has more than that in a year."

Now the priest looked at Brendan out of the corner of his eye. "What did he say?"

"Who?"

"Father Reilly."

"Among other things, he said that the Madonna here in your church now weeps so much that he has to have a maintenance worker mop up the floor every morning."

"Did he say anything about me?"

"What people tell me is held in strictest confidence, Father. I probably shouldn't have shared with you what I just did."

"But everybody knows that that Madonna weeps all the time."

"Indeed."

"You can see for yourself."

"I have."

Father Gary Walsh swallowed hard, licked his lips, then said, "Okay, what do you want to ask me?"

Brendan opened the briefcase he carried, took out a small tape recorder and a five-page questionnaire, placed the items on the desk in front of the curate. "Actually, I'd prefer not to ask you much of anything. I'd like you to fill out this questionnaire, and then I'd like you to relate your story into the tape recorder. You can take as much time as you like."

Walsh nodded, reached out and pulled the questionnaire toward him. Brendan sat down in the only other chair in the room, leaned back, crossed his legs and waited as the other man leafed through the questionnaire.

"Some of this stuff is really personal," the young priest said, his face reddening. "In fact, I'd have sinned if I'd done some of these things."

"All of us have sinned, Father, and there's no admission you can make on that form that will threaten your mortal soul. I guarantee your privacy. You'll be assigned a code number, and your name will not appear on any report. It's important that you answer all the questions. If you can't do that, I'd prefer to end the interview now."

"I have to do it," the other man mumbled. "Father Reilly made it clear that I should cooperate."

"What happens in this room is between you and me."

Walsh shook his head, then hunched his shoulders and began to rapidly check off the boxes on the questionnaire. When he had finished he shoved the form to the edge of the desk. Brendan rose, slipped the questionnaire into his briefcase, then turned on the recorder and sat back down. He waited as the priest stared at the recorder. Walsh cleared his throat several times, but said nothing.

"Father Gary . . . ?"

"It's . . . uh . . . it's kind of hard to get started."

Brendan uncrossed his legs and leaned forward in the chair, resting his elbows on his knees. "Father Gary," he said in a neutral tone, "about three months ago you walked into this church and saw the Madonna in the apse outside the sanctuary, weeping. The statue is still weeping—literally in buckets. Since that time you've suffered stigmata twice.

"The Madonna in your parents' home weeps; in fact, there are weeping Madonnas everywhere you go. Since that first incident you've performed dozens of healings, and dozens of others have been performed in your name. People all over town have seen visions of Mary, and two families have seen the sun begin to spin and radiate all the colors of the rainbow. There have been six murders, three times the number Craiggville has had in the past decade, and a rash of teenage suicides. Considering—"

"The murders and suicides can't have anything to do with

the signs from God!"

"—all that's happened since you saw the first weeping Madonna, I would think you could spend hours recollecting your experiences and feelings."

"It's . . . just kind of hard. Maybe you could ask me questions?"

"All right. Tell me how it began."

"I came into church one morning and saw the Madonna weeping," the priest replied, averting his gaze.

"And?"

"I went to Father Reilly and brought him back to see it. He didn't know what to make of it. Then it happened again the next day."

"And you began to suffer stigmata."

"Yes."

"It happened twice. The last time, your palms started bleeding when you were giving a homily before your congregation."

"Yes."

"And?"

The curate shrugged. "Word got out. Reporters started showing up to interview me, and then thousands of people started coming to town to see the weeping Madonna."

"And then the Madonna in your parents' home began to weep. And then there were others. It seems that everywhere you went, you would cause Madonnas to start weeping."

"Yes."

"And?"

"Then Father Reilly told me that the bishop disapproved of all the attention we were getting, that it was unhealthy. I can't imagine why he thought that. I was to stop giving interviews, and I was temporarily suspended from assisting in the Mass. Without the publicity, we didn't get the same number of people coming to town and Mass."

"But the Madonnas continue to weep."

"Yes."

Brendan waited, but the young priest with the pompadour continued to stare at the top of his desk in silence. "That's it? That's all you have to say?"

Gary Walsh nodded.

"All right, Father Gary," Brendan continued as he rose, shut off the tape recorder and put it back into his briefcase. "Thank you for your time."

Suddenly Walsh looked up, and Brendan was surprised to see what looked like fear in the other man's eyes. "Brendan?"

"What is it, Father?"

"Can I talk to you?"

Brendan suppressed a smile. "Of course. That's precisely what I've been trying to get you to do, Father."

The priest pointed to Brendan's half-open briefcase. "Without . . . that."

"Is it personal, or does it have something to do with what's happened in Craiggville?"

"It's . . . uh, both."

"Then I'd like to tape what you have to say."

"Do you have to?"

"If it has to do with what are perceived as these miracles, yes. That's why I'm here, Father. It's my job."

"But you did say it would be confidential."

"Absolutely."

"Like confession."

"No, Father, not like confession. The tapes won't have the legal shield enjoyed by confession, but I don't see how that would be relevant. I guarantee your privacy. The tape will be transcribed into a written report that's correlated to the answers on your questionnaire. Then your name disappears. Certain people who occasionally check the accuracy of my work may hear your voice, but they won't know who you are."

The young priest's face had gone pale. He licked his lips as he thought about it, then finally nodded. Brendan took out the tape recorder again, turned it on and replaced it on the desk. Gary Walsh rose, walked to the far end of the room and bowed his head slightly. He took a deep breath, then said to the wall, "Craiggville is very economically depressed."

"I know," Brendan replied evenly.

"Coal mining is virtually our only industry. We were doing just fine up to a couple of years ago, until new EPA laws went into effect. The coal that comes from here has too high a sulfur content to meet the new environmental standards, so the mines were shut down. Hundreds of people lost jobs. When their unemployment benefits ran out, they had to go on welfare. There was no money to support the other businesses in town, so they began to fail. People were losing their faith."

"So you decided to do something about it."

"God decided to do something about it!" Walsh said in a voice that had suddenly become clear and loud. He abruptly turned to face Brendan. His eyes had grown bright. "I had a dream, Brendan. I've never had a dream like it before—it was so clear, so real. God spoke to me in that dream. He told me He wanted to send a sign to the people of Craiggville to give them hope and bolster their faith, and I was to be His messenger."

"So you faked the tears on the Madonna."

"No!" the curate exclaimed, shaking his head so hard that his hair fell around the sides of his face. Color rose in his cheeks. "You can't call something which is God's will 'fake'!"

"You put water in the Madonna's eyes and on her face because God told you to."

"Yes."

"How many times?"

"Only twice. After that, God provided the signs Himself."

"What about your stigmata? Did God tell you to use phony blood?"

"It was real blood. I cut myself with broken glass. But then other people around here began to exhibit genuine stigmata."

"The healings?"

"They really happened. I know these people, and they were sick. They came to me for help. I put my hands on them, and they got better. I swear I'm telling you the truth, Brendan."

"I believe you, Father," Brendan said quietly, turning off the recorder and replacing it in his briefcase, which he snapped shut.

"Brendan . . . ?"

"Is there something else, Father Gary?"

The curate walked closer to Brendan, said in a small voice, "It isn't working out like it was supposed to."

"How was it supposed to work out?"

"At the beginning, things went just the way God said they would. The church was full every Sunday. People came to town and spent money. God had smiled on us. Then the bishop and Father Reilly discouraged people from thinking these were really miracles. They rejected God's signs, and now God has turned His face from us again."

"I'm not the one to talk to about that, Father."

"You're well known. People trust you. If you were to say that you believed most of the miracles were real, then people would—"

"I can't do that, Father Gary."

"Why not? I swear it's the truth. The Madonna here is still weeping. You've seen it."

"God spoke to you, Father Gary, not me. I can't tell people what to believe or not to believe. All I can do is my job, and part of that job is not expressing opinions on the events I observe, or intervening in any other way. You have to find your own way to deal with the forces you've unleashed, good or bad."

The priest sighed, then turned and went back to his desk, where he sat and put his face in his hands. Brendan stepped forward and put his hand on the man's shoulder, then turned and walked from the office, closing the door behind him.

Marla was waiting for him in the sanctuary. The six-foot, statuesque blond woman with the velvety brown eyes was standing in a side aisle, head tilted back and hands clasped behind her back as she studied a stained-glass depiction of one of the Stations of the Cross. In her short, plaid skirt and yellow blouse, she looked like a college student, giving no indication of the deadly skills she possessed.

Someone else was also waiting for him. Father John Reilly, a balding, portly, kind-faced man who was perhaps in his mid-fifties, rose from the front pew where he had been sitting as Brendan entered the sanctuary through a door next to the altar.

"Brendan, may I speak with you?"

"Of course, Father," Brendan replied, smiling as he motioned for the priest to sit back down. Then he sat beside him. "What can I do for you?"

"I'd like your advice."

Brendan turned to look at the other man, who was staring straight ahead of him at a crucifix affixed to the wall behind the altar. "I can't imagine what useful advice I could give you," he said quietly.

"I've known you only a week, Brendan, but you still seem like a priest to me."

"I take that as a compliment. Thank you, Father."

"A very good priest. I can't imagine why you were excommunicated."

Brendan did not reply.

"Brendan, Craiggville is a very troubled town. Some of the things that have happened here aren't good."

"No. Murder and suicide are certainly never good."

"Do you think miracles have really occurred here in Craiggville?"

"I can't answer that, Father."

"But you have an opinion?"

"I'm not allowed to have an opinion on that."

"I don't know what to do, Brendan. Things have gotten out of hand. I feel like I'm caught in the middle between very powerful opposing forces."

"The middle isn't where you should be, Father. You have to lead. I think people are waiting to see what you say and do. Silence isn't a viable option."

"I don't know how to lead, Brendan. On the one hand I have a young priest who makes statues weep wherever he goes, and on the other I have a Church hierarchy which just wants the whole thing to go away. They're scared to death that all this talk of miracles will blow up in the Church's face. But what if these things are miracles, signs from God of His presence? How can we ignore them? Is it right to encourage people not to believe in miracles?"

"I don't see the point."

Now the priest turned to look at Brendan, frowned slightly. "I don't understand."

"There are millions of weeping children all over the world, Father. I've seen more than my share of them. They're not made of plaster. They weep from hunger, pain, disease, and terror."

"Then you don't believe the things that have happened here are miracles?"

"I didn't say that, Father."

"You don't seem impressed."

"On the contrary, I'm very impressed by the events in Craiggville. But if God were to send us a sign of His or Her presence, I would have preferred manna from heaven, food and medicine for those children, not tears on statues. I would have preferred She sent us a cure for AIDS."

The older man stared at Brendan for some time, and then his oval face broke into a smile. "I think you've given me the subject for next Sunday's homily."

"I'm sorry I can't be in town to hear it."

"I—"

"Excuse me for interrupting, Father. I need to speak with this man."

Brendan looked up at the group of men who had suddenly appeared in front of them. The man who had spoken and who seemed to be their leader was in his late thirties or early forties, lean, just under six feet, with hard gray eyes. He wore boots and matching khaki shirt and trousers. He wore his hair combed and slicked over the bald patch on top of his head. He had thin lips, and the rosy nose of a heavy drinker.

"Pardon me, Brendan," John Reilly said in a low voice, then abruptly rose and walked quickly away without making any introductions.

"You're Brendan Furie," the man with the hard eyes said. "I'm Frank York. I'm a lay deacon of this church. These are friends of mine."

Brendan rose to shake Frank York's hand; he glanced over the man's shoulder to see that Marla had turned and was watching them. A little girl who was perhaps four or five sat very stiffly, hands clasped tightly in her lap, in the first pew across the aisle. The child was dressed neatly in a white dress and saddle shoes, but there were Band-Aids on both legs and a smudge on her left cheek that might be a bruise. "What can I do for you, Mr. York?"

"I hear you've been asking people about the miracles that have been happening around here." The man had a rasping quality to his voice that Brendan found unpleasant.

"You heard right, Mr. York."

"Some people say you're famous."

"Do they? I can't imagine why."

"What are you doing here?"

"I was talking to Father Reilly."

"I mean, what are you doing in Craiggville? Why are you asking questions?"

"I'm conducting a research survey of people's reactions to the weeping Madonna."

Movement across the aisle caught Brendan's eye, and he glanced in that direction and was surprised to see the little girl, unbidden, get up and walk over to where Marla was standing. She said something to Marla, and the blond woman picked the child up in her arms and began to gently caress the girl's bruised cheek. York turned, flushed angrily. "Hey, you!" he shouted. "That's not your kid! Put her down!"

Marla hesitated, then hugged the girl and put her back on the floor. Clearly frightened, the child ran back to her place, where she sat and once again clasped her hands in her lap.

"I want you to talk to me and my friends, Furie," Frank York continued, turning back to Brendan. "We've got lots of stories to tell you about the miracles. As a deacon, I spend a lot of time here in the church. One time I actually heard the Virgin sob and call out my name."

"That's very interesting, Mr. York. I'm sure all of you have fascinating stories to tell. There seem to be hundreds of people who live here or visited Craiggville who've seen the Madonna weep, or visions of the Virgin. I've already talked to a good number of them, and I have all the interviews I need. But I do appreciate your volunteering."

"You're going to get the word out, right? You'll be writing articles and telling reporters about the miracles that have happened here?"

"No, Mr. York. That isn't what I'll be doing."

The puzzled expression on York's face wrinkled into an angry frown. "Then what's the point of talking to people?"

"I'm involved in an academic survey," Brendan replied, glancing at his watch. "Excuse me. I have to be going."

He caught Marla's eye, and they walked quickly down the parallel aisles, meeting at the rear and exiting from the church together. Suddenly Brendan felt a hand grip his shoulder, and he was pulled around. He found himself staring into the angry face of Frank York, who was standing so close that Brendan could smell the morning beer on his breath. His friends were standing a few yards behind him, at the entrance to the church, looking thoroughly embarrassed.

"You can't just walk away from me like that, Furie! I wanted to tell you about the miracles I've witnessed! People around the world have a right to know what's happening here, and you're a big shot; people will listen to you!"

"I did walk away from you before, Mr. York," Brendan replied evenly, "and now I'm about to do it again."

Brendan started to turn away, and York grabbed the front of his shirt. "Listen, big shot—!"

It was all he managed to get out before Marla abruptly stepped forward and gripped his elbow with her fingertips, pressing into the nerve cluster there. Frank York's gray, angry eyes went wide with pain and surprise as his fingers, clutching Brendan's shirt, opened of their own accord. York cursed and tried to shove Marla away with his free hand. Marla's response was to grab that wrist and twist. Her face with its exquisite, chiseled features showed no emotion as York's mouth dropped open. As he started to go down to his knees, Marla shoved him back.

"Jesus," York said, cradling his twisted wrist as his gaze shifted back and forth between Marla and Brendan. "What is she, your bodyguard?"

"She's my arbiter of etiquette, and she doesn't like it when people put their hands on me. Try to have a nice day, Mr. York."

They drove out of town for lunch at a restaurant overlooking a lake they had come to enjoy, and then returned to their motel. Marla went to her room, and Brendan to his. He took out his laptop computer and began the task of assigning codes to the names on the questionnaires, then transferring the answers from the forms into the computer. When he had finished doing that, he would start doing the same with the tapes. He hoped to have most of his work done by midnight, so that he could go on to his next assignment with the paperwork for this one almost completed.

At four thirty there was a knock on the door. Brendan did not rise, for he assumed it was Marla, who would come in after she had knocked. When there was a second knock, Brendan got up and opened the door to find a man in a sheriff's uniform standing outside. He was a burly man, heavily muscled, and his two-tone blue uniform fit him tightly. He wore a trooper's hat low on his forehead, just above green eyes that were watchful but not hostile.

"You Brendan Furie?"

"Yes."

"I'm Sheriff Warwick. I'd like to talk to you."

"Why?"

"Would you mind coming back with me to the station house?"

"Actually, I would mind," Brendan said, moving out of the doorway and pointing to his computer and the forms and tapes piled beside it. "I'll be leaving tomorrow, and I have a great deal of work to finish up. What's the problem?"

"There's been a . . . death."

Brendan frowned. "Who?"

"Father Reilly. It looks like a suicide. I understand you were among the last people to talk to him, which is why I'm here to talk to you."

Brendan felt his stomach muscles tighten as a wave of sadness washed through him. Something cold touched his heart. "Come in, Sheriff," he said, opening the door wider. The sheriff entered the room, then turned when Marla suddenly appeared behind him in the doorway. "This is my associate, Marla," Brendan continued. "She's mute, but she'll answer any questions you may have in writing. As for me, I don't believe Father Reilly committed suicide. First of all, he's Catholic, and suicide is a mortal sin. When I last saw him, he was in a good mood and looking forward to preparing his homily for Sunday."

The sheriff took off his hat and nodded to Marla, then turned back to Brendan. "I don't believe he committed suicide either."

"When did it happen?"

"The coroner's guess is somewhere between eleven thirty and one thirty, just after you finished talking with him. You mind telling me where you were then?"

"Marla and I were having lunch at the Lakeside Inn. We got there about eleven forty-five. We were just leaving about one thirty."

"Witnesses?"

"Sure. There were about a dozen other diners, and the owner knows us. We've been eating lunch and dinner there all week."

The sheriff sighed, then reached up and ran a hand back through his short-cut brown hair. "Yeah, well, I didn't think there was much chance you did it, but I have to touch all the bases. You two are the only strangers in town."

Brendan pulled the chair out from under the tiny desk and motioned for the sheriff to sit down. The other man hesitated, then did so. He looked tired. Brendan asked, "How was he killed, Sheriff?"

"He cut the end off an extension cord and stripped the wires. Then he plugged in the cord and put the wires in his mouth. Or it was made to look like that's what he did."

Brendan winced. "Why would you think there was any possibility that I killed him?"

"There was a note."

"Handwritten and signed?"

"Nah. Written on a typewriter. Whoever wrote it can't spell, and Father Reilly was a literary man. He didn't write it."

"What did the note say?"

"It kind of rambled, but the gist of it was that he'd been wrong to choke off publicity about the miracles. It said he'd been cooperating with the Antichrist and woman demon who'd come to town—which I assumed referred to the two of you. It said he understood now what God's purpose had been in providing the miracles, that God wanted Craiggville to become the Lourdes of America so that people from all over the world would come to Craiggville to be healed. Lourdes was spelled wrong, by the way."

"It sounds like whoever killed Father Reilly may have a strong economic interest in getting a new wave of publicity for Craiggville."

The sheriff grunted. "That would include just about everyone in town. What were the two of you talking about this morning?"

"Father Reilly was very concerned about the atmosphere that has developed and events that have transpired since these so-called miracles started taking place."

The other man narrowed his eyes. "So-called?"

"Poor choice of words. I should have said apparent."

"How can they be 'so-called' or 'apparent'? Man, you've got statues all over town crying tears by the bucketful, people whose palms start bleeding spontaneously, and the healing of sick people through prayer. If these aren't miracles, what are?"

Brendan looked at Marla, who was leaning against the door jamb, arms crossed over her chest, listening. She raised her eyebrows slightly and shrugged.

"You aren't one of the people I interviewed, Sheriff, so I can be a little more forthcoming with you. There are any number of ways to make a statue weep."

Now it was the sheriff's turn to raise his eyebrows. "You don't say?"

"I do say. You can smear cold grease, oil or lard, on the eyes, and the grease will begin to drip as it warms to room temperature. Calcium chloride will cause water vapor to condense. If you're mechanically minded and want to get fancy, you could run a tube up the inside of the statue, attach it to a small water pump behind a wall or under floorboards, and have your Madonna weep on cue. If you'd like, I'll introduce you to a physicist who'll explain to you in detail how he can make anything in sight start to shed water the moment he enters a room. A simple squirt gun will do the trick, especially if you're good at using the magician's trick of misdirection. Stigmata are easily faked—all you need is something sharp and a tolerance for pain, or even fake blood from a theatrical supply shop. There have been verified cases of actual stigmata and spiritual healings, but psychiatrists and other doctors will tell you these are examples of a phenomenon called psychogenesis, not miracles."

"Jesus," the other man said quietly.

"Jesus has nothing to do with it, Sheriff."

"How the hell do you know so much, Furie? Who are you working for?"

Once again Brendan glanced over at Marla, who this time gave him a nod of encouragement. Brendan turned back to the sheriff, said, "We work for a private foundation made up of scientists, philanthropists, sociologists, and maybe one or two retired intelligence agents. These people think they have good reason to believe the human race will become extinct within the next few decades, probably before the middle of the next century."

"What? That's crazy."

"Let's hope so. They base their opinions on a mathematical model that can track and project human behavior on a global scale—something like long-range weather prediction. According to their data, large masses of people all over the world will become increasingly anxious, tense, and irrational as the millennium nears. This spreading neurosis could, if their supercomputer knows what it's talking about, lead to mass hysteria and a sort of global nervous breakdown that will lead to mass destruction and death, most likely from new plagues that will ravage the planet when medical facilities break down. My job is to collect data from places where some form of mass hysteria has already taken place, or where lethal belief systems have taken shape. Their hope is to gather enough data to feed the equations, which in turn may spit out some solution to the problem, say a finely tuned psychological and educational program that can be used by national and world health organizations. That's the nickel tour of what I do and who I work for."

The burly sheriff sighed heavily, shook his head. "Well, you've certainly got a lot of craziness here—statues crying, the sun spinning, sightings of flying saucers, people killing each other, and kids killing themselves. And it seems to be getting worse, not better.

People thinking and acting nutty because they believe God's rented a condo here, or something. The other day I overheard two of my deputies talking about how maybe we didn't need law enforcement any longer because Jesus is coming back any day. How can I trust them to do their jobs? I'm afraid Father Reilly's death could lead to a lot more bad stuff, and I'm not sure how I can deal with it. I can't stay on duty twenty-four hours a day."

"If this town has a fever, maybe you have to lance the boil that's causing it," Brendan said carefully.

The other man blinked slowly. "What do you mean?"

"The fever started with the weeping Madonnas. Maybe you should look into that as a public health issue."

"You mean prove they're phony?"

"If they are phony."

"But you believe they're phony."

"I'll stand by what I said."

"You really think Father Gary has been faking all these weeping Madonnas? In case you didn't notice, he's not the brightest bulb in the hardware store. He grew up in this town, and he never much impressed anybody—not even when he came back here as a priest. Before this weeping Madonna and stigmata business, most people thought of him as a kind of joke in a clerical collar."

"I'm not offering up any suspects, Sheriff. It's possible there's more than one person involved, and they're all operating independently of one another. They might even have different motives, but the majority, most likely, would have a vested interest in seeing Craiggville become the Lourdes of America mentioned in that suicide note we both agree is fake." Brendan paused, then continued. "Look, Sheriff, you'll never convince some people—sincere people—that every one of the incidents isn't a miracle, and these people will continue to be enraptured and unpredictable. But you might convince enough that what's happened here is earthbound, and the results demonstrably dangerous to the mental health of the community. They could convince others, and then the heated atmosphere around here might cool down."

"Why can't you issue a statement telling people what you just told me?"

"Because this isn't my town, these aren't my people, and it isn't my job. I've already been labeled the Antichrist, remember? This is your job, Sheriff. Analyze some of the 'tears' from these weeping Madonnas, and I'll bet you any sum you like that you'll find they're common tap water. Check the faces for any residual traces of grease; take a couple of them apart and see what's inside. Investigate these so-called miracles, and you may even turn up your killer along the way. You'll be working in an official capacity, investigating a suspicious death, so you won't need anyone's permission or cooperation."

"Jesus, Furie. People will hate me. They'll try to run me out of town. They want to believe."

Brendan sat down on the edge of the bed, spoke in a low, deliberate tone as he stared hard at the other man. "Listen to me carefully, Sheriff. I can't be certain of it, but my guess is that the people I work for are going to be watching very carefully what happens here in Craiggville over the next few weeks and months. This town is a kind of model for what they believe is going to happen in other communities all over this country and the world as the millenium approaches. You no longer trust some of your own deputies to keep the peace because, in a virtually literal sense, their heads are in the clouds as they anticipate the Second Coming.

"We've already had a Secretary of the Interior who was giving away public lands because he thought Jesus' landing on earth was imminent. He may have been a harbinger of the future. How long before the people elect a president who may harbor the same beliefs and who thinks it may not be such a bad idea to lob a few nuclear warheads into trouble spots around the world so as to make Jesus' job easier when He does arrive?

"This is only one of dozens of scenarios produced by this mathematical model I mentioned. Impossible? My employers not only think it possible that something like this is going to happen, but probable, and they're putting their money where their minds are. They estimate it will take hundreds of millions of dollars to develop an educational program and train mental health officials to administer it in order to bring our species back from the abyss."

"But maybe they're wrong. Maybe all it takes in each community is a single person—someone like yourself—who is respected, clear-headed, and courageous enough to say that these miracles are only a miasma, and the real demons in our midst are the Bible- and Koran-thumping demagogues. I plan to include this conversation in my report—I have to. With your permission, and only with your permission, I'd like to identify you by name as the person I said these things to."

The sheriff was silent for some time. Finally he rose, put his hat back on his head. "I don't care what you put in your report, Furie. What I do care about is doing my job."

"An excellent response."

"There's one more base I have to touch, Furie. I know you interviewed Father Reilly at the beginning of the week. I'd like to hear what he had to say to you."

"There's nothing on that tape that will help you find his killer."

"I can't take your word for that."

Now Brendan rose to his feet, stiffened slightly. "I can't allow you to listen to the tape, Sheriff."

"Why not?"

"I guaranteed that whatever he said to me would be held in confidence."

"He's dead."

"His family, friends, and colleagues in the Church aren't, and he may not have wanted to share his thoughts on this matter with them. I assure that nothing he said gave the slightest indication that he wanted to kill himself."

"I'll get a court order."

Brendan shrugged resignedly. "There's nothing I can do about that. Serve me with papers, and I'll have to play the tape for you. When you verify that I've told you the truth, I trust you'll respect his privacy."

"I'll be back in the morning," the sheriff said, moving toward the door as Marla stepped to one side. He paused in the doorway, turned back, continued quietly. "I'll give some thought to what you said, Furie."

Brendan nodded, and the other man walked quickly to his car. Marla smiled at Brendan, then left, closing the door behind her.

Brendan was deeply saddened by the death of Father John Reilly, but he forced himself to go back to work at the small desk in the motel room. He had made his way through about a third of the material when he glanced at his watch and found it was after seven, an hour past their regular dinnertime.

Normally, Marla would have come and gotten him. He turned off the computer, splashed his face and put on a clean shirt, jacket, and tie, then went out of the room. The first thing he noticed was that their car, which had been parked in front of Marla's room, was gone. When he knocked at her door, there was no answer. It was decidedly odd, he thought—odd that she would go anywhere without telling him, and even odder that she had not returned by dinnertime.

He was not overly concerned about her safety. The beautiful, silent, blond woman that the mysterious Mr. Lipid, to whom Brendan reported, had assigned to travel with him was, he had discovered early on and to his considerable amazement, not only a judo master, but an expert with both knives and guns. He often wondered what her previous occupation had been, and how she had met Mr. Lipid, but he had never inquired. One reason being that he suspected she would not tell him. He returned to his room and phoned for a pizza to be delivered, then went back to work.

At ten fifteen there was a soft knock on the door. A moment later the door opened and Marla, dressed in black leather jacket and pants, entered the room.

"Marla . . . ?"

The woman came over to him and squeezed his shoulder. She picked up his briefcase from the floor, took out the tape recorder and a questionnaire. She put the items into his hands, then motioned him toward the door.

"Marla, it's past ten o'clock at night. Where the hell do you want us to go?"

The woman's response was to gesture toward the door even more urgently. When Brendan did not move, she pulled him to his feet, smiled sweetly, and gave him a hard push. Shaking his head, Brendan walked from the room to their car, which was now parked outside his room.

In the six months they had worked together, the woman had already saved his life three times, and was an expert at quickly shepherding him out of situations that threatened to grow ugly. But it was not for these reasons that Brendan was willing to go out with her at night on an unspecified task. Above all, he had come to trust Marla's instincts and judgment, and if she wanted him to come with her now, it was for a very good reason.

As always, Marla slipped behind the wheel. She drove them back into and through Craiggville, to a gas station and convenience store on the highway at the edge of town. She drove into the darkened parking area, stopped beside a gas pump and motioned for him to get out.

Now thoroughly puzzled, Brendan looked through the window, surveying the scene. Hung above the row of three outdated gas pumps was a freshly painted, hand-lettered sign that read, MIRACLE GAS STATION AND CONVENIENCE STORE.

The prices posted on the pumps were about the same as at gas stations throughout the region, even a cent or two lower. But stacked haphazardly next to the pumps were other, crudely lettered signs with different prices indicating that, at some time in the past, this particular station had charged upward of fifty cents more per gallon. The owner had started to paint the exterior of the otherwise shabby convenience store, where signs advertising exorbitant prices had not been taken from the windows, but had apparently abandoned the job halfway through. Piled on the sidewalk outside were rain-soaked cartons of merchandise that had not been sold.

Marla reached over his shoulder and pointed off to his right, then gave him a not-so-gentle nudge in the back. Brendan opened the door and got out, angling through the gas pump parking area toward the corner of the convenience store.

When he rounded the corner he could see light spilling from living quarters, little more than a shack, behind the store. He glanced down at the tape recorder he carried, and was surprised to see that Marla had flipped a switch changing its recording mode from manual to voice-activated, which he never used.

He reached out to switch the mode back to manual, then dropped his hand back to his side. Hefting the recorder, which now felt like a weapon, in his palm, he walked up to the door.

He stiffened in alarm when he heard the screaming of a woman and the crying of a little girl coming from inside, then the harsh sound of a palm striking flesh. More screams. Brendan knocked hard on the door, and when the screaming and crying did not stop he began to pound.

Suddenly there was silence. The silence lasted almost half a minute, and then the door opened a crack to reveal the flushed, suspicious face of Frank York, who reeked of bourbon.

York blinked his bloodshot gray eyes a few times, and then recognition came. "What the hell do you want?" he growled, slurring his words.

"You said you wanted to be interviewed," Brendan replied evenly. "I'm here to interview you."

"It's eleven o'clock at night!"

Brendan glanced over the man's shoulder, and between the door jamb and the man's head he could see the startled and terrified face of a woman whom he judged to be no more than middle-aged, although her hair was snow white. Her bruised face was puffy and streaked with tears, and one of her eyes was turning purple. Clinging to the woman's torn dress was the little girl Brendan had seen in the church.

"God doesn't keep a timetable," Brendan said, looking back into Frank York's face with its alcohol-ruptured veins.

"You comparing yourself to God?"

"I'm saying you're a man who claims he not only saw the Madonna weep, but heard her cry out and call your name. As I was sitting in my motel room, it occurred to me that this was just too important to leave out of my report. I have to leave town in the morning, so I came right over. Considering the sign God sent to you, I didn't think it would matter to you what time it was."

"How'd you find me?"

"I'm a crack private investigator," Brendan answered dryly.

York's bloodshot eyes opened and closed a few times while he thought about it. "Just a minute," he said, and closed the door.

Brendan heard him shouting at the woman and child, ordering them to leave the room, and a few seconds later the door opened again.

"C'mon in," York said, stumbling slightly as he moved to one side.

Brendan entered the cramped living room that smelled of cooking grease and body odor, stopped in the middle of the room.

"You're gonna' make sure people in the country hear about all the miracles happening here, aren't ya?" York continued.

"A report will be made, Mr. York."

"Why don't you sit down?"

"No, thank you. This won't take long. I don't want to take up any more of your time than is necessary."

York slumped in a torn, overstuffed chair, belched, then reached out for a can of beer on a dust-streaked side table. "So, you want me to tell you how the Virgin talked to me?"

"First I want you to fill out this form," Brendan said, taking the questionnaire from his pocket and handing it to the other man.

"When you finish, you can talk about your experiences into the tape recorder."

York took the five-page questionnaire and held it close to his face. His lips moved as he scanned the questions on the first page. He had read halfway through the second page when he suddenly looked up sharply. "What's all this business about bed-wetting, masturbation, and sexual fantasies? What the hell does that have to do with the Virgin talking to me?"

"I don't make up the questions, Mr. York."

"Yeah? Who does?"

"A team of psychologists and social scientists. They're quite insistent that anyone I interview completely fill out that questionnaire."

Frank York slowly and deliberately tore the form in half, dropped the pieces to the floor. "Well, you and your psychologists and social scientists know what you can do with this. I ain't answering none of these questions. I don't need you. By this time tomorrow night Craiggville's going to be in the news again. Everybody's gonna to know about the miracles happening here. There'll be television reporters all over the place, and then word will get out again."

Brendan felt a chill, and he stared hard at the other man. "Why is that, Mr. York? Why will reporters be coming to Craiggville tomorrow?"

York leered, revealing bad teeth. "You'll know soon enough, big shot. Wait'll you see the papers tomorrow."

"It doesn't make any difference whether you answer the questions or not, Mr. York," Brendan said quietly, putting the tape recorder in his pocket. "I realize now why I was sent here."

York frowned. "What do you mean, 'sent here'? Who sent you here?"

"I'm here to stop you from abusing your wife and child."

York's face darkened even more. He tipped over the can of beer, then lurched to his feet, where he swayed unsteadily. "You got a hell of a nerve, mister! My family ain't none of your business!"

"An abused child is everybody's business."

"I got a good mind to—I..."

"Shut up," Brendan said evenly. "Here's the drill. After I talk to your wife and daughter, I think they'll agree to come with me. There must be a woman's shelter somewhere in the county; if there isn't, I'll find someplace else to put them for the night. In the morning I'll make some calls and see if I can't arrange some help for all three of you."

"It'll be a cold day in hell before I let my wife and kid walk out of here with you. They won't want to."

"In that case, you're going to help me convince them that it's the right thing to do. Because, if you don't, I'm going to make sure that Frank York gets more publicity than he can handle. I'll tell all those reporters who'll be gathering here tomorrow about how a lay deacon of the local church where the Madonna first wept, a man who actually heard the Madonna speak to him, still couldn't find it in his heart to stop brutalizing his wife and child. We'll see what miracle they make of that."

"I'm going to kick your ass," York mumbled, staggering toward Brendan.

"Frank, stop it!"

Brendan glanced to his right to see Frank York's wife standing in the room, having just entered from the kitchen. Her white hair was still disheveled, and dried blood stained her lips, but her head was held high and her mouth was set in a firm line as her pale eyes blazed. The terror Brendan had glimpsed in her before was gone, replaced by an air of steely determination. Her daughter was with her. Standing between them, an arm around each of them, was the source of the woman's strength: Marla.

It took York a few moments to comprehend the situation, and then he bellowed, "I told you two to stay in the kitchen! What's that bitch doing in my house?"

The woman ignored him, spoke directly to Brendan. "I heard

that you were a man of God, mister, and who else but God could have sent you and this woman to this house tonight?"

"It's a miracle, and I'm going to listen to God and thank Him for sending you to save us. I realize now that we don't have to live like this."

"God wants us to be safe and happy. Dotty and I will be grateful if you'll take us with you. Frank did something real bad today; I know it. He started to get drunk even earlier than usual, and he started ranting about teaching some priest a lesson. Finally he started beating on me and Dotty, like always. This time I thought he was going to kill me, but then you and this woman came."

"Now I will kill you, bitch!" York roared, and stumbled toward his wife.

Marla stepped in front of the woman and child and brought the heel of her right hand up sharply under the man's chin. Frank York's head snapped back and he slumped to the floor, unconscious.

The woman started to go to him, but Marla held her back, gently folding her in one arm at the same time as she caressed the cheek of the child standing next to her. Brendan went to the phone and dialed the sheriff's office. As the phone began to ring he turned and smiled at Marla, who smiled back at him.

Craiggville was the last place on earth he would have expected to feel the breath of God.

JACQUELINE FIEDLER

∞ ∞ ∞

Jacqueline Fiedler writes the Caroline Canfield mystery series featuring a wildlife artist with an eye for crime. Each book in the series focuses on a different animal species. Her first book, *Tiger's Palette*, received nominations for the Agatha, Anthony and Macavity Awards for Best First Mystery of 1998. Jacqueline is currently at work on her third mystery, *Bamboozled.*

AMISH BUTTER

A Caroline Canfield Story

BY JACQUELINE FIEDLER

If it hadn't been for the flash of lightning, I might never have seen her that night. In the downpour, the woman in the white bonnet and gray dress looked like a drenched opossum on the side of the Indiana back road.

Another bolt of white ripped the sky and lit the road ahead. A covered buggy's back end rested in the mud. Its rear axle must have broken. I pulled my car next to the woman standing beneath the black silhouette of a massive oak tree.

Reaching over, I cranked down the passenger-side window. Raindrops angled through the gap. "How 'bout a ride home?" What could be the harm? This was Amish country, for godsake.

The woman hesitated, perhaps waiting for the thunder to subside. "But I am not going home."

"Then how about a ride to wherever you are going? There must be a garage in the next town." I glanced at the buggy. "Or a livery."

"Sam Nielson's Buggy Shop is closed by now," she said. "Besides, Mr. Nielson has been far too kind already."

What did kindness have to do with it? Wasn't fixing buggies a buggy shop's business? I'd heard the Amish were polite, but this was ridiculous. "Then how may I help you?"

Lightning flickered and illuminated the lines that time had drawn on her face. "Please, do not concern yourself. *Der Herr ist mein Hirte.*"

The Lord is my shepherd. The German words appeared on many of the headstones in the tiny Lutheran cemetery next to my home.

"You can't stay out here in the storm," I called. "And certainly not under this tree. You'll get struck by lightning."

The sky rumbled, and she glanced up. "If it is God's will." Heavy drops of rain beat the roof of the car. She closed her eyes. "He leadeth me beside still waters."

Rain streamed through the car's open window. I couldn't simply drive off and leave her there. I'd have to try another approach. "I'm lost on these back roads. Could you show me the way to the nearest town?" That idea seemed more acceptable to her.

"Lesterville, is not far, but . . ." She studied me, then her eyes shifted away to assess the fresh dent in my fender.

"I clipped a fence post," I explained. "Swerved to miss a deer."

Smiling for the first time, she appeared to need one final nudge.

I reached over and unlocked the passenger door. "Come on. Hop in."

She gestured toward the back of her buggy. "My belongings."

"There's room in my trunk." I popped the door and got out while she returned to her buggy. Raindrops pummeled me as I scurried to the rear of the Camaro. I opened the trunk, then shoved aside my portable French easel and paint box to make room for her things that I'd assumed would be minimal.

But when I looked up, she had managed to drag a huge steamer trunk through the mud to the back of the car. Holes riddled the side of the steamer, and an odor reminiscent of a barnyard emanated from it. She must have seen my nose crinkle.

"Butter," she explained. "Very fresh. The holes let it breathe."

"Okay, let's lift it together. On three." I gripped the opposite handle. "One . . .two . . ."

"*Nein.*"

"Nine?"

She nudged my hand away. "I can manage it alone, if you will get the churn from the back of the carriage, *bitte.*" Her weathered hands and rounded shoulders looked accustomed to hard, physical labor.

Knowing firsthand that strong women often decline help, I didn't insist but plowed through the gooey mud to retrieve the churn. The smooth, dark wood of the churn's handle had witnessed multiple generations of hands. When I returned to the car with it, the woman had indeed lifted the steamer into the trunk. From the sound of her heavy breathing, it hadn't been easy, even though she stood a head taller and outweighed me by fifty pounds. I jammed the butter churn into the remaining space, but the lid of the trunk wouldn't close.

"Go ahead and get in the car," I said. No use in both of us continuing to get wet. Using a bungie cord, I secured the half-open trunk, then hurried head-down to the driver's side of the car. Yanking open the door, I glanced across the roof of the car.

She waited outside the passenger door as though afraid to open it.

"What's wrong?" A whinny answered my question. I should have realized where there's a buggy, there's usually a horse. I scanned the dark landscape until I located it, tethered to a tree down the road. "Is there someone we can call to come get your horse?"

"I can't think of anyone," she said, "except for Mr. Nielson, and he's already—"

"I know. He's already been far too kind. Well, we'll call the local police, then."

"Oh, no, you mustn't." Fear filled her eyes. "Not the police."

All I knew about the Amish came from viewing the movie, *Witness*. They wanted nothing to do with the police, not even cops who looked like Harrison Ford.

"Don't worry," I said. Raindrops beat my scalp and dripped off my face. "I can't call anyone right now. I'm probably the only woman alive who doesn't have a cell phone." I laughed, then remembered who I was talking to. Great. None of her friends or family would probably have a phone, either—including Mr. Nielson.

The horse danced in terror with the next combination punch the storm threw. What else could I do? Given the opportunity, I'd brake for deer ticks. "Okay. We'll take the horse with us."

"*Gott* bless you." She opened the car door and got in. The door banged shut.

What the hell. I was soaked to the bone anyway.

The mare backed away as I approached in an ungainly slip and slide motion through the mud. I patted her neck to assure her I meant no harm, then unhitched and led her back to the car. I tied the reins to the passenger side-view mirror so she could walk along the road next to her owner.

Behind the raindrops that trailed down the window, the Amish woman wore a worried look. In the darkness, with the window framing her rounded features and rosy cheeks, she looked like a portrait by the Dutch Master, Frans Hals.

"We'll drive slowly," I shouted through the glass. With the horse present and accounted for, I returned to the interior of the car.

Using a plain white hanky, the woman dabbed at the remnants of raindrops on her forehead. "That ol' buggy just weren't meant to go another mile."

"I know what you mean." My vehicle was nearly as old as hers. I wiped my face with a sleeve and used the thighs of my jeans to dry my palms. They left brown streaks on the denim, probably from the rusted iron bands that encircled the butter churn. "You'd better buckle up," I said. When she stared at me blankly, I reached over and pulled the belt across her chest and secured it. I fastened my own, then put the car in drive. "Now, which way to Lesterville?"

"Down the road, then I will show you where to turn."

The back wheels spun in the mud, then grabbed. We jolted forward. I eased off the gas. The car splashed through pools of water. We hit a pothole and bounced. A loud thump pounded in the back end. I checked the road in the rear-view mirror to make sure I hadn't lost anything. "Bad shocks," I guessed. Like that meant anything to her.

She shifted uncomfortably—probably more used to a buckboard than a bucket seat.

Between the broad sweeps of the wipers, I caught only glimpses of the road. "Some storm, huh?"

"Rain is the Lord's gift. I give thanks for it." She stared down at her folded hands.

Making small talk with an Amish woman wouldn't be easy. I waited for her prayer to end. "Perhaps we should introduce ourselves," I said. "My name's Caroline." Thunder rumbled. Or was the car making more noise? "And your name?"

"I'm Agnes . . . Sister Agnes. And that's Tilly." She nodded at the horse and kept nodding as if to fill the silence with motion.

We'd quickly hit the conversational wall.

She leaned forward to peer through the windshield beaten by the rain. "You need to turn right onto the next road."

I glimpsed the crossroad and made the turn. *Bang!* Tilly jerked at the noise. The back of the car quivered. "What the hell—heck—was that?" I glared into the rear-view mirror, as though a glare could penetrate the raised trunk lid.

"It is just the butter," she said. "It likely fell over in the trunk."

From the sound of it, those bricks of butter were heavy enough to kill somebody.

"Would this be a radio?" Without waiting for a reply, she reached forward and spun the dials. "*Das ist gut,*" she said, settling back. "Very good."

The loud rock music she'd selected made the little hairs in my ears stand up. Maybe she thought it was Amish rock—of ages. Or did she hope the radio would cover any other noise? When the dashboard began to vibrate with the heavy bass, I turned down the volume, then punched the buttons, settling for the local farm report on another station. The announcer's voice made me feel less isolated, until another short, swift blow thudded in the trunk.

"There it goes again." I sat up straighter in my seat. We hadn't made a turn and we hadn't hit a hole. "What is that?" My gut instinct said there was something—or somebody—alive back there. My heart pounded in tempo with the windshield wipers.

"*Es ist nichts.* Nothing," she said. "Just the butter. I didn't take care to pack it well . . . in my hurry to outrun the storm." She smiled at me.

What was I thinking? She looked like somebody's grandmother—even my own—even down to the fuzz on her upper lip. "Just the same," I said, "I better stop and check the—"

"*Nein.*" She jammed her hand into the pocket of her apron. "You will keep going." Her tone struck me as over the edge for the average Amish woman—but not for the average serial killer. Lightning flickered. The dark and stormy night galloped away with my imagination.

I'd been stupid to break my rule on hitchhikers. Who died and made me the Good Samaritan? My throat constricted. Maybe she wasn't Amish at all. She'd been standing there waiting for a mark to come along. Sure, she put up a mild protest over accepting a ride, but she probably thought I'd be suspicious if she hadn't. I'd fallen for the oldest trick in the Criminal Hitchhiker's Bible—a seemingly harmless, pathetic figure on the side of the road. Her hand remained ominously tucked inside her pocket. Concealing a weapon?

"The Lord is with us," she said. "I thank Him for sending your help in my hour of need." She must have realized that she'd spooked me. Or was her piety just an act?

Tilly trudged forward, head down, doing battle with the storm. The car moved ahead slowly. The radio announcer droned on. Where was Lesterville? I pressed my foot against the accelerator, but a protesting whinny forced me to slow once again. "Have you thought about where I can drop you in town? You and your horse?" I wanted to dump her right there on the side of the road. But I couldn't exactly make a fast getaway with the horse tied to the car.

She twisted the hanky in her hands as though it were wringing wet. "I'm afraid I will have to impose on Mr. Nielson once more." She stared out the window, watching Tilly march along the road. "He is a kind man," she continued, as though thinking out loud, "yet he has a firm hand too. He will know what to do with Mr. G." She seemed to take each plodding footstep with the horse.

"I thought you said your horse's name was Tilly."

"What? Oh, yes, of course, I meant Tilly."

How could she forget her own horse's name? I bit my lower lip. I'd foolishly assumed she owned the horse and buggy. What if she'd hijacked it for some reason? What if the buggy's real owner was locked in the steamer? It would be a tight fit, unless the person were small . . . like me. My eyes darted back and forth across the road looking for answers—and help. I clicked on the bright lights, but the beams illuminated little beyond fifty feet ahead. I let my vision drop to the odometer. We'd gone a half mile—with no signposts for Lesterville.

"I wonder if there's a map in the glove compartment," I said, knowing full well there wasn't. "Excuse me." I leaned over and popped the little door at her knees. I'd seen enough crime shows to know an impostor might switch clothes but often kept his or her own shoes. The dim bulb barely illuminated her feet resting on the floor mat, but the sight sent some relief. Only a true ascetic would choose the austere black shoes and opaque hose that she wore.

I slammed the door shut. "Nope, no map." No defensive weapon, either. And except for the stark silhouette of a barn or silo, we might have been driving on the moon for all the visible signs of life.

As though reading my thoughts, she bowed her head and whispered, "Yea, though I walk through the valley of the shadow of death, I shall fear no evil."

Wasn't that used at funerals? I swallowed—twice.

The radio announcer gave the station's call letters. "And now our top local story."

I turned up the volume in the hopes his voice would reassure me that I wasn't alone in the car with her.

> *A search is under way tonight for a local couple in their late sixties reported missing from their farm on Highway 19. Karl Grunwald is described as short, bald and thin, and his wife, Harriet, tall and heavy-set with gray hair. Anyone with information on their where abouts . . .*

The woman leaned forward quickly. "*Musik?*" With index finger pointed, she leaned forward to switch to another station.

"Please." I caught her hand. Her fingers felt like ice. For someone with little concern for modern fashion, she had a huge interest in contemporary music. "I'd like to listen for a weather report or news of any road closures."

I fixed my eyes on the road. I'd been searching for Highway 19 when I'd picked her up. She clearly matched the broad description of Harriet Grunwald, but the newscaster had made no reference to her being Amish.

Her fingers tapped a nervous beat on the armrest. When she realized I'd noticed, she stuffed her hand back into her apron's pocket.

> *. . . switch now to our reporter on the scene, Howard Mathes. Howard, has the sheriff's department released any more infor-mation?*
>
> *Very little, Terry. But there's a lot of activity out here at the*

Grunwald farm tonight. The barn is clearly considered a crime scene. Forensic investigators arrived moments ago, as did the county coroner. A source close to the investigation tells me there's evidence that Karl Grunwald may have been murdered inside the barn, but the sheriff has yet to confirm finding a body. Nevertheless, the department has now issued an all-points bulletin for Harriet Grunwald. They maintain she is not regarded as a suspect at this time, and they only want to question her.

Yeah, right. I didn't like where I was going—mentally or physically.

Bang. Another thump came from the trunk. Tilly jerked on her reins.

Of course they hadn't found Karl Grunwald's body. Mr. G—Karl Grunwald—wasn't dead, just stuffed in the steamer trunk. Maybe she only thought she'd killed him. No wonder she hadn't let me help her lift it. Hadn't the announcer described Grunwald as short and thin? With her sturdy build and her adrenaline pumping, Harriet could have lifted him.

The woman withdrew her hand from her pocket. I heard the tinkle of metal and tensed. A chain? Brass knuckles? Handcuffs?

She held a wadded hanky in her fist and slowly wiped her forehead with it. A washed-out and smeared rusty stain had penetrated the fabric of her dress. Blood? The radio crackled.

I . . . let's see if we can talk to the man who owns the farm across the road here from Grunwald . . . Sir . . . Sir . . .
Howard Mathes, All-News Radio. Will you speak with us?
S'pose I can. Sheriff didn't say I couldn't.
What's your name, sir?
Hopkins.
What's your relationship to Karl Grunwald? Are you friends?
Grunwald don't have no friends. Even his own kind

don't like him. They kicked him out of their group.
   What group?
   The Amish. They, what do you call it, shunned him.

I tightened my grip on the steering wheel. Amish—the final nail in the coffin. My coffin? My passenger was none other than Harriet Grunwald.

   Do you know why the Amish shunned Karl Grunwald, Mr. Hopkins?
   How do I know? But I'll say this much. He didn't deserve to be called a farmer. Served him right when one of his bulls gored him last summer.
   Why do you say that?
   Ever seen his livestock? Overgrown hooves, welts from being whipped, and some of them are malnourished.

"Man treats animals that way, you can fig're how he treats a wife," the woman said.

"Isn't it the other way around?" What was I trying to do? Start an argument? "You're right. No living creature deserves to be beaten."

"That's true enough. The good Lord knows Mr. G had cause for what he done." She lowered her head. The red welt on her chin would soon be a bruise.

My expertise in injuries, however, came from being accident-prone, not beaten. So Karl had abused Harriet. But her victim's mentality continued to make excuses for him.

   Can you tell us exactly what you saw out here today, Mr. Hopkins?
   Well, sir, I was bringing my tractor in for the night, coming down the highway here, when I seen Harriet Grunwald tear out onto the road in the buggy. Nearly collided with me,

she come out so fast. I thought the wheels would spin right
off her buggy. Didn't know that old nag could move so fast.
The horse, I mean, not Harriet.

   You sure it was her?
   Sure looked like her in those clothes they wear.
   Was she alone?
   Yep, except for a big old trunk in the back of her buggy.
Sheriff seemed mighty interested when I told him that.

The radio snapped with the flashes in the sky. Did I need to
get struck by lightning to be convinced of her identity? As
though Tilly sensed my anxiety, she tried to rear, forcing me to
slow the car even more. I kept my eyes fixed on the road. The less
Harriet thought I suspected, the better.

   What did you do then, Mr. Hopkins?
   Well, I figured something must be wrong. Harriet
never leaves their farm. Karl don't let her. So I pulled my
tractor over and went in to find out.
   What did you find in the Grunwald barn?
   Lotta blood. Shotgun laying there. All the livestock
seemed to be in the barn for the night, but no sign of Karl.
   So, you called the sheriff?
   Seeing splattered blood didn't surprise me none.
Grunwald used to butcher his own meat in there. But his
shotgun laying in the dirt like that, well sir, that's when I
knew something was wrong. He took better care of his tools
than he did anything else.

I wiped my sweaty palms on my pants, then returned them
to the slippery steering wheel. Grunwald was lying wounded
inside the trunk, possibly dying. The holes in the side of the
steamer had provided him enough air to breathe. Even though I
didn't exactly like what I'd heard about him, I had to help him.

But if Harriet had tried to kill her husband, what might she do to a stranger and a potential witness? What if she were taking us both somewhere to dispose of our bodies?

"I can tell what you're thinking," the woman said.

I swallowed. "You can?"

"Karl beat her, it's true, but you're thinking she finally took her revenge."

Bingo. "No . . . no, I'm not, but I . . . I . . . I can sympathize with—"

"Because I don't abide by that," she said. "Don't agree with an eye for an eye. Vengeance is mine, saith the Lord."

So she did retain a sense of right and wrong.

"But if we rely on the Lord, He will see us through."

I was saying a little prayer about that myself.

Terry, this just in. The sheriff's department has now confirmed the discovery of Karl Grunwald's body hidden under a stack of hay in the barn.

I swallowed hard. If Karl Grunwald wasn't in the trunk, then who was? An eyewitness?

At approximately six o'clock tonight, Karl Grunwald died of a crushing blow to the top of his head. It was delivered with enough force to split his skull open. Preliminary tests have eliminated the rifle butt as the murder weapon, and so far, no other blunt instrument at the scene has tested positive for blood.

I glanced down at the brown stains on my thighs where I'd wiped my hands earlier. Not rust, but blood. The butter churn. A clumsy weapon, but Karl Grunwald would think nothing of seeing it in Harriet's hands, until she raised it over his head and—

I cringed inwardly.

A reliable source tells me, Terry, that a clump of gray hair found at the scene is considered the best lead in this case.

I didn't have to look to recall the color of her hair, but I glanced over anyway to make sure the seat belt held her captive. I noted with relief that it did.

Did the Grunwalds have any kids, Howard?
Sorry, I didn't copy that, Terry. Interference. Bad storm.
I asked if there were any kids?
Children? No, Terry, I'm told they were childless.

"The good Lord protects the innocents, like kids," she said.

I hoped he hadn't stopped now—and that I still qualified. Confident that she wouldn't know how to unfasten the seat beat quickly, I pulled to a stop.

"Okay." My voice quavered. "It's time to take care of what's in the trunk." If it came to it, I was certain I could outrun her.

"But I've told you," she said. "It is only the butter. Believe me." Her fingers lightly tapped her lips as she stared through the windshield.

I took the keys from the ignition and got out of the car. Fortunately, the rain had turned into a sprinkle. While she remained sitting in the front seat, I walked to the back of the vehicle. Under the glow of red taillights, I released the bungie cord and set the butter churn on the ground. I leaned deep inside the car trunk to reach the clasp on the steamer. It was locked. She probably had the key in her pocket. That's what had made the tinkling sound earlier.

Wham! The unexpected crash inside the steamer jarred me into an upright position. I felt the sharp blow to my head and winced in pain. My God, she'd clubbed me. Opening my eyes, I fully expected to see Harriet standing there with the butter churn in her hands. When she wasn't, I realized I'd merely hit my skull on the top of the trunk. Rubbing my head, I peered above the lid of the trunk. Harriet remained sitting meekly in the passenger seat.

Just to be safe, I picked up the tire iron. Holding it behind my back, I returned to the passenger side. After patting Tilly, I gestured to Harriet to roll down the window. "Give me the key to the steamer, Harriet."

"What?" Her eyes were filled with fear and guilt. "Why?"

"You know why." As she reached into her dress pocket, I held my breath and tightened my grip on the tire iron. "Slowly," I cautioned.

There was the tinkling sound again as she fished in her pocket. "I believe in protecting the innocent, don't you?" she said.

"Innocent, yes."

She withdrew her hand from her pocket, delicately opened the corners of the hanky, then slowly displayed the single key wrapped inside. So it couldn't have made the tinkling noise, but something else. Something I should have identified earlier with the murderer. Along with the smell from the trunk, the bruise on her chin, the gray hair, and Mr. G, it all added up.

I hurried back to the rear of the car. The pounding inside the trunk had increased.

"Hold on," I said. "You'll be free in a minute." My hunch had better be right. I inserted the key in the steamer's lock and turned it. Taking a deep breath, I lifted the lid. "Mr. G, I presume."

The gray goat lifted its head and scrambled to its feet inside the crate. I unwrapped the fabric tried around his snout. Bleating filled the night. His legs had been bound, too, but he'd kicked off the loosely tied bindings. Blood stained the bristly, gray hair on the top of his bony head. I didn't want to speculate about the gray matter on his horns. The radio's rear-mounted speakers echoed in the trunk.

*Police now confirm they have made a preliminary
match of the gray hair found as evidence in this case. It's
goat hair, Terry. That's right. Police believe that a billy goat
attacked and killed Grunwald, but it must have wandered
off afterward with the gate open. The coroner confirms that
Grunwald's fractured skull could indeed have come as the
result of the full-force impact of a goat's charge.*

When I looked up, the woman stood beside me. Between her
fingers, she held a dirty collar with a rusted metal bell attached.

"Mr. G killed Karl?" I asked.

"It was self-defense. Karl was fixing to shoot him." She
reached forward and lifted the wiry, gray goat out of the trunk
and set him on the ground. He bucked in her arms. His head hit
her chin. "Lord knows he is a handful, but it's no cause to kill
him."

She tied the rope around Mr. G's neck to the car's rear end.
In the red glow of the taillights, we watched him lower his head
and repeatedly charge the car's back bumper. When he couldn't
dent the fiberglass bumper, he tried to eat it instead.

"Did you train him to kill?"

"Oh, my heavens, no," she said. "Mr. G was only doing what
male goats do—protecting his females. Mr. G considered Harriet
one of his harem. He forced Karl to back down more than once
when Harriet was in danger."

"But I thought you were Harriet."

"Me?" She laughed. "I told you. I'm Sister Agnes. I wouldn't
lie."

"Then where is Harriet Grunwald?"

"Staying with Sam Nielson and his family—until I could
relocate her to a community where Karl Grunwald couldn't find
her."

The goat began to urinate in the road. I shifted my foot out
of his line of fire.

"You see," she continued, "a few of us are working to rescue those in unholy marriages within our faith. Karl said he'd see Harriet dead before she left him, but I finally convinced her to leave this morning while he was in town. She left all her possessions behind."

"But if you got her out safely, why did you go back to the farm this evening?"

"Harriet wouldn't leave Lesterville without two things: her mother's butter churn and Mr. G. She named the goat after her father, Gottlieb. Means God's love. She knew Karl would shoot Mr. G in her place. Mr. G had protected her, so she felt she needed to protect him too. I couldn't let Harriet go back to the farm, so I went instead. When Karl came into the barn, I hid. I listened to him take our Lord's name in vain while quoting Leviticus sixteen about the goat being a symbol of the devil. Just like Harriet said, he intended to shoot all the female goats and Mr. G tonight. He had gathered them all in the barn to slaughter them."

"So what happened?" I asked.

"Karl let his guard down and bent over to pick up his shotgun. Mr. G took the opportunity to charge."

"And killed Karl in a head-on crash."

She nodded. "The Lord moves in mysterious ways. I knew Harriet was innocent, but it wouldn't stop your lawmen from trying to arrest her before I could get her out of Elkhart County. So I hid Karl's body to give me time."

"Wouldn't it have been better to leave Mr. G there, so the sheriff would immediately find evidence that the goat, not Harriet, had killed Karl?"

"I worried they might shoot Mr. G on the spot for killing a man. Or put him down later. What would I tell Harriet? So I hid him in the steamer trunk, so Mr. Hopkins wouldn't think I was stealing livestock. Then I left as fast as I could in the buggy. But, as you saw, it broke down."

"You risked your life tonight to save a goat?"

"I did it to save Harriet. You said earlier you risked your life to miss a deer. When you wouldn't abandon Tilly back there, I knew I could trust you."

"Harriet will be able to go back to her farm safely now. But first, you'll need to talk to the sheriff."

"I answer only to God's laws, my dear. You can explain it. But I pray that you keep Mr. Nielson's name out of this. Our group could be exposed. Then where will women like Harriet get help?"

"You should have more faith in our law enforcement."

"And you should have more faith in the Lord. He is truly our shepherd. He led you to me." She reached out and touched my arm. "Don't look so troubled, my dear. Justice has been served."

What a night. I shook my head. "You gave me a real scare, you know. Why didn't you tell me there was nothing more than a goat in the trunk?"

"But I did, my dear," Sister Agnes replied. "I told you all along it was just the butter."

KATE CHARLES

∞∞ ∞∞ ∞∞

Kate Charles, former Chairman of Crime Writers Association, is best known for her Book of Psalms mystery series. Her stories are set against the background of the Church of England. Born in the U.S., she has lived in England for many years. Currently she is chair of the Barbara Pym Society.

THAT OLD
ETERNAL TRIANGLE

BY KATE CHARLES

The trouble with murdering one's husband is . . . but I'm getting ahead of myself. Let me start at the beginning.

It was during Mass on Trinity Sunday that I first decided to murder Hugh. That may seem an irrelevant and possibly even sacrilegious way to begin my story, but I can assure you that it is important. For one thing, the Holy Trinity itself has to do with triangles—the oldest Eternal Triangle in the book. As my beautiful Jonathan stood there, giving the absolution in the name of "the Father, the Son, and the Holy Spirit," making the sign of the cross with that exquisite white hand, I knew that our own personal triangle had to come to an end. And there was only one possible ending: Hugh had to die.

It was not, you understand, that I hated my husband. Even dislike is too strong a word for the feelings aroused by him. Hugh, I assure you, was a good man, liked and respected by all who knew him. He was moderately intelligent, moderately good looking, moderately successful. He was kind to dumb animals. He was never, I am quite sure, unfaithful to me. But he was—and here I speak as the one who knew him best—utterly, terminally, and mind-numbingly dull.

Once, I suppose, I was actually quite fond of him, before I'd heard all of his stories and become accustomed to all of his ways. It's difficult to remember back ten years or so to the early days of our marriage. All I can say is that if there had ever been any romance in our life together, it had long since departed.

I'd always been a good wife to Hugh, of course. I kept his house for him, and looked after him as a wife should. We never had children, but tests showed that it was his fault, not mine. And though I've had plenty of chances to have affairs with other men, I remained faithful to him. We could have gone on for quite a few more years in that fashion, I suppose, if it hadn't been for Jonathan. Jonathan. He came to be our parish priest just after the beginning of the year, in that time between the white and gold vestments of Christmas and the purple of Lent. Most people in the parish, of course, give him his proper title of Father Jonathan, but to me he will always be just Jonathan.

I'd never seen anyone so beautiful, as he stood there that first Sunday celebrating the Mass. No description can do him justice, but I must try. Shortly after we were married, Hugh and I spent a week at the Aldeburgh Festival in Suffolk. We walked for hours in the marshes around Snape—always during daylight and carefully avoiding the treacherous water's edge—and found there some colors which struck me at the time as being almost unrepeated anywhere else in nature. I have always remembered those colors, at the same time both incredibly pale and incredibly intense, and that is the only way, really, to describe Jonathan. His hair was the bleached gold of the dried rushes at Snape, and his eyes the clear, transparent blue of the East Anglian sky. It would be no exaggeration to say that I loved him completely and with all of my being from the moment I saw him.

That was six months ago. It didn't take long for our relationship to develop. At first, of course, Hugh and I were just one of the many couples who invited the new priest around for a meal, displaying hospitality and curiosity in equal measures. But once the obligatory first round of parish visits was over, Jonathan returned to us. Made welcome, he began to drop in regularly. Initially it was once or twice a week, but in time he came by almost every evening, sometimes early and sometimes late, after a meeting or a pastoral call. We rarely knew when to expect him—only that he would almost certainly come. I, of course, lived for those visits, and I think that Hugh appreciated them too. After all, Jonathan was a new audience for Hugh's stories, which he always listened to with seeming enjoyment. Clergymen, I suppose, are used to dealing with tedious people.

Those evenings all blur together now in my mind into one long haze of delight. The doorbell would ring and my heartbeat would skip. Deep breath; open the door. On the doorstep Jonathan, smiling. "Do you think that that husband of yours would offer me a drink?" he'd ask with a twinkle. Breathlessly I'd say yes, and he would follow me into the drawing room. Hugh would sit on one side of the fire, fiddling with his pipe in a way that I've always found irritating. But I scarcely noticed him, for on the other side of the fire would be Jonathan, twisting his glass in his long pale fingers, the firelight glinting off the amber liquid, the faceted crystal, and Jonathan's fine, straight hair. He would watch me, surreptitiously, when he thought I didn't know, always with an excitingly speculative look in his eye. But when Jonathan was in the room, though I might have seemed to be looking somewhere else, I was always acutely, intensely aware of him and him alone.

The poor dear man was, of course, very highly strung by nature. I liked to think that his evenings with us were a calming influence on him, a respite from his stressful life and calling. I told myself that he needed someone like me to look after him. And I knew that he realized it too: After all, he kept coming back, as drawn to me as I was to him.

I think I knew from the beginning that there was no question of my divorcing Hugh, even if he had agreed.

Although clergymen who marry divorced women are no longer defrocked, or whatever its modern equivalent may be, such things are certainly frowned upon, especially for those who wish to rise in the Church. And I had no doubt that Jonathan would rise—his gifts marked him out as a possible future bishop, or at least archdeacon.

There was no possibility, either, of an affair with Jonathan. He was a clergyman, a priest in the Church of England, and his high moral standards would never slip to permit such a thing. Not that I wanted an affair: My love for him was, from the very beginning, far too exalted an emotion to be satisfied with a transitory physical relationship. And I knew, as I sensed his eyes on me night after night, that he felt the same.

It was all pretty hopeless, I was beginning to realize. My happy, formless dreams of love seemed to have no future until the night—the only night—that we spoke of our love. It happened during the week between Pentecost and Trinity Sunday, on an evening when Hugh's train had been delayed by a crank bomb-scare and I was unexpectedly and uncharacteristically alone. As I look back, I realize that that was the only occasion—until after, of course—that Jonathan and I were ever alone together, a twosome instead of a threesome.

He was uncomfortable to find me alone, I recall. That pleased me. It meant that he was concerned for my reputation in the village. It could also mean, I thought with a little thrill, that he was afraid that he would be unable to resist me—that in spite of his resolution, and my virtue, we would somehow be swept into each others' arms by the force of our mutual passion. That possibility seemed to loom between as we talked over drinks.

"You're not very often alone in the evenings," Jonathan began awkwardly.

"No," I replied, looking at him with downcast eyes, suddenly shy. "You're used to being alone, I suppose," I added.

"I haven't felt alone since I've moved here," he said. After a long pause he went on. "Cressida, I do hope you realize how much I value your friendship—yours and Hugh's. It means more to me than I can say. But if you ever feel that I'm spending too much time here, please do tell me."

"Oh, no!" I assured him, alarmed, then moved on to even more dangerous ground, changing the subject slightly. "I can't understand why you should be alone, Jonathan. You must have had plenty of chances to get married.

"We all know how silly spinsters can be over unmarried priests, throwing themselves at them at every opportunity. And surely every mother in every church you've ever served has thrust her eligible, nubile daughters in your direction." I laughed nervously, aware of my thudding heart.

Jonathan looked at me for a long moment before he replied; at least I sensed that he was looking at me, though I didn't dare to return his gaze.

"Of course I've had plenty of chances," he said at last. "But you must know, Cressida—surely you must know that I'm not interested in silly spinsters or nubile daughters. I need someone mature, someone dependable and strong."

I swallowed hard, and raised my eyes to meet his. They were the most incredibly translucent blue, and they looked straight through me to my heart. "Yes," I said. "I know. You don't have to say anything more. I know exactly how you feel."

"You know?"

"Yes."

He sighed then, a long drawn-out sigh of relief. "And you don't mind?"

I smiled my love at him. "No, of course I don't mind." I reached out my hand to him, but he drew back.

"I want you to know, Cressida, that it will never go further than this," he said stiffly, painfully. "You have my word of honor on that. I would never come between a man and his wife."

I was right, then. A divorce was out of the question. "But you can't help the way you feel!" I protested.

Jonathan raised his white fingers to his brow and stroked it. "Of course I can't help the way I feel. But it's wrong, Cressida. I'm a priest. My life—even my thoughts—must be above reproach. I can never forget that."

"You're a man, too!" My voice sounded urgent, agonized. "You're not just a priest—you're a man!"

"No!" Suddenly he was on his feet. "You mustn't say that! And we must never speak of this again, Cressida. Never." Mutely I followed him to the door. "Promise me that you'll never mention it again," he insisted.

"But if—"

"No! And Hugh must never know. Promise me that you will do everything you can to keep Hugh from even suspecting. Or," he added, chillingly, "my visits here will have to stop. Surely you realize that."

"Yes," I said, numb with misery. And so it was on the following Sunday, during the Prayer of Absolution, that I apprehended the only way out of the dilemma: the one way to ensure that Hugh would never know. Hugh had to die.

∞ ∞ ∞

I need not go into detail about my plans and calculations for killing Hugh.

I thought about it for several weeks, but in the end the deed was remarkably simple, and accomplished without any complications.

Fittingly, it happened at Snape. Fittingly, also, Hugh himself made the plans that facilitated it. "I have a little surprise for you, darling," he said to me one evening after

Jonathan had gone, as we prepared for bed.

"I've never forgotten how much you enjoyed that week we spent at Aldeburgh the first year we were married."

"Yes?" I said indifferently. Hugh was nothing to me now: In my mind he was already dead. Only the time, the place, and the means had yet to be determined, but it wouldn't—couldn't—be long.

"I've booked tickets for next weekend!" He grinned, pleased with himself.

"And I've even booked the accommodation—the same place we stayed before, Cressida! It will be like a second honeymoon, won't it?"

As I nodded, my mind was already working. The marshes, and the River Alde. Hugh had never learned to swim.

The largest hurdle was forcing myself to be away that weekend, to miss not only Jonathan's visits but also seeing him at church, watching him celebrating the Mass, and receiving the consecrated host from his beautiful pale hands. Once that had been got through, it was easy. Late on Sunday evening, after the concert, we walked along the path beside the marshes, just another couple enjoying the warm June air and the sound of the susurrating reeds in the gloaming darkness. There was no moon, and the tide was high. When we reached the river, just a quick shove and it was all over. Hugh never knew what had happened, I tell myself. He called my name only once, and after a few splashes, there was nothing.

A tragic accident, they said. After Hugh's body had been found and identified (and that bit was much more horrible than I'd imagined, believe me) I was able to avoid Jonathan until the funeral. Quite frankly I wasn't ready to face him yet, and although it seemed only natural that my parish priest should call to comfort me, when he did so I sent my mother to the door to turn him away. It would seem that a grief-stricken widow's wishes are usually respected, and he left without demur. "Tell Cressida," he said to my mother, "that I am grieving with her, and that whenever she is ready to see me, I am available." But I wasn't ready, and the funeral arrangements were made by my mother on my behalf.

The funeral was splendid—a Solemn Requiem Mass. The church was packed—as I've said, Hugh was universally liked and respected—and Jonathan conducted the service with great decorum and a passable simulation of grief. Or perhaps, I thought, he was concerned for my eternal soul: Surely he would know in his heart that Hugh's death had been no accident, and could guess why. Dressed somberly in a black chasuble, he was, I noted, even paler than pale, the blue of his eyes almost invisible in the intensity of their pale-ness. My poor dear Jonathan. Soon the need for pretense would be over.

We met, at last, in the churchyard, after the forlorn clods of dirt had been scattered on the coffin, and after the rest of the mourners had withdrawn discreetly to allow the widow her moment of grief, her moment of comfort from her priest. Jonathan took my hand; his was icy cold. For a moment he didn't speak. Then, brokenly, "My dear Cressida, I'm sure it must comfort you to know that Hugh loved you very much. That's something you mustn't ever allow yourself to doubt."

"He never knew," I assured him quietly.

His look was searching. "No, I didn't think so. At least he was spared that, poor Hugh."

"Yes."

To my horror, Jonathan completely lost his composure; his hand clutched at mine as if for comfort, and he drew his breath in a shuddering sob. "Hugh was so good, so decent. So gentle, but so strong." Tears ran from his pale eyes and streaked his pale cheeks. "I couldn't help loving him. You understood that, Cressida. It was so marvelous of you not to mind."

The hand that he held was without feeling, a dead thing, and I heard myself speaking in a voice that I didn't recognize as my own. "Yes," I said.

"Hugh was a good man. We shall both miss him very much."

TERENCE FAHERTY

❦ ❦ ❦

Terence Faherty has written 8 books; his most recent are *The Ordained*, *Raise The Devil*—winner of the Shamus Award—and *Orion Rising*.

GOD'S INSTRUMENT

BY TERENCE FAHERTY

Many residents of Indianapolis can tell you where they were on November 19, 1979, when they first heard of the Mitchell Street Disaster, a freight train explosion that killed over twenty people. A few will also remember a macabre detail of the tragedy, the story of a victim who phoned home to say he was all right—after he had died. Ten years later, when I was told to write an anniversary piece on the accident for the *Star Republic*, the mystery of that long-distance call was still unsolved.

I could have written a story on the Mitchell Street explosion without leaving the office, using my own memories and the thick file of clippings from special editions of the *Star Republic*. But Mr. Boxleiter, my editor, wanted the human element, a term he considered his own coinage, so I reread the old clippings looking for human elements to interview. I selected a fireman, two survivors, and the father who had received the call from his dead son.

I began with Lieutenant Clyde Aikers of the Indianapolis Fire Department. He was one of scores of fireman who had responded after the explosion, and he had been decorated for bravery in the fight against the huge fire touched off by the accident.

"You ever been on a train that derailed?" Aikers asked me. His dark skin was dull under the fluorescent light in his windowless office and his eyes were tired. I'd caught him at the end of a long shift. "I was once. Years ago. The train was just pulling out of the Union Station in Saint Louis. You think of a train derailing as a big thing, like an earthquake or a plane crash, but to me it just felt like a bump. Course, we weren't moving very fast.

"That must have been what it was like the day of the Mitchell Street thing. This long freight was coming into town from the east, just passing through Indy, not stopping at all. The train had slowed way down for all the street crossings out on the east side of town. Barely moving. Then, at the Mitchell Street crossing, a tanker car jumped the track. Just a bump, right? That car dragged along for half a block, spilling more and more gasoline as it twisted, with its wheels throwing up sparks from the roadbed. Then blam! That car went up. It was like a blockbuster bomb had hit square on the tracks.

"Cryer's Lumberyard was right there next to the crossing. Nobody inside the building had a chance. Six dead. The only survivors were some guys working out back in the open lot. On the other side of the tracks was a packing house, Heineman's. Flattened, practically. Twelve dead."

Aikers sank deeper into his chair. "We fought that fire in the lumberyard and then in the warehouse next to it and then in the factory next to that. When it was over, late the next day, three more were dead. Firemen. Twenty-one killed in all, and a lot more hurt."

"Oh, yeah, that," Aikers said when I asked about his medal. "That was mostly for just being on my feet at the end of the fight. Toughest fire I ever worked, Mitchell Street."

He sat for a while, looking back, his heavy-lidded eyes slowly closing.

By way of wrapping up, I asked him if he remembered the story of a dead man who had called his father.

"I remember three dead fireman," Aikers said. "That's enough." He recited their names for me from memory.

As Lieutenant Aikers had recalled, some of the men working outside in the lumberyard that day had escaped the explosion. I had already gleaned the names of those lucky few from the *Star Republic* clippings and compared the list to a current city directory. There had been two matches. Now, I used a pay phone to track the first man, Tommy Lee Taber, to the discount tire store where he worked. I judged from its address that the store wasn't more than a mile from the former site of Cryer's Lumberyard. The store's manager answered my call and went off in search of Taber. I held the line for five minutes and received nothing for my trouble. Taber hung up with emphasis as soon as I mentioned Mitchell Street.

The second survivor, Douglas Hayes, was more cooperative. I called his home and was referred by Mrs. Hayes to a small insurance office that her husband owned and operated. "He'll be very happy to talk with you," Mrs. Hayes predicted.

She was right. "I'm your man," Hayes told me over the phone. "Come on over."

His directions took me to Castleton, a once-quiet area of northeastern Indianapolis, now awash in the city's rising tide of shopping centers and office parks. In a modest office building off Shadeland Avenue, I found the Hayes Insurance Agency. Douglas Hayes was a tall, lean man of about thirty with thinning light brown hair and a practiced handshake. He wore a sports coat with a plaid of brown and white and sky blue. The blue was repeated in his tie, which he tugged absentmindedly as he spoke.

"If you're looking for human interest on the Mitchell Street tragedy, I guess I qualify," Hayes said. "That day turned my life around, that's for sure. I've spoken of it often at church functions and motivational seminars. It was the bolt of lightning that knocked me from my horse, you might say."

"I was the original dead-end kid in those days. Born and raised down in Kentucky, outside Louisville. Sort of raised, that is. Product of a broken home. No father. My mom kicked me out about the same time I dropped out of high school. I had six or seven jobs here and there around southern Indiana before I arrived in Indy and hired on at Cryer's. I worked a forklift out in the yard with a pal of mine, Tom Taber."

I told Hayes of my phone call to Taber and his reaction.

Hayes shook his head. "Tom always was a little short-fused. Drunk when he had the money and mean when he didn't. I was the same way back then. There but for the grace of God, you know what I mean?

"The day of the accident, Tom and I were way in the back, in among some old stacks of lumber. Catching a smoke, to tell you the truth, and trying to stay warm. I can't remember hearing the train. Trains came by the yard so often that you stopped noticing. There was nothing like a warning. The first explosion knocked us down, and we looked up to see a fireball coming right at us. I still see an orange wall of fire against a gray sky some nights in my dreams.

"Tom and I didn't think or look around or plan. We just ran away from that fire. We were only a few steps from the chain-link fence that bordered the yard. Ten feet tall that fence was, with barbed wire on top, and we went over it like it wasn't there. I could feel the heat from the fire on my back through my coat. That kept me moving.

"You could say that I've been running from that fire ever since," Hayes said. His smooth transition reminded me that I was hearing a well-rehearsed speech. "Seeing friends and co-workers taken like that, in the wink of an eye, it woke me up. I realized that I had been spared by God, that He had more in mind for me than I knew. I finished high school, went into the army, and then worked my way through Earlham College, where I met my Peggy." He turned a framed photograph that stood on his desk around to face me. It showed a smiling woman and two smiling children.

Hayes was smiling an identical smile when I looked back to him. "So you see," he said, "the Mitchell Street Disaster was really the Mitchell Street Miracle for me."

His use of the word *miracle* provided me with a smooth

transition of my own. I asked Hayes if he remembered the story of the dead man who had called his father.

Hayes nodded, his smile suddenly gone. "That was another friend of mine, Art Kealing. He'd worked out in the yard with Tom and me until a week or so before the accident. Then he'd been promoted to the office. I'd thought it was a great thing for him, but . . ." His voice trailed off. When he resumed his story he spoke slowly, searching for each new word. I understood that we had strayed beyond the material he used in his motivational seminars.

"Mr. Kealing showed up about an hour after the explosion. He told everybody that he'd heard from Art, that Art was okay. I thought that Art must have been out running an errand or something when the train had come through. I helped Mr. Kealing search the crowd that had gathered to watch the fire. He ended up going to all the hospitals in the city, searching. He was sure he'd find him. He didn't stop looking until they identified Art's body using dental records.

"Art had died in the first blast. No way he made any call. No way." I asked Hayes if he could explain the call.

"No," he said. "Mr. Kealing may have dreamed it, or maybe . . ."

I waited out his silence.

"God works in mysterious ways," Hayes finally said.

My next stop was the apartment where Mr. and Mrs. James Kealing now lived. It was on the south side of town in a retirement community that called itself a village but was actually a large brick building. The Kealing apartment was on the fourth floor, and I climbed to it on a stairway that rose up one side of the building in its own glass-walled enclosure. I hadn't called ahead for an interview. Judging from the old stories I'd studied, the Kealings hadn't been appreciative of the press at the time of the accident. I had no way of knowing whether their attitude had changed.

It had not. The door of their apartment was opened by Mrs. Kealing. Over the top of her closely clipped gray head I had a brief glimpse of a color television set and the back of a man who sat watching it. When I introduced myself and my business, Mrs. Kealing took a step toward me and shut the apartment door quietly behind her. Without speaking, she took hold of the sleeve of my coat and led me back down the hallway and into the glass stairwell.

When the hallway door had slammed to, she stood with her back against it, facing me. "Not one word," she said. "Not one word do you say to my husband about Arthur." She was a plump woman dressed in a brightly colored exercise suit and athletic shoes. Her angry expression was contradicted by a tiny gold butterfly pasted to one lens of her glasses. "Leave us alone," she said. "Please. I knew you people would be stirring things up again, I just knew it. Ten years. Ten years, and only in the last few months has Jim found peace. If you only knew how haunted Jim had been through all those long years, you'd never bring that awful day into his mind again."

I asked Mrs. Kealing if it was the unexplained phone call that had haunted her husband.

"No," she said scornfully. "Not that. I don't know if I've ever believed in that call. Jim swore by it: a two-second call— 'Dad, I'm okay—'and then nothing but the sound of fire sirens. I've always felt Jim must have imagined it. Or misunderstood someone. He doesn't hear so well.

"No, it wasn't that call that troubled him." She stared at me for a long time. When I didn't disappear, she sighed. "There was bad blood between Jim and Art just before the end. They'd been great pals until Art fell in with a wild crowd after high school. Then he and his dad had some terrible fights. Just arguments, I mean. Except for the last one. Art struck his father that night. They never spoke again."

Mrs. Kealing held her arms crossed against her chest. I

could see her breath in the cold air of the stairwell. "That's what bothered Jim so, that Art died without ever saying he was sorry, and, worse, that Jim never had a chance to forgive him. Art would have come around, I know. It was just a stage a boy has to get through. Only Art never had the chance.

"Anyway, like I told you, Jim finally put it behind him a few months ago. I don't know how he did it, but God knows I've prayed and prayed that he would. Now that he's found peace, I won't let anything hurt him again."

Or anybody. I thanked Mrs. Kealing and returned to my car. I left the south side, heading nowhere in particular. I'd found enough of the human element for several stories, but I wasn't satisfied. The mystery of Art Kealing's last phone call was still unsolved. I'd been handed several theories. It had been a dream or a misunderstanding or perhaps an act of God. That last idea was the most attractive, but it was undermined by a tiny concrete detail that Mrs. Kealing had tossed my way. Jim Kealing had heard a siren during that call. That placed the caller at the Mitchell Street site.

My tired Chevrolet was way ahead of me. It had found its way onto I-465, the beltway that circles Indianapolis. It's the road to take if you want to end up where you started, which seemed appropriate suddenly. I followed the highway north again to Castleton. It was after business hours, but the front door of the Hayes Insurance Agency was unlocked. The door to Douglas Hayes's inner office stood open. Hayes still sat at the desk where I'd left him, but he'd lost his jacket and tie. In exchange, he'd acquired a bottle of Jim Beam and two glasses. He held one glass out to me as I entered.

"You see," he said. "I knew you'd be back."

That was more than I'd known myself, but I didn't argue with him. Hayes had the look of a man who wanted to talk. I sat down to listen.

"You talked to Tom, I'll bet," Hayes said. "I knew old

Tommy Lee couldn't keep his mouth shut. Probably didn't see any reason to. Probably still thinks it's funny, God help him.

"I don't. I knew the second I'd hung up from calling Mr. Kealing that day that I'd done the worst thing I'd ever do in this life. The meanest, most inhuman thing."

The office was dark, except for the area lit by a tiny desk lamp. Hayes sat at the edge of its circle of light. "It was supposed to be a joke, if you can call something that hateful a joke. We knew Art was dead—we were pretty damn sure, anyway—and we weren't too broken up about it. We hated his guts, thought he was a traitor, you know, promoted up to the office and giving us orders. My first idea was just to call his father and give him the news, be the one to stick the knife in him. I must have hated Mr. Kealing, too, just for being around. Then I got a better idea, a really terrible one. It came into my head while the phone was ringing. I pretended to be Art.

"When Mr. Kealing showed up looking for his son, I felt a sick cold run through me. I wandered through the crowd that day more frightened than I'd been after the explosion, certain that if the people around me found out what I'd done, they'd throw me into the fire and cheer it on."

"I went through some bad days after the accident. I was really close to the edge of the pit. Then I got the idea that saved my life." Hayes leaned toward me across the desk. "It came to me that maybe I hadn't been acting for the devil that day. Maybe, after all, I'd been acting for God. Maybe He'd used me to get a message through to Mr. Kealing from his son, the message that Art was all right, that he was safe, wherever he was.

"That thought is what really redeemed me and put me on the right path. Whenever I talk to people now about Mitchell Street—I can't help talking about it—whenever I say that I was spared by God, that's what I'm really thinking inside. That God turned the most hateful thing I ever did into a service, by making me His instrument."

Hayes's words were more confident than his delivery. I understood that he wanted me to confirm his rationalization. Unfortunately, I'd spoken with Mrs. Kealing. I knew that her husband had not been comforted by the long-ago message that his son was "okay."

Hayes seemed to read my thoughts. As I rose to leave, he said, "Mr. Kealing's forgiven me. He really has."

When I hesitated, he plunged on. "I called him a few months ago to confess. This ten-year mark coming up had Mitchell Street on my mind again. I was drunk and all worked up when I called. All I could say was, 'I'm sorry. I'm so sorry for hurting you.' Then Mr. Kealing cut me off. He started saying, 'I forgive you,' over and over. Shouting it almost. I swear he did. It was like he'd been waiting all these years for me to call."

I asked Hayes if he had identified himself.

"No," he said. "I was crying too hard. Couldn't talk. Mr. Kealing was crying too. After a little while, I just hung up."

I stood there in the doorway of the darkened office for a time, feeling a cold wind through the paneled walls. Then I told Hayes that I thought he was right. He had spoken for Arthur Kealing. I didn't mention that he'd done it nearly ten years after Kealing's death.

I left Hayes crying at his desk and went back to my own to write the story of Clyde Aikers and the three dead firemen.

MARY MONICA PULVER

∞ ∞ ∞

Mary Monica Pulver is the author of numerous historical mysteries both on her own and with Gail Frazer.
Royal Whodunits is another anthology to which she
contributes. Ms. Pulver sold her first short story to
Alfred Hitchcock's Mystery Magazine in 1983. Her first
novel, *Murder at the War*, appeared in 1987. She has
sold fifteen novels and twenty short stories, some also
published in German and French.

FATHER HUGH AND THE KETTLE OF ST. FRIDESWIDE

BY MARY MONICA PULVER

The chapter meeting was going smoothly despite the absence of our Mass Priest, Father Hugh Paddington. When he came panting in, late as usual, it was more a disruption than a completion of our number.

Father Hugh was a small man, and his monk's robe was too big. The hood of his monk's robe hung down to his bottom, and the hem dragged on the floor behind—also as usual. This time there was also a smear of egg on the side of his mouth and a tumble of breadcrumbs down his front. Really, the fellow has no sense of his own dignity as a holy priest of God and Mass priest of the royal abbey of nuns he serves.

He bowed to me and hurried to his stool on my right, barely noticing the slender book waiting for him before he sat on it.

"Er-hmmm!" he said in his light tenor and put one sandaled foot on top of the other. My nine nuns and two novices hid their laughing mouths behind their sleeves.

"Good morning, Father Hugh," I said repressively.

"Good morning, Domina," replied my priest as cheerfully as if I had sincerely wished him well. "It is a great pity I am so fond of eggs," he went on, "especially eggs in onion sauce, because our cook somehow can't get the hang of them, so I have to help her, and so it makes me late. And I know you do not like tardiness."

"Perhaps if you could find it in your heart to like eggs for dinner instead of breakfast, you would not find it necessary to keep us all behind our time while you teach the cook how to prepare them." Which was very nearly a lie, as we had long ago given up expecting him to come to morning Chapter on time and went on with the business meeting until he should arrive with his readings and prayers.

I'm sure he knew this; doubtless he had heard us discussing abbey business as he came up the cloister walk. But he drew up his shoulders and dropped his tonsured head and said very meekly, "You are in the right, Domina, and I beg your pardon."

His meekness was a rebuke, so my tone remained gruff. "Still, since you have arrived, perhaps you could read today's portion of the Holy Rule."

He opened the book and spent a paternoster while searching for the day's reading before he noticed the slip of ribbon marking it, and made a grimace so humorous and deprecating that again my nuns covered their mouths, and even I had to clear my throat.

"Today is October nineteenth, the Feastday of St. Frideswide. She is the patron saint of Oxford, and was a wonderful abbess and builder, but did you know she lived in a pigsty for three years, hiding from Prince Algar? Such was her determination not to be forced into marriage—and such was her brave example that two companions joined her in those foul surroundings, to support and protect her from the prince, who thought to kidnap her. Frideswide was determined to become a Bride of Christ, not of Prince Algar, so she prayed daily to St. Lucy—"

I cleared my throat to stop him. His stories tend toward the earthy, and I wanted my nuns to keep their minds on more lofty things. I sometimes think he should have become a friar, their good-humored humility and racy sermons would have suited him down to the ground.

At my warning he broke off immediately, cleared his own throat, and set off again, "The reading from the Holy Rule of St. Benedict for today is as follows," and continued in fluent Latin. Unfortunately I am the only member of this little flock with even a small grasp of Latin, so when he finished, he offered a translation. The segment was a simple instruction on the use of "Alleluia" in the psalms and responsories from Pentecost to the beginning of Lent, and my ladies, who had already heard this segment in February and again in June—the Rule is so brief we hear it in full three times a year—tried to look edified.

He then offered a prayer for guidance from the Holy Ghost that should have been offered at the beginning of Chapter (and which was sorely needed), and said, "Do continue with your meeting."

"Thank you, Father," I said. "Where were we?"

"I believe it is my turn to make a report," said Sister Mildred, my sturdy cellarer, rising from her stool.

"No, no," said Sister Alys, "we still haven't decided whether to send a christening gift to the son just born to Queen Margaret."

"I say no," murmured Sister Harley, with a sideways glance at me, which meant she was going to say something rude or gossipy or both. "Everyone says that King Henry VI is a celibate saint and has lived chaste from early childhood. So what if this child is not a princeling at all?"

My nuns goggled at her words—not that what she said was news, but that she dared to speak so openly. We had all heard the rumors, of course; there had been talk for months that the king was surprised at her pregnancy and declared it to be of the Holy Ghost, not his own getting. But then he had gone completely mad and still lay witless at Windsor, so no one knew yet if this babe would be acknowledged as his or not. On the other hand, the political situation in this Year of Our Lord 1453 was such that a misstep could bring the fury of the powerful queen down on even such political innocents as we.

Everyone started speaking at once—these are all gently bred women, except those who are actually of noble blood, and each had been corresponding with family and thereby keeping up with all the news from court. "Enough!" I declared at last, and called for a vote on the various possible actions we might take.

The decision was to send a small present, a silver-gilt cup we had gotten as a chance gift from Sir Thomas of Banbury, and a letter pleading poverty.

"Now!" declared Sister Mildred, rising to her feet again. "I have a matter of importance to bring before this meeting."

My cellarer was a tall woman of nearly thirty-five summers, with broad shoulders, a high stomach, and a chin not to be trifled with. She was a most excellent second-in-command, in charge of land and buildings, lay labor, and everything concerning them, from plow oxen to granaries. She had a deep voice and a commanding presence. Yet for all that, no one would ever take her for a man. Perhaps it was her blue eyes, which rarely lost their twinkle.

They were not twinkling at present.

"Is it something so serious you cannot handle it yourself?" I asked.

"Madame, I wish to report that there is a thief at the abbey!"

There was an astonished murmur, quickly stifled as my nuns looked at Mildred for an explanation. "Who among us do you suspect?" I asked.

"None of us, of course, my lady!" snapped Mildred impatiently. "I mean among the servants we employ!"

Ah. "Is John Freemantle aware of this thief?" I asked. He was our steward and a more capable and intelligent manager of our property I could not have wished for.

"Of course. It was he who brought the matter to my attention when he could not himself determine who among them was guilty of theft."

"What has been stolen?" I asked. "And when was it taken?"

"It's been a series of thefts, over the past six or seven weeks. Just one or two at a time, so Cissy didn't notice for a while that there were fewer eggs because there were fewer chickens."

"Chickens? Oh, by St. Loy, Mildred, I thought you were talking about something really serious!"

"It *is* serious," said Mildred. "We had nearly fifty laying hens and the eggs we didn't eat ourselves were sold to help support the kitchen. There are only thirty-seven left, and the ones stolen were our best layers. We may have less to sell, and indeed fewer eggs to eat ourselves, unless this thievery is stopped."

"No more eggs in onion sauce?" said Father Hugh. "Unhappy fate! Has John any idea who might be stealing the hens?"

"He thinks it is one of four people, but he can't pick who among the four is the guilty one."

"I suggest he dismiss all four, then," I said, impatient with this discussion.

"But that wouldn't be fair," protested Father Hugh. "Even in these times, when hired labor is scarce, an employer might hesitate to hire someone under suspicion of theft. You would not make three beggars of three innocent men, surely."

"Indeed not!" I said, trying to sound indignant that he thought so. "Therefore, you go and assist John in finding out which of the four is guilty, so he may be punished and you may continue to have eggs in onion sauce for breakfast."

Father Hugh stood and bowed. "Yes, Domina. At once, Domina." He hurried out of the room.

I should have been warned by his eagerness.

It was just after the prayers of None, about mid-afternoon, when I received word that Father Hugh was going to work a miracle down by the smaller storage shed. A miracle to be worked by Father Hugh Paddington: For a moment I sat with my eyes closed and prayed for strength. Then I announced I had better go see.

Father Hugh is a kind man and a good one. But he is small and he is clumsy. If he were a saint, which he is not, his miracles would be the sort that change wine into water. This news was exasperating, and I was determined to quash any absurdity he might be getting up to.

Surely, I thought as I left the cloister, crossed the inner courtyard and went through the big double doors that led to the outer court that held our barns, stables, granaries, sheds and servants' quarters, Father Hugh knows better than to mock God and his saints.

I was wrong.

Father Hugh had put on his second-best alb because of the mud in the yard, but he wore his good purple stole with the gold fringe that reached below his ankles. He was standing over an upended old kettle, making the sign of the cross and intoning the beginning of the Gospel of John in Latin. He was up to the part about lighting shining in darkness.

When he glanced up and saw me, he immediately switched recitations to the first line of a psalm: *"Domine, ne in furore tuo arguas me, negue in ira tua corripias me."* Lord, rebuke me not in Thy anger, and chastise me not in Thy wrath. He sounded very serious, and I stifled the rebuke that was about to spill from my mouth.

He nodded approval at my comprehension and went back to the Gospel of John, holding his hands out over the kettle as if it were an altar. There was not a sound in the yard; even the animals that inhabit it had fallen silent under the glaring sun.

A knot of villeins had gathered at a safe distance, heads bowed.

John Freemantle stood nearer, and in front of him were four villeins trying to put a brave face on the proceedings. Sister Mildred stood a little behind John, her face stiff and formal, a bright brown rooster hanging down from one hand, wings slightly spread.

Father Hugh finished his recitation, then gestured for Mildred to bring the rooster to him. He blessed it before taking it from her, then held it aloft. "Help us, St. Frideswide!" he cried, and everyone, except the four, responded, "Amen!"

Mildred had seen me when she handed over the rooster, and now came to stand beside me. "This is a formal occasion," she murmured. "You should have brought your crozier."

"Please don't tell me he has turned pagan and is going to sacrifice that rooster," I replied.

"Of course not!" She sounded scandalized. "Father Hugh has asked St. Frideswide to identify the thief."

"What has a rooster got to do with her?"

"He is going to put Chanticleer under St. Frideswide's kettle, the one she cooked in while hiding from Prince Algar in the pigsty. Each man will put his hand on the kettle, and when the one who is the thief does that, the rooster will crow."

"St. Frideswide's kettle?" I exclaimed.

"Oh, please, madame, hush," pleaded Mildred.

"But that is not St. Frideswide's kettle!" I said, more quietly. "There is no such relic here or even in her city of Oxford. What he has got is the oldest kettle from our kitchen—I recognize it by the crooked handle. He must have taken it directly off the fire, it is filthy."

"Yes, I know. Isn't he clever?"

"Of all the witless, impossible—"

"Please, madame, it will work. Trust me. Trust him. Trust God and St. Frideswide."

I threw up my hands and was silent.

I saw John Freemantle give a tiny nudge to one of the four suspects, whom I suddenly recognized as Old Hob, our village reeve, who could not possibly be a thief. Hob raised a work-hardened hand and said, "Beggin' yer pardon, Father Hugh, but that be an unsteady old pot, sir, upside down an' all. Seems to me that if I put me hand on it, it might wobble to one side like. And if that rooster sees a bit o' light come under the lifted edge, sir, he might think it were the sun comin' up, and crow at it, y'see. And God bless 'ee, sir, I don't want to be taken for a thief when I'm no such a thing, sir."

"That's a good point, Hob," said Father Hugh, and John nodded. "John, close the shutter on the window of that shed. We'll put St. Frideswide's kettle in there, and the rooster under it, and send these fellows in one at a time to test the saint. That way, if we hear the crow, we will know it is not a stray sunbeam but St. Frideswide herself stirring him up, and we will have our thief."

And while John obeyed, Father Hugh broke into the *Dies Irae*, which with its description of the terrors of the Final Judgment made even my blood run cold. I crossed myself and saw Mildred and the villeins do the same. Hob fell to his knees and his wife in the little crowd began to wail. The other three villeins quaked.

Hob went into the shed first while Father Hugh stood outside praying in a loud voice. Then he stopped and everyone could hear Hob inside the shed say, "St. Frideswide as my witness, I stole no chicken." There was a little pause as everyone waiting for the sound of a cock crow.

Which didn't come.

Hob came out of the shed with a grin you could see a mile.

But neither did the rooster crow for any of the other villeins.

The last villein came out of the shed wiping his brow with relief, and the group of villein witnesses murmured in disappointment and looked askance at Father Hugh.

"You think St. Frideswide would disappoint me?" cried the little priest. "I think not! You", he continued, turning to the four, who immediately stopped grinning and nudging one another, "hold out your hands, palm up."

Puzzled, the villeins obeyed, each displaying one relatively clean hand and one blackened by contact with the kettle. Except the third one. Both of his hands were unmarred by soot. He saw Father Hugh's gaze settle on him, and then saw why, and put his hands behind his back.

"Aha, I knew it!" cried Father Hugh. "It was you, Willem, who took the chickens. And you were afraid to test the powers of St. Frideswide! You knew if you touched the pot, Chanticleer would crow and tell us you are the thief!"

John Freemantle's large hand descended on the luckless villein's shoulder, forestalling an attempt to flee. He turned the man to face me and said, "I have a thief who is in your mercy, my lady!"

Now I tell this story not to show how clever Father Hugh was after all, or to lay to rest the stories that circulate nowadays of his saintliness, but because I have heard this self-same story attributed to a clever farmer from Kent after a pig thief, a friar from outside of Ely after a cutpurse, and even the bishop of York after a murderer; and I want to set the record true before it enters forever the realm of folklore. It was Father Hugh Paddington, Mass priest at the Abbey of St. Mary, who set a trap to catch a chicken thief at the instance of me, Margaret Fitzduke, Abbess.

RALPH MCINERNY

❧ ❧ ❧

Ralph McInerny is a professor of philosophy at the University of Notre Dame and the writer of the Father Dowling Mystery Stories. His current mysteries have Notre Dame for their setting, and the latest in that series is *Grave Undertakings*, which has been selected by the Mystery Guild.

THE DUNNE DEAL

BY RALPH McINERNY

The necklace that had been slipped into the poor box had to be artificial pearls.

"How can you tell?" Phil Keegan asked Marie Murkin, who had just returned from the church with the contents of the poor box.

Marie adopted a patient expression. "Who would put real pearls in a poor box?"

"Who would put fake pearls in a poor box?"

Father Dowling intervened. The three were seated at the kitchen table enjoying some of Marie's pineapple upside-down cake. "Maybe someone thought it was lost-and-found."

Marie accepted that, since it left the genuineness of the pearls an open question. She drafted a little notice for insertion in the bulletin, stating that the owner of a missing necklace could claim it at the rectory.

"You didn't mention that it was a pearl necklace," Father Dowling observed. "Whether artificial or genuine," he added.

"They're fake," Phil said.

"We don't know that," Marie said.

The notice appeared. No one claimed the necklace, but two weeks later Marie came and stood in the pastor's study door, waiting to be noticed.

"What is it, Marie?"

"How much is a hundred thousand lire worth?"

"Lire?"

She took a colorful bill from the pocket of her apron and tried to read the legend on it but gave up. "I can read the numbers anyway. One hundred thousand lire."

"Was it in the collection?"

Marie shook her head. And waited. Either he asked her or she would wait until spring before saying more.

"Where did you find it?"

"It wasn't lost. It was in the poor box."

"Hmmm. Better check with the bank."

"Don't you think it's real?"

"I meant, find out what it's worth."

Marie made the call in the kitchen and returned to say the bill was worth between seventy and eighty dollars. She was clearly disappointed.

"That's a very generous contribution, Marie."

It was also unprecedented. The poor box was seldom the recipient of large amounts. People dropped in a few coins on the way out of church on Sunday, but there was such a press that few of the departing congregation got near enough to the poor box to have the chance if they had the intention.

"I'll put it with the necklace."

The pastor had to think before he remembered the pearl necklace that had been dropped through the slot of the poor box some weeks before.

"Put eighty dollars into the poor box account."

"What for?"

"I thought you wanted to keep the Italian money."

"Father Dowling, do you think for a moment that was meant for the poor? It's some kind of joke."

"Well, it will certainly bring a smile to some unfortunate person."

It was nearly a month later that the Krugerrand was put in the poor box. Marie just laid it beside the pastor's plate and waited for him to notice and ask about it. But it was Phil Keegan, who had attended the noon Mass and been invited to lunch, whose eye fell immediately on the shiny object. He picked it up and whistled.

"What is it, some kind of jewelry?" he asked.

"It's pure gold," Marie said.

"Come on."

Marie, having served the soup, took a chair at the table. "What do you think it's worth?"

"Was that in the poor box, Marie?"

"It was, Father. And I'm glad Captain Keegan is here. He will remember the necklace."

But Phil needed reminding. "Oh, those fake pearls."

"Is that fake gold? Was the Italian money fake?"

"What Italian money?"

It would not require Marie Murkin to seek a connection between the necklace, the lire, and the Krugerrand even if the only thing that linked them was the fact that they had been found in the poor box at the back of St. Hilary's church. The two men finished their soup and she brought in the pasta and salad and then stood at attention beside the table.

"Join us, Marie."

"I've eaten."

"When?"

"What are we going to do about the poor box?" She put the question to Phil Keegan, appealing to his professional curiosity. As Captain of Detectives in the Fox River Police Department he could expect to have his suspicions aroused by the odd contributions recently made to the parish poor box. But not while he was enjoying Marie's pasta. When he had finished and was having coffee he seemed to have forgotten Marie's question. She conquered her annoyance and repeated the question.

"Put it in the bulletin."

"Put what in the bulletin?"

"Marie has already mentioned the pearl necklace."

"That proves they're fake. If they were genuine, someone would have claimed them."

"The question is, what are you going to do about it, Captain Keegan. I am reporting these facts to you."

"You say you found these items in the poor box?"

"I've said that."

"Were there any witnesses?"

"Witnesses to what?"

"To the alleged fact that you found them in the poor box?"

"Do you think I made this up!"

"Are those pearls you're wearing?"

Marie's hand flew to her throat and she emitted a little yelp. "I just tried them on. I forgot I was wearing them."

"No reason why you shouldn't," Phil said magnanimously and Marie withdrew in confusion. But the field became level again some hours later.

"They're genuine."

Father Dowling, at his desk with Dante open before him, looked up. He had heard Marie speak but had not understood the question.

"Those pearls are genuine." She put them carefully on the pastor's desk. "Montrose the jeweler says they are real and perfectly matched."

"Well, well."

"He gave me an estimate of their value. Now, if we add up the value of the gold and the Italian lire . . ."

"It makes a very handsome contribution to the poor."

"No one would put that much in the poor box just to give something to the poor."

"Oh, I don't know."

In a burst of thanksgiving or contrition people were capable of unusual acts of generosity. It did seem hard to believe that different individuals had put these items in the poor box, however, and the variety and manner of giving were more than odd. Still, the pastor told Marie, he was prepared to live with a measure of oddness.

"Well, I'm not."

"Are you giving notice?"

"Don't you wish."

"No, I don't. However, if you think you can better yourself . . ."

"I have been here longer that you have."

"And now you're bored."

Marie waved away this red herring. "I think you should make a formal complaint to Captain Keegan."

"Complain that someone has been helping the poor?"

"Ask him to find out who it is."

"Would that be fair?"

"Don't you think he could do it?"

"I was thinking of the donor."

"Will you ask him?"

"I don't like to promise."

The matter became moot when Phil Keegan telephoned to say that he thought he knew from whom the items in the poor box had been stolen.

"Stolen!"

"Someone has filled a complaint of theft. Among the missing items were a large Italian bill, a Krugerrand, and a pearl necklace."

"Other things were missing as well?"

"One other thing. A Purple Heart."

"A Purple Heart!"

"The medal awarded to those wounded in action."

"I wonder if it's in the poor box."

"Wait until I get there."

Phil Keegan had lost his wife but only after the girls were raised, thank God, and his life ever since had been lonely. He was, Father Dowling had told him, a naturally uxorious man and if that meant he didn't care to live alone, Phil agreed. If it hadn't been the renewal of his old friendship with Roger Dowling, he didn't know what he would have done. Visits to the St. Hilary rectory were frequent and long and he knew he was welcome there, even by the crusty housekeeper, Marie Murkin. Nonetheless, he didn't work far longer hours than needed, involving himself in various investigations if only to cut down on those blank hours when he had little to do but watch television. His eye was caught by the theft report for two reasons. One, the complainant, Mrs. Dorothea Dunne, was the prominent widow of Fergus Dunne, who had made a fortune, married late and died early, leaving Dorothea with the earthly goods he had accumulated. She had been in her thirties when they married and not twenty years had passed since the happy day, but ever afterwards she had been the phenomenally attractive and eminently eligible Widow Dunne, not that anyone would presume to call her such a thing to her face.

"We were in school together," Lieutenant Cy Horvath said. Keegan had been bent over the counter, reading the report, but at this remark he straightened and turned to face Cy.

"You were in school with Dorothea Dunne?"

"She was just Dorothy then. Dotty Elmore."

"Where was this?"

"St. Casimir's."

"The grade school."

"She was no beauty then. Pigtails, a little fat . . . "

"Did you take the call when she reported this theft?"

"No, but I thought I'd follow up on it."

"For old time's sake?"

"She didn't come to the reunion."

"I'll tag along with you."

"I wonder where she went to high school?" Cy said when they were in the car.

"You can ask her."

"Good idea."

You never knew with Cy. He had only the one expression and nothing had ever been able to change it. He'd had his ups and downs, among them a thwarted football career. Injuring his knee during the first game of his sophomore year at Champaign had been the end of a dream. Not having any kids was another. These and other slings and arrows of outrageous fortune Cy had borne without a facial flicker. It was unlikely that his expression now would reveal whether or not he was joking. Phil decided to read the report again, aloud and carefully.

Mrs. Dorothea Dunne had registered a complaint and asked her lawyer Amos Cadbury to prod the police into action. Several items were missing from her home overlooking the Fox River. She was unsure when they had been taken; she was certain only that they were missing and she had no idea where they had gone. The thought that she had been robbed had eventually suggested itself. She wished the police to conduct a quiet and discrete investigation.

"Why didn't she hire a private detective?"

"I asked Cadbury that. She wants investigators who can arrest if they find the guilty party."

"Sounds like she has some one in mind."

Cy said nothing. The list of missing items was as follows: one matched pearl necklace; one large Italian bill, a memento of her honeymoon; one Krugerrand, suitable for wearing, if one were given to that sort of ostentation . . .

"Are these her comments, Cy?"

"Apparently she insisted that they be written down."

The fourth item was the Purple Heart her husband had won in Korea.

⁊ ⁊ ⁊

Given the size of the mansion and the imposing look of the main entrance it was something of a surprise to have the door open by the lady of the house. Her eyes fixed on Cy.

"Police, ma'am."

"I know you."

"Cyril Horvath."

Her heavily mascared eyes narrowed. Her chin lifted higher. The great mass of her silver hair, freed from her shoulders by this movement of her head, cascaded down her rigid back. She tossed her head. If she was waiting for Cy to say more, she had a long wait coming.

"St. Casimir's?" she asked.

Cy nodded. "Nineteen . . ." he began, but her hand flew out, grasped his wrist, and pulled him inside before he could complete the date. Feeling superfluous, Phil Keegan followed.

Phil's wife used to subscribe to magazines that featured homes like this one. They moved through the vestibule, on through a large living room with a great fireplace, and into the sunporch where a tropical garden flourished despite the winter outside. She waved Cy to a chair but he remained standing.

"Captain Keegan and I are here to investigate a theft."

"I hope I'm not being an alarmist, Cyril, but some of the missing items are of great sentimental value."

"The Purple Heart?"

She turned her lovely head and looked at Cy from the corner of her eye. She hoped she didn't have to explain the significance of such a medal. Cy said he understood. Phil Keegan also had earned one. A wintry little smile was directed briefly at Phil but it was clear that Cy commanded her complete attention.

"Are you alone in the house, Mrs. Dunne?" Phil asked.

"How do you mean?"

"Do you live alone?" Cy said.

"Of course I live alone."

"No one else in the house?"

"There is old Mrs. Dunne, Fergus's mother. Her apartment is over the garages. And there's Thelma."

"Who is Thelma?"

"She takes care of things."

"Housekeeper?"

"You could call her that."

"What would you call her?"

"Companion wouldn't be right. She has worked here since before I married Mr. Dunne. There has never been any question of her not staying."

"What Captain Keegan is after is, who might have stolen the things."

"Well, certainly not Thelma. It was she who made me aware that the things were gone."

"Ah."

"She insisted I call Mr. Cadbury."

Phil left Cy with his old classmate and went to talk to Thelma. She might have been a twin, or at least a cousin, of Marie Murkin. She sat in a rocking chair in the kitchen, listening to music. Phil told her who he was.

"Good. Maybe now we'll get to the bottom of this."

"Mrs. Dunne said you discovered that things were missing."

Thelma looked as if she might want to amend the remark. "I urged her to call Mr. Cadbury."

"What would you say the value of the missing items is?"

"Their monetary value? I have no idea."

Do you have any idea what happened to them?"

She inhaled deeply. "At first I thought Mrs. Dunne had simply been careless. If only one or two things had been missing, it would not perhaps have seemed so important. But the Purple Heart?"

"Mr. Dunne must have been proud of that."

"It was, he said, his tainted nature's solitary boast. Wordsworth."

"Wordsworth?"

"The poet. The phrase is his. He used it in another connection."

"Was there any sign of a break-in?"

"None. Casey was quite definite."

"Who is Casey?"

"He drives and looks after the yard."

Phil nodded. "Would there be any point in speaking with the older Mrs. Dunne?"

"It is an experience you should not deny yourself."

That could have meant anything. Thelma led Phil through a breezeway to where a stairway outfitted with an invalid's elevator rose to the area over the garage. Upstairs, Thelma just opened the door and went in. The apartment, unlike the main house, was a study of modernity. Clean lines, walls forming right angles with the ceiling, no molding, pastels, silver frames on the pictures and, in the living room where they found the old lady, a picture window that gave a wonderful view of the back lawn. When Thelma announced him a fragile hand lifted from a wing chair and its occupant sat forward. Keegan shook her hand but had the impression she had expected him to kiss it.

"I can't hear a thing," the elder Mrs. Dunne said, although Phil hadn't said anything yet.

"She won't wear her hearing aid," Thelma remarked.

"They don't work."

"You heard that," Phil said.

Thelma said, "She reads lips."

Thelma's help was indispensable in the interview that followed. The old lady grew animated as they discussed the theft. "Were those my pearls?"

"You gave them to Dorothea, dear."

"Did I say I didn't? Are those the ones that were stolen?"

"Fergus' Purple Heart was taken too."

"Officer, get those things back."

"That's our job."

"Fergus was a great admirer of the black archbishop with the ballet name."

"In Chicago?"

"No, in Africa."

"Tutu," Thelma explained.

Hence the Krugerrand? Phil was becoming confused. Everyone in this house seemed sane enough, but he couldn't make head or tail of what they said. He took Mrs. Dunne's pad and wrote THANK YOU on it.

"For what?"

He left Thelma to explain and went in search of Casey in the garage below.

There was the faintest odor of grease and oil, but the floor of the garage looked as if you could eat off it. Four cars were parked in a row, all of sober color except the white sports car. There was a door with a glazed window at the far end of the garage. On it was painted in Gothic script F. X. CASEY. Keegan knocked.

"It's open."

Phil stepped inside. Theman's back was to the door, he had his feet on the desk and was buffing his nails. "They gone?" he asked.

"No, they're still here."

The man turned his head and looked at Phil. Then he uncrossed his legs and took his feet from the desktop one at a time. Finally he turned in his chair.

"I'm Frank Casey."

"I know. I read your door. Now I recognize you. I wondered where you ended up."

"That was a long time ago."

"Years ago."

Casey had spent a checkered youth and as a man had been convicted of dealing drugs. Keegan figured Casey had been a free man for perhaps a half-dozen years. The fact that he had kept out of the way of the police was a recommendation.

"How long you been here?"

"Since I got out."

"You know why we're here?"

"I know what Thelma told me."

"Theft wasn't in your repertoire, was it?"

"No way."

"What do you think happened?"

"For too many years I lived only with men. I didn't understand many of them. Here there are only women. I don't understand any of them. They are very different from men."

"Can I quote you on that?"

"These three are playing three-way tag, and I'm never sure who's it."

"You drive them all?"

"When they let me. Mainly I take Thelma to the mall. To shop."

"The young Mrs. Dunne has reported missing items. She wanted us to investigate so an arrest could be made if we find a suspect."

"She never liked me."

"Neither did I." But Phil smiled when he said it. "For the record, did you steal those items?"

"No. What were they anyway?"

"Odds and ends. A necklace, an Italian banknote, a South African gold piece. A Purple Heart."

Casey shook his head at the list.

"If it's an inside job and you're out, who did it?"

Casey displayed his palms. "Hey, I'm no fink."

"So you have a suspicion?"

"No! I didn't say that. And I don't. Why would any of these ladies steal? The have everything they want."

"Maybe you're a bad influence."

Father Dowling waited until Phil came before he let Marie open the poor box. There among the coins was a military ribbon, the distinctive Purple Heart.

"So nothing's missing after all."

"Did you tell Mrs. Dunne that some of her things had shown up in our poor box?"

Phil shook his head. "Not yet. Could any of them have put these items in the poor box? And don't ask me why they would. They are all unusual people."

"So what was the upshot?"

"Cy took Casey downtown for further questioning."

"Is he a suspect?"

"Of what? Putting things in the poor box? No. But Cy thought he would be a good source to find out about the others."

"I should think you would ask Amos Cadbury."

"I was hoping you would do that."

Father Dowling agreed to talk with his parishioner and friend about the supposed theft from the Dunne house. He offered to come downtown to Amos' office, but the lawyer would not hear of inconveniencing the pastor of St. Hilary's. Father Dowling had learned not to quarrel with Amos' exaggerated respect for the cloth. It was quite impersonal. It was the priesthood Amos honored. But Father Dowling liked to think that they were friends as well.

"Now if Mrs. Murkin would make some of her tea . . ." Amos said after insisting that he would come to the rectory.

Father Dowling promised that tea would be made. Marie was delighted at the prospect of Amos Cadbury's visit. He was deferential to the gentle sex, as he continued to call women, and had flattered Marie Murkin's culinary capacities to such a degree that Father Dowling sometimes feared that Amos might lure Marie away. If the lawyer was not so patently sincere, Father Dowling would think him a flatterer. Another of his enthusiasms was the paragraphs the pastor wrote each Sunday for the parish bulletin. "I have kept them all, Father. At the end of the year, I have them bound."

Amos arrived in homburg and black overcoat with a fur collar. The pleats of his trousers were razor sharp, the shoes that emerged from his galoshes were shiny, his suit jacket was open to reveal the buttoned vest across which a chain stretched. It held the Phi Beta Kappa key he had earned at Notre Dame. Marie took the lawyer's coat as if she were an acolyte and Amos a celebrant. Father Dowling had come to the door as well and now led Amos to his study.

"Tea will be ready in a minute," Marie chirped.

"*Deo gratias!*" said Amos.

There would have been no way to avoid the ensuing ceremony even if Father Dowling had been inclined to. They moved into the dining room at Marie's call, and the lawyer tasted with closed eyes and then having opened them praised the result of Marie's brewing. He also oh'd and ah'd appropriately over the sandwiches and fruitcake she served. For half an hour it would have seemed that the purpose of Amos Cadbury's visit was to take tea with Marie. But eventually the pastor and his guest withdrew to the study and to the topic of the theft from the Dunne house.

"I warned against hiring that man," Amos murmured. "I speak, Father Dowling, strictly *entre nous*. Dorothea Dunne would not be the first person to pay for a misguided compassion. Note that I speak quite generically. I do not know this man. Casey is his name. But it is a sad rule of human nature that one who has fallen once may fall again. But I need not explain such things to you."

"Do you think Mrs. Dunne suspects the man?"

"The elder Mrs. Dunne?"

The question seemed to be a species of answer. In any case, Amos wanted to speak of Fergus Dunne, whom he described as an equivocal fellow.

"How so?"

"How to put it? He was his own greatest admirer. But there was so much to admire. He was a very gifted man, a very generous man, a very driven man. He started from nothing and amassed a fortune."

"What exactly did he do?"

"What didn't he do? Business, sports entrepreneur, pilot."

"Pilot?"

"He was in the Air National Guard reserve. He was inordinately proud of it."

"And he won a Purple Heart?"

"He was not reluctant to say so."

"There is something I want to tell you, Amos. All those missing items turned up in the poor box at the back of the church. Including the Purple Heart."

"You don't say."

"First, there was the necklace, and then the other items, one by one at intervals. If they were stolen, the thief did not keep them."

"If?"

"It seems a way to draw attention, doesn't it?"

"To the theft?"

"Or to the fact that it wasn't a theft."

"Are they in your parish, the Dunnes?"

"Yes."

"This is quite mysterious, Father Dowling."

"Any ideas?"

"I am speechless."

❈ ❈ ❈

Things that might have seemed insignificant before took on significance now, and Marie Murkin always kept a sharp eye out. She must have noticed that the two Mrs. Dunnes were driven to Mass each Sunday in a very noticeable car. The driver did not wear a uniform, but he did everything but tug at his forelock when he opened the back door for the ladies. He saw them safely into church and then sauntered back to the car where he spent the next hour smoking and reading the paper. Ten minutes before Mass ended, he aired out the car and had a final cigarette standing in the entrance of the school, a recessed area that afforded him some protection from the winter winds.

"They must come to Mass weekdays too," Edna Hospers said.

"I've never seen them there," Marie said.

"The car you describe has parked in the lot on weekdays too."

"Are you sure?"

"There are not many Jaguars of that style cluttering up the parking lot."

"Is that the kind of car it is?"

"I checked with my son Carl."

Marie was certain she had seen neither of the Mrs. Dunnes at daily Mass. She took it as one of the duties of her job to notice such things. That must mean that the driver had come alone. His background and his apparent presence on the parish grounds painted inevitably to a conclusion. He would not be coming for Mass, since he skipped that on Sunday when he had an obligation to attend. She drew her conclusion explicitly for the pastor.

"Have you told Phil Keegan?"

"Do you think I should?"

"He may be a little less grateful to you for doing his job for him than I am."

Marie refused to be gotten off on a tangent by his teasing. "I don't like to be the cause of another's trouble, Father."

"It's not your role to grant clemency, Marie."

"Are you saying I have an obligation?"

"I have every confidence you will do the right thing."

Try as she would, Marie could not get Father Dowling to tell her in so many words that she should tell Phil Keegan what she had learned about F. X. Casey, the Dunne driver. When the pest Tuttle, the lawyer, came by and actually said he had an appointment with the pastor, Marie was about to tell a little white lie but Father Dowling looked out of his study.

"Ah, Mr. Tuttle. I thought I heard your voice. Come in."

The door closed on them and Marie, without exactly pressing her ear to the door, still could not discover what they were talking of. The door was still shut an hour and a half later. Her curiosity overwhelmed her and armed with a plate of cookies, she knocked on the study door.

"Come in."

She breezed across the room and put the cookies on the desk, then looked around.

"Where is he?"

"Where is who?"

"Tuttle!"

"He left hours ago."

Marie was so astounded, she dropped into a chair. How could that man get out of the house without her hearing him? But there was a more important question.

"Why was he here?"

"Are you sure you want to know?" She hesitated at so easy a victory. "If you think I should."

"I hope I didn't do the wrong thing."

Marie waited, silently counting, dying to know.

"He asked if you ever thought of marrying again. His is a modest practice, but his eye has been on you for some time. . . ."

She leapt to her feet and was so miffed she took the cookies with her when she left. Honestly, she didn't know why she put herself in the way she put herself in the way of such teasing.

Phil Keegan came by that evening and Marie did not have to be the one to turn his professional attention to F.X. Casey.

"What put you on to him, Phil?"

"Edna Hospers has a pair of sharp eyes, Roger. She has seen one of the Dunne cars here. Probably when he came to drop things in the poor box."

"I was the one who saw that car!" Marie cried.

"You can corroborate Edna's testimony?"

It had been a dreadful day and Marie was glad to creep away to her apartment over the back part of the house. Her thunder had been stolen.

And she still did not know why the pastor had wanted to talk to Tuttle. It was one of those moments when she really knew that God was her only refuge.

When Marie Murkin came to tell Father Dowling that a woman named Thelma Spooner was in the front parlor she wore a quizzical look, as if she had just seen a ghost, or a lost cousin. Father Dowling went into the parlor where the woman sat slumped in a chair. She looked up but did not stand when the pastor entered.

"I work for the Dunnes."

"Ah."

"Amos Cadbury has been to see you."

"Yes, he has."

"Frank Casey is still in jail."

She seemed a treasury of items he already knew.

He said "I understand he refuses to talk."

"They have bound him over to the grand jury!"

"I think that is the usual procedure."

"He didn't do anything wrong."

"Let's hope that will become clearer than it is. One of the Dunne cars was seen here at about the time that items were left in the church."

"That was me."

"You?"

She nodded. She sat forward and looked at the door. "Is that woman still out there?"

Father Dowling got up to close the parlor door, cutting off the sound of Marie's departure down the hallway.

"Tell me about it."

She was embarrassed to tell the tale. Three women living together, none much caring for the others. The elder Mrs. Dunne had not hired Thelma, her husband had.

"She'd throw me out in a minute but she's afraid he would come and haunt her."

The two Mrs. Dunne barely tolerated one another. The bond was the memory of Fergus Dunne.

"A complete blowhard, Father, but they worship his memory."

"Why would you have left those things in the church?"

"Spite. The pearls were the older woman's. Dorothea had convinced her that she had made a present of them to her."

A drama of petty vindictiveness emerged from the story. Thelma had resented her employers for years, but the only retaliation she had thought of was petty theft.

"I am surprised that Frank Casey has kept quiet."

Thelma seemed to be about to explain that, but then her mouth formed a straight line and she rocked back and forth for a moment.

"I suppose they'll arrest me now."

Father Dowling's solution was to call Phil Keegan and Amos Cadbury and ask them to come to the rectory. They had no sooner arrived and got settled in the parlor, when Marie appeared, wearing a look of annoyance.

"Tuttle," she said to the pastor.

"Put him in the study."

Rebellion sparked in her eyes but she went off to do as she was asked.

"Thelma, why don't you tell Captain Keegan and Mr. Cadbury what you have told me."

He excused himself for a moment and went into the study to talk with Tuttle. When he returned to the parlor, Thelma was just finishing her account to a sympathetic Amos Cadbury and a skeptical Phil Keegan.

"It doesn't make any sense," Phil said.

"You have to imagine yourself living in that house," Amos suggested.

"Why the Purple Heart?"

Father Dowling intervened. "Should I tell them, Thelma?"

She studied the pastor's face. "Do you know?"

"I have just learned."

"Learned what?" Phil said, exasperated.

"Fergus Dunne never earned a Purple Heart. He never saw action and he never shed blood for his country, that being the *sine qua non* of the Purple Heart. As I needn't tell you, Phil."

A cloud formed on Phil Keegan's face, but the face of Thelma was a mask of relief and almost joy.

"He was a phony," she said. "From the time he was a boy. Doing what he did was never enough, he had to claim to do more."

"How did you find out, Father Dowling?" Amos asked.

"Tuttle found it out for me."

At the mention of Fox River's least distinguished member of the bar, Amos Cadbury winced.

"I'm not going to charge you for misplacing a few items," Phil Keegan said to Thelma.

"Then why did you arrest Frank Casey?"

"He has a record."

"That's not fair."

"Frank has been telling me the same thing."

"Will you let him go now?"

"Why don't you release him to Thelma's custody, Phil?" Thelma actually threw up her hands in surprise. But she agreed. Phil took her with him when he left but Amos stayed on, seduced by the offer of a cup of Marie Murkin's tea.

"Spooner is her married name," Father Dowling said, when tea had been poured. Amos Cadbury's patrician brows lifted and he glanced at the pastor.

"You found that out too?"

"And that her maiden name was Casey. I assume she is Frank's sister."

"Aunt."

"Ah."

Amos sipped his tea. "Dorothea never let Casey forget his criminal past. That, coupled with her almost oriental devotion to the memory of her heroic husband, eventually weighed Thelma down. She knew the Purple Heart had not been earned.

"She wanted to discredit the memory of Fergus Dunne."

"Let us say she wanted revenge on his widow."

Silence fell over the parlor as the two men pondered the antics that take place on the stage of life.

"The means were ignoble, but her intention was not."

Father Dowling said, "She didn't put those things in the poor box."

Amos rattled his cup into its saucer. "Why do you say that?"

"I think you know, Amos."

Another silence set in. "What told you?"

"You expressed surprise about the necklace, but there had been a notice in the parish bulletin."

Amos opened his mouth, then closed it. He had no wish to deny that he was a close reader and collector of the bulletin. Father Dowling tried to imagine the stately lawyer slipping those items into the poor box.

"It was Fergus' claim to be a hero that explains my deed. To become involved in the quarrels of a nest of women—that I would never done. But Thelma's cause seemed just to me." His eyes darted to the priest's, then fell. "I suggested the other things, to lead up to the pièce de résistance."

"No crime has been committed."

"Just sins? I am worse than those women. Father, I want you to say some Masses for the repose of the soul of Fergus Dunne. I sincerely hope he has achieved the only reward that really matters."

ഗ്ഗോ ഗ്ഗോ ഗ്ഗോ

"What about the Jaguar?" Phil asked some days later during a lull in the Bulls' game. "The weekday visits."

"That was Dorothea."

"What was she up to?"

"Why do people come to church?"

Marie humphed. "To put things in the poor box."

"Exactly. We have been so distracted by those items that we failed to notice that some larger bills were stuffed into the box during those weeks. American bills. And she also lit a candle for her husband."

"The hero," Marie said, but her heart was not in it.

"Do you know how some people got their Purple Hearts?" Phil asked.

But Marie did not want to know. The thought of Dorothea Dunne as a grieving widow had softened her. As for Phil, he hunched forward when play resumed. Tomorrow Father Dowling would say the first of a series of Masses for Fergus Dunne, with a commemoration of other sinners, present company included.

CAROLYN WHEAT

⚮ ⚮ ⚮

Carolyn Wheat, winner of the Agatha, Anthony, Macavity, and Shamus awards for her short stories, is the author of the Cass Jameson mysteries. She is also the editor of *Murder on Route 66*, in which murder rides the Mother Road. She currently makes her home in Southern California.

REMEMBERED ZION

BY CAROLYN WHEAT

By the rivers of Babylon
We laid us down.
And there we wept
When we remembered Zion.

The time of hating had lasted so long that it was hard for the old woman to recall the time of—of what, exactly? Not love, no, there had never really been a time of love, but maybe of tolerance or of getting along all right or of just being able to go to the bakery for bread without fearing for your life. A time when you didn't even know what religion your neighbors practiced; you might think, 'Oh, that sounds like a Muslim name,' or 'My grandfather's name was Vaso,' but few women wore the veil and a lot of men liked little round hats, so you couldn't tell by their clothes or their names, and in truth, you didn't really care whether they went to St. Stanislaus on Sunday or the mosque on Friday, so long as they kept a neat yard and didn't cook revolting food.

After all, you could live next door to people who went to your church and smell rotten cabbage and see children half-dressed and running around like wild Indians; nobody had a monopoly on virtue just because they wore a saint's medal underneath a filthy shirt.

But that was the old way of thinking. The new way was that anybody different was evil and evil had to be destroyed. Men with guns came in the night and pulled people from their homes and lit the houses on fire, laughing and cursing and drinking, loud and scary even though they invited the Christian neighbors to come watch the bonfire. A lot of them did; "Some Christians," thought the old lady with a snort, but then her son, her middle son, the one she'd always worried about, he was so angry, so full of something to prove, resentments that flared with the slightest of insults, that son insisted she leave her warm bed with its hand-embroidered quilt to stand in the icy night and bask in the glow of the fire.

She didn't bask. She stood solid as a potato, her shawl wrapped around her, a woolen scarf on her head, looking for all the world like a statue of Mother Russia herself, all of Eastern Europe wrapped in a gray dress, as she gazed emotionless at the wreck of her neighbors' house. What was the use of telling Darko what a fool he was? What was the point of arguing with the red-faced men shooting their guns into the air, taunting the neighbors as they ran away, clutching whatever possessions they could scrape together before the fire destroyed the home they'd lived in these last forty years?

The stupid, ugly men who looked just like her son would only tell her they were doing it for her. Purity. Cleansing. Making the country free for old women like herself, taking out the garbage—whatever disgusting euphemism they used, she knew the truth, knew it in her bones because she'd been here before. She'd seen men just like these drunken savages, only the men who lived in her nightmares had twisted crosses on their sleeves and the people they were sweeping into camps included her best friend Esma.

So long ago. So recent in memory. So unforgettable.

Esma the shy, Esma the sunny, Esma who shared her honey cake at school and could do math as well as any boy. She had one photograph of her best friend, a shiny black-and-white image, as tiny as a postage stamp, fading now but there she stood in front of her brown gingerbread house, her mouth open in a gap-toothed grin, a too-short dress handed down from an older sister hanging on her skinny frame.

Esma, dead and gone these fifty years. She'd made her friend a promise—the promise echoed around the world by any number of people horrified by what they'd witnessed: Never Again. *Never again will I let them take you, my Esma.*

Yet here she was standing like a stone, like a loaf of bread, saying nothing and doing less, allowing her own flesh and blood to rampage with drunken glee as the home next door burned to ashes.

The battered tricycle on the front lawn said it all. The men were so intoxicated with hate that none of them thought to take it for a child of their own. It was a pretty good tricycle when the looting began, when the television and the dining room table and the brass bed were carried in triumph out of the house. But the search for valuables to "confiscate" ended abruptly when someone—was it Darko?—ordered the burning. It was better in this new time of madness to destroy than to take and use.

The neighbors had been quiet people; she didn't know them well, but she'd given a crust of bread and honey to the child with the tricycle and she'd nodded to the young mother hanging her wash on the line. The mother-in-law was an invalid who walked with a cane and the old grandfather, who'd moved in with his bride at the same time the old woman and her late husband bought the house next door, worked in the garden every day, rain or shine. An ordinary family. People who cooked meals and took baths and read books and played the television a little too loud because the grandfather was losing his hearing.

Now they were on the road, their possessions wrapped in a blanket, walking to the border. The old woman had a premonition that the crippled mother-in-law wouldn't make it. The grandfather was a tough old bird who'd been through the same war she'd endured; he'd survive and he'd make damned sure his granddaughter and great-grand-child did too. The old woman shook her head slowly; war was unkind to those without strength.

The little boy with the big dark eyes who rode his tri-cycle around in circles, chasing the birds—what would happen to him?

She'd been a few years older than him when the men with the twisted crosses on their uniforms came for Esma's family.

What would happen to him? Would he wake, forty and fifty, sixty and seventy years later, soaked in sweat and breathing too fast, heart beating a mile a minute, clutching his breast because he thought maybe he heard a knock at the door, and a knock on the door in the middle of the night could only mean one thing?

༝ ༝ ༝

She had to do something. Wrong as the drunken pil-laging, cursing, pushing, fire-lighting men were, to stand silently by was also wrong.

Yet challenging the bullies carried a heavy price. Old man Karejian, the Armenian fruit vendor, stood up to the mob one night. Spit on the street when the loudest of them kicked an old woman into the gutter. Called the bully a Turk—under his breath—just an old man mutter-ing, no threat to the men with the guns, but it was enough to earn him a gun butt in the mouth, which dis-located his jaw and sent him sprawling into the street, where steel-toed boots kicked the life out of him while the mob clapped and cheered.

That was perhaps the worst of it. She knew people who were there that night, who saw it all, who now whispered that the mob had gone too far, that it wasn't right to treat an old man that way.

They said that now, and they told stories of other neighbors who joined in the jeering and got in a kick or two, but what they couldn't admit was that they, too, had gone mad for that single moment, had danced in the fireglow from burning stores and looted lives, had clapped and kicked and cheered on the glorious liberators. Good people, ordinary people, people who gave coins to beggars and prayed all day on Sunday, suddenly erotically thrilled by the sight of naked power in the hands of thugs.

"They want to turn the country into a Muslim state," they said afterward.

"If they had the power, they'd do the same to us," others agreed.

"No, they'd do far worse. We're not killing them, we're letting them go back where they belong. If they had the power, they'd slit our throats in our beds. We're just protecting ourselves."

The old woman listened and nodded as if the words made sense, as if, after all, there was a purpose to the madness.

She knew there wasn't, knew it for the deepest and darkest of reasons.

∞ ∞ ∞

Her uncle told the story many times, told it so often the words were worn and shiny with use, like the handle of his cane. Something to lean on, something smooth to wrap your hands around when the world felt wobbly.

A story of heroes, of fighting against unbearable oppression, of downtrodden people feeling their strength and facing the enemy with only weapons of righteousness. David confronting Goliath.

Night of Diamonds, he called it. A night of twinkling lights and giant fires that glowed with the purpose of the people. A night that changed the world, a night that those who lived it would never forget. A night of decision and bravery, of anger and purifying flames.

She later learned—

Oh, much later, and not from her uncle, long dead by then, but from her oldest cousin, the one who went to university, the name the rest of the world used to describe that night:

Kristallnacht.

Her uncle's Night of Diamonds was the night of broken glass; the heroic German people throwing off the yoke of oppression were really just drunken Nazi bullies breaking the store windows of Jewish merchants, like naughty schoolboys.

Where were the heroes? Where was the glory?

Her uncle's solution to the men with the crooked crosses was to join them, to become one of them, to call them heroes and tell the story backward, so that wrong became right and bullies became victims and evil became good.

But there was another story from that long-ago time of horror and sadness, a story that lifted her soul even as it seared her with guilt. A king—but then a king has power; what a king could do, a peasant would be killed for thinking about—a king stepped into the square of his royal city wearing a yellow star, the same yellow star the Nazis made the Jews wear. And the rest of the city woke up and went about its business, and every single person in the town, Jew and Christian, wore the same yellow star.

She loved that story, loved to picture herself a child no older than Esma, proudly stepping out of her doorway with the yellow star pinned to her winter coat. She'd stand before the Nazis and gaze into hard eyes without a tremor, knowing she was safe because all her people were with her and the king on his horse wore the same yellow star.

This time it would be different. She and Esma would walk the streets together, both wearing their stars, both unafraid and happy, growing old together, meeting for a cup of tea and talking of the old days instead of the way it really was, with Esma never reaching her twelfth birthday.

If only they'd been Danish.

There were two more Muslim families on her street. Their time was coming, of this the old woman was certain. They'd been warned already, but for some reason they stayed, stubborn and fearful. The women went to the market like frightened mice, scuttling round-shouldered and head-bowed, looking from left to right like birds, hoping to make themselves invisible to the men who glared at them and sometimes called out obscenities.

She'd heard stories—hadn't seen for herself, thank the living God—that the soldiers raped Muslim women over and over again, deliberately trying to make them pregnant. What if the men of her village, her own son, ravished that innocent little girl with the budding breasts?

She had to do something.

The next time the men came, carrying torches and shouting, she stepped out of her house and walked silently toward them. She wore a veil of black cotton that wrapped her head and covered her mouth. She looked like a Muslim woman walking to the mosque, and she was not alone. Most of her neighbors, not all, they were not saints, her neighbors, just ordinary people trying to make sense of the times they lived in, but most of them were tired of the bullies and the fires and the hatred, and the women joined her, veiled and silent.

They stood like a black wall between the ugly shouting men and the trembling little family in the yellow house.

Was she doing it because the teenage girl with the black hair and gap-toothed smile reminded her of Esma?

Perhaps.

The first stone struck her squarely on the breast. It hurt and she winced, but what really hurt was that the man who threw it, face distorted with rage, was her own son.

And she saw by his eyes that he knew who she was. His anger wasn't just directed at Muslims or women who tried to protect Muslims—he wanted to hurt her. His rage encompassed worlds, it was red-hot and icy cold and it would be appeased only by the sight of the little yellow house burning in the night sky and the family humbled and expelled.

As the second stone hit, this time striking her head, she saw again that awful day, the day they took Esma away from her, Nazi soldiers rounding up all the Jews and putting them on trains.

And she saw herself, wearing her Sunday dress, standing with the other children of the village, chanting—

Oh, God, the pain. The pain, not from sharp stones or the sharper realization that her own son wanted her dead, but the pain of that long-ago day, the pain of remembering day after day of her long life, the last words she'd shouted at her best friend:

Good-bye, Jews.

Die, Jews.

Everyone was saying it. Everyone had told her she and Esma could no longer be friends, and she had believed them. They told her Esma was evil because Jews killed Jesus and she loved Jesus, didn't she?

Well, of course she did. And if Jesus didn't want her to be friends with Esma, then she wouldn't be. She stopped talking to Esma and she refused an invitation to her friend's birthday party, and pretty soon she forgot that Esma made her laugh like nobody else in the world.

When the gun butt struck her and she fell onto the cobblestones, knowing she would never get up, a smile crossed her face, a smile that maddened the already enraged men and forced them to kick her until the smile vanished along with her breath.

I'm coming, Esma.

Forgive me.

SERITA STEVENS

ⳉ ⳉ ⳉ

Serita Stevens is the author of 26 books including *Deadly Doses: A Writer's Guide to Poisons*. As a forensic nurse she has been trained in domestic violence counseling, sexual assault exams and death investigation. Her series character, Fanny Zindel, everyone's favorite Jewish grandmother, carries an everything bag with tricks to help her. *Red Sea*, *Dead Sea* and *Bagels For Tea*, Fanny's first two adventures, will be released in e book format. Her newest book is about forensic nurses who solve crimes. Serita and her adopted Romanian daughter, Alexzandra, live in Southern California with their dog, Pupperazi, cats Edgar A. Poe, Charlie Dickens, Marky Twain and Goldie Meir. Serita is on the board of directors for Hearts for Romania and has written the story of her daughter's adoption as well as information on the charity. Her website is http://home.earthlink.net/~alexmom/

IN A JEWISH VEIN

BY SERITA STEVENS

"Romania? Why would anyone want to go there?" I asked my granddaughter, Susan, when she told me that her former sixth-grade teacher, Rachel Fink, a single woman, was planning on adopting a child from Eastern Europe.

"She can't find someone around here? Pretty girl. You know, *Susa-le*," I said using the Yiddish diminutive for her name, "Menachem Levy is her age. She's thirty-five, yes? Maybe we should have them over for *Shabbos* lunch?"

Susan shrugged. *"Bubbe!* Rachel . . . uh . . . Ms. Fink, doesn't want to go out with Menachem."

"Why not? He's a doctor. An anesthesiologist no less. Hardly any call."

"*Bub-be*, please. Rachel does not want to be fixed up. I think she went out with Menachem anyway."

"Well, then, there I—"

"*Bubbe.* Rachel Fink just finished that horrid divorce. She doesn't want to get married again yet . . . maybe not ever. But her hourglass is draining of sand. She told me that if she wanted to find someone again it wouldn't be soon enough for her to get to know him and . . . and get . . . uh . . . something going." Susan waved her hand to and fro. "You know what I mean, before the last bit of sand ran out."

I sighed. My trademark you should know, at least that is what my family tells me. "*Susa-le*, raising a child alone is . . ."

"An awesome thing. But how else is she going to become a mother?"

It was my turn to shrug. "She could always marry someone

with kids."

Susan gave me the look. "I don't think that would pass. Anyway, *Bubbe*, I told her that we'd be happy to go with her and give moral support."

I could only stare. Surely my ears had aged. My hearing not always as good as it was twenty, even ten, better yet five years ago. "Susan . . . ?"

"*Bubbe* . . . she didn't have anyone to accompany her. You wouldn't want her going alone. After all, you knew her mother. Didn't you guys go to school together?" Just only out of her teens and my granddaughter was an expert in Jewish guilt.

"*Oy vay*. I should be so young. The Finks actually lived in my old neighborhood. I used to baby-sit for her mother." Such a thought can make you age ten years at least.

"Anyway"—Susan rushed on ignoring my correction,— "aren't you always telling me about Grandma Vera escaping the pogroms and fleeing across the river by seducing a Romanian soldier?."

My face turned redder than horseradish at Passover. "*Susale*, I don't remember"—I swallowed hard—"besides, what do you know . . . ?"

Susan gave me a sly smile and shrugged. "Anyway, I want to see where my great-grandmother was born. And," she added hastily, "I can do a paper for my Jewish studies on the plight of the Romanian Jews."

"There's Jews there yet?"

"Sure." Susan smiled and produced an article from the *Daily Forward* English edition talking about the chief rabbi of Bucharest and the old synagogue.

Tsk-tsk. My tongue made clucking noises as if it had a life its own. "Barely ten thousand left in a country that used to have over two million." Most of them, the paper said, were centered in the main city, Bucharest, but there were a few in outlying communities.

"So, tell me, *Susa-le*. Just why were we volunteered? Besides my knowing Mrs. Fink, I mean?" I gave my granddaughter the eye.

Susan shrugged. It was her turn to cook in the sun. "I told the rabbi that I would bring over a few religious items for the families there. And . . . being that it is Eastern Europe, well, I mean . . ." Her hands were doing their dance again.

My sigh again. "When do we leave?"

My granddaughter hugged me and ran for the phone.

Little did I know what we were getting ourselves into. *Oy vay.* A "Buffy the Vampire Slayer" I wasn't, but my wooden knitting needles I took, just in case. Not that I believed in vampires, but one never knew. Remembering my adventure with Sergi in Tiberias, Israel, I packed a few metal ones too.

My parents, may their names and memories be blessed, had left the *shtetl*, a small ghettolike town, on the Russian-Romanian border far away . . . just like the song: "May the Lord keep the Tzar . . . far away from us."

While mildly curious, Romania wasn't high on my shopping list. Still, my learning the recipe for *mamaleka*, the cornmeal sour cream staple used by the Romanians in a variety of ways, would please the palate of my old uncle Yaakov. Nursing home material he wasn't yet, but who knew how much longer he had? A few pictures I had also promised him. Since I was going, why not?

Before we left Uncle Yaakov warned me to take plenty of garlic "to keep the vampires away," he had laughed.

Not until we reached the airport at 1 A.M. for our connecting fight to New York did I finally meet Rachel Fink in person. Pleasant, but plain and perhaps a bit *zoftig*, pleasingly plump, though I should talk. It was easy to see why she had decided to adopt rather than wait for her Prince Charming.

Eighteen-plus hours of nonstop talk. Enough it was to know anyone, but especially Rachel Fink. Like a teapot she was pouring—sometimes steam and sometimes hot water. Such a family. Easy to see how she might *chollish*, hunger, for a child of her own just as I had a deep hunger right now for a few hour's shut-eye. Lucky for Susan she could sleep anywhere.

Barely awake I was when we landed at half past eleven, several hours later than we had expected, due to some gusting winds near Vienna. I had said *tefilath ha-derech*, the traveler's prayer, only once, but from fear of crashing the *Shema* I said several times.

As we landed I wanted to kiss the Delta pilot, but I took one look at the guard's *punim*, face, customizing our line. Such a face not even a mother could love. A fuss here I didn't need to make.

I thought about *Susa-le's* buried treasures she had brought as gifts for the Jewish community. Hard, almost impossible to get here, they were: a few High Holiday *matchzors*, for the special annual prayers; two shofars, rams' horns for blowing on Rosh Hashanah; *havdalah* sets for concluding the end of the Sabbath; menorahs for the Hanukkah holiday: Shabbat candlabras; some *tallaysim*, prayer shawls for covering during the Davening; *tzitzit*, which the men wore to remind them of the 613 commandments; *tefillin*, and prayer books.

One of each maybe she could claim but four or five...but how did she get away with the things like *tzitzit*, *tallaysim*, and *tefillin* that only Jewish men would need? She was looking for a husband maybe? My mind started to create the recipe we would need for an eatable cake—a good excuse for the guards. I only hoped none of the guards had nibbled at Judaism before or else we would all be in a stew.

At least there would be two less suitcases coming home. Such a *shlep* but thanks I gave to *HaShem* for my granddaughter's passion for Judaism and our traditions.

The few minutes we had before reaching customs I observed the others in line with us. Harry and Belinda Barr, a nicely dressed couple with whom I had shared a coffee and chatted while we waited in the washroom line. Some business they planned to set up in Romania, but what business I didn't know.

Now they stood two ahead of us. Her, I liked. Him, I wasn't so sure. A bit too confident and boisterous he seemed. He strutted toward the guards like a turkey about to be plucked.

I could see they were having an argument of some kind.

Rather he argued, she tried to talk, but was a slow simmer next to his boil. He pinched her quiet. I saw the fire in her die down immediately. Like the boiling water, his voice raised the temperature in the room. *"Glump!* Stupid, he's talking to me." He boiled up to full steam.

I winced for me and for her. From such Jews, the Romanians didn't need to know.

Beside me, Rachel Fink inhaled sharply. "Something ought to be done about men like him."

Shrinking into my coat, I heard him "discussing" with the guards about his status as a lawyer and how important his work was here in Romania. Already, I had seen how he treated his wife. A client of his I didn't want to be.

Harry was becoming angrier and more irate as the customs officers became intent on examining his luggage. Just when it looked like they were about to haul him off to who knew where, a pale blond young man in a black coat and black fur hat appeared.

Total silence. Next to me, Rachel Fink and my granddaughter had stopped talking. Rachel stared at him. He, too, was looking at her—a slight smile on his lips.

"You know him, Rachel?"

"I . . . uh . . . no." She glanced away and down, modestly averting her gaze.

A second glance I had to take at the fellow. From the past he looked like a Chassidic yeshiva student of old complete with a fur hat and garter.

No older than twenty, to be sure. But an air he carried, one of worldly authority. All the customs guards stopped when he appeared. He nodded toward the lawyer. The big hand on the scruff of Barr's neck was dropped.

Irritated and angry the attorney straightened his jacket. Apparently he didn't see the interaction. He assumed his own power had broken the spell.

"Har—"

"Shut up, *glump*. Idiot. When I want your input I will ask for it." He brushed his wife away and then turned.

The young man, slight like a toothpick, tapped the beast. "I believe you owe your wife an apology." The English rolled off his tongue like Yorkshire beef. Oxford? Now I was doubly confused.

"Who the hell . . . ?" Harry Barr, the turkey, spun around ready to fly off without his wings again. "Maybe you want to mind your own business?"

"The Torah's honoring of our brethren, especially our spouses, is my business." The young man stared into the eyes of the lawyer. As if the fire had suddenly been shut off under the boiling water, Mr. Barr lost his voice. What spices had he seen that I had not detected?

"I suggest you watch yourself while in this country, sir. The consequences can be quite deadly."

What could his business be? A marriage counselor I didn't think he was. Hardly old enough to be a groom, himself. Intriguing, like a recipe with ingredients I couldn't quite label.

"You'll find cabs just outside." The young man pointed to the exit.

"Come on, Belinda." He grabbed his wife's arm. "Let's get done what we need in this primitive country and leave."

From being a prime roast, she had become a piece of hamburger. She gave me a glance and then a shrug. Pressing her lips together to keep the tears at bay, she hurried after him. Her I didn't envy. Money they obviously had, but love and consideration, she didn't. Maybe later I could give her the name of the hotline that helped women like her get away.

"I believe you are next, madam," the young man reminded me. For a moment our eyes met. Brooding and oh so sad. I almost reached out to touch and comfort him, but then I realized that if he was a yeshiva *boucher*, a touch from a lady he wouldn't want.

He glanced away quickly, as if there was something he didn't want me to see. What I didn't know, but it was just beyond my taste buds. The flavor was . . . something dark and painful.

"Oh, yes. Right. *Susa-le*, here." I motioned to my granddaughter and to Rachel Fink, who had moved off to the side. Despite the laws of *tznis*, modesty, Rachel seemed unable to stop watching our new companion.

"Allow me," he said, in a voice so soothing it was almost seductive. Mature, not pipsqueak, as one might imagine for a face so youthful. Strong, he was, too, as he lifted Susan's suitcase filled with contraband.

I inhaled sharply in fear. If one of the latches popped open, we would all be exposed. What did they do to black marketers here? Nothing good I was sure. It wasn't even as if we were selling the items, but, at one time, they had been illegal here and maybe they still were.

"It's yours?" the young man asked. He had lifted the two-ton suitcase as if it were lighter than my grandsons's cloth Torah toy. X-ray vision he didn't have. Yet somehow I had the feeling he knew what the suitcase contained.

"No, . . . it's my . . . " I glanced around for the girls.

"*Aceasta e valiza mea.*" Rachel Fink stepped up. "It's mine—clothes and other items for the baby I am about to adopt," she said quickly and smiled her thanks while putting her hand on the handle to make sure it didn't snap open. "Thank you for your help."

"You're welcome," he said, moving his fingers quickly so that they would not touch. Religious, I thought? Had to be. But here in post-Communist Romania? Anything was possible and yet . . . "Baruch is my name. You're Romanian?" A regular Valentino, this one was. He smiled so brilliantly and such perfect teeth. My son-in-law the dentist would be jealous.

"And you're Jewish?" I countered.

He smiled.

Rachel flushed like a schoolgirl. "My grandmother was. I learned from her. Fanny"—she turned to me—"maybe you can finish the details with our passports?"

The customs guard moved to take documents from Rachel, Susan, and myself. I caught a quick look pass between him and our new protector. Without even looking, the guards handed us back our documents. Maybe some secret code? Could the guard also be a Jew? Was he letting the young man's assessment of us guide him?

So who was this fellow? Son of one of the government people, maybe? Whoever he was, he wielded some power. I was grateful that we did not have to go through a search of our luggage or a long drawn-out interrogation as I feared we might. From airport police, I had had my fill—and then some.

"If you ladies will come with me, I would be most happy to see you to your accommodations."

"I . . . " Rachel was speechless. "The adoption attorney was supposed to . . ."

"It is fine." Now I heard the foreign twinge in his voice, but it was ever so slight. "I often help Vivian Ileausu with her meetings."

"So you knew we were coming?" I asked. More ingredients in this secret recipe.

He merely smiled. "I knew."

Perhaps it was the colder night air, or the lack of sleep, but the shivers that ran up my spine were not ones I could easily ignore.

෴ ෴ ෴

Midnight had nearly arrived. November in Romania was almost as cold as November in Chicago. The Barrs were outside still waiting for the car Harry had rented. Baruch pulled up in a car.

"Allow me. I believe you both are staying on Calle Victoria."

"What are you? Some kind of government spy? Whom do you work with?" Harry asked. I could see he was looking for some chink in the armor.

Baruch shrugged. "Will you join us?" He asked again without answering.

"Sorry, garlic peasant. I do my own driving."

"As you wish."

So that was the last time we saw Harry Barr alive.

෴ ෴ ෴

The apartment in the heart of the city near several of the major boulevards was a cozy furnished one-bedroom. Baruch handed over the keys to us and showed us where the necessary things were.

He seemed pleased that Rachel, because of the *kashrut* laws, had insisted we bring our own cheap pots, paper plates, and utensils.

"So. You have no husband?" Baruch asked Rachel.

"Uh, no." Even in the dark I could see her blush. "I am doing this alone because I want to help a child and I want very much to be a mother." Rachel paused. "Are you Vivian's assistant?"

From romance, I knew plenty. An interesting situation. Maybe before we left here Ms. Fink might be considering another title. He appeared so mature for someone so young.

He shrugged. "Not exactly. But I will see you anon." He paused. "Take care to get proper rest. Vivian will be calling to situate you in the morning. The Rav, our chief rabbi, will be most pleased to meet with you tomorrow. If you'll excuse me, I must now settle up my own accounts."

With that he disappeared like a whiff of steam into the dimly lit corridor, leaving us to wonder. It only occurred to me later that we had said nothing about going to the synagogue or meeting with the rabbi, but somehow he had known.

With the time change, it was hard to sleep. My body told me it was night, my mind told me it was day. Outside our window the marketplace was already busy. Shopping was something I knew how to do. So when I want to think, I shop.

The Romanian market square was an experience, but not unlike shopping the Arab market in Tel Aviv. I busied myself with buying us some fruit, vegetables, and eggs. I couldn't resist the string of garlic to hang in the kitchen.

Our apartment was near Mendelev Street, obviously once the heart of Jewish Bucharest. The synagogue building at the end of the block, still standing, now bore the name of a government agency. A silent reminder of the brutal past.

I had just turned the key to our apartment when I heard the sound of crying from inside.

"What happened?" I threw the door open and hurried into the living area where Rachel had set up for her and the baby.

Belinda Barr sat on our sofa, sobbing. When she saw me she glanced up for just a moment. "Har . . . Harry's dead."

It seemed that her husband hadn't been able to settle down. From the looks of her right eye, he had done more than talk.

Still angry after the airport he had taken a walk, she said. The
body had been found in the hotel parking lot. A heart attack
was the official cause of death.

"I hope you don't mind," Belinda Barr sobbed. "I just did-
n't know where to turn. The police suggested I come here rather
than be alone."

The phone shrilled at 9 A.M. Our agency contact, Vivian
profusely apologized for not meeting us at the airport, but she
hoped we had gotten the message.

"Oh, yes," I told her. "Your assistant Baruch was very helpful. We didn't even have to check through customs. He did
something or said something, I don't know what, but they let
us through without even looking at our luggage."

Through the pause I could hear crackling and distant voic-
es on the line. Like a bad connection it was, but even though I
wanted to doubt my hearing, I still heard Vivian's words echo-
ing. She knew no one named Baruch. She had called the airport
and asked them to arrange for a cab for us. Yet she was close-
mouthed about the fellow who had met us and too quickly she
dismissed the subject.

A fool I wasn't, but there was a lot not being said. I briefly
told her about our new friend and her predicament and suggested that maybe Belinda could stay with us while we were
here . . . unless of course the police needed her at the hotel.

Vivian agreed that Belinda shouldn't be alone and said she
would be over shortly to take care of Rachel's account. Then we
would be free until tomorrow when we would drive to Brasov,
the mountain area in Transylvania, where the orphanage was.
Rachel would, for the first time, see the child she was adopting.

Susan was insistent that we call the shul and speak to the
rabbi about bringing over the items she had brought with us.

"All in good time, *faygeleh*," I said, using my pet name for her. "We came here to help Rachel and I would think we need to get her straightened away first."

I had expected Rachel to be pleased, but instead she seemed distant and preoccupied. She hadn't even finished all her unpacking.

It was then I noticed the fresh mud on her shoes. "Didn't you sleep well either?"

She glanced at me and shrugged. A guilty look I knew from. "I'm going to make some coffee." She took out the can of instant that she had brought, unsure if they would have kosher coffee here. "Vivian will be here soon."

"Good idea." I pulled out the creamer packets we had taken from the plane. These we knew were kosher. "Still on jet lag?" I asked her as we sipped our coffees waiting for Vivian's arrival.

"I guess." She kept looking at the sofa where we had tucked the covers around a now sleeping Belinda. "She reminds me of my past."

"Oh?" I looked at her now with different glasses. I had been right. Pretty she was, but hiding it.

"Your ex-husband, he was like Harry Barr?"

Rachel shrugged. "Hard to say. I saw the Barrs for a only bit on the plane and at the airport, but yes, there were similarities."

"And that is why you gained weight? Didn't want to date again?"

"You're very insightful, Fanny. Susan is lucky to have a grandmother like you."

"So you should know, Rachel, not all men are Harry Barrs. Some are like my Morris, kind, considerate . . . or even like Nathan," I said, thinking of my Mossad friend whom I had not heard from in some time.

She didn't get a chance to answer because the bell rang.

⚬✤⚬ ⚬✤⚬ ⚬✤⚬

Our morning business with the adoption agency concluded, we all four decided to visit the synagogue. The chief rabbi of Romania, Rabbi Dr. David Rosen, was not in, but his associate would be happy to speak with us and give Susan the facts she needed for her paper.

Finding a taxi driver who claimed he knew where the synagogue was another treat in of itself.

"Maybe we shouldn't be making such a point of our being Jewish here," I said, a bit concerned from the history of Romania. Pogroms had been plenty in Romania as well as Russia. "Anti-Semitism is the policy of the country, isn't it?"

"Not anymore. At least, not officially. I think we're okay, Fanny," Rachel said. "Baruch told me—"

"You talked to him about us?" When, I wondered, had they conversed?

"Well, sure. He's a student at the yeshiva. He told me as long as we are not obnoxious about who we are"—she glanced back at Belinda talking with Susan as they looked in one of the store windows—"we should be all right."

So I had been right about something. "You didn't by any chance ask him how he happened to be helping Vivian last night?" I paused for effect. "She says she never sent him. Doesn't know who he is."

Rachel just looked at me and shrugged.

The two-story yellow brick synagogue was on a small side street, 9-11 Sfantul Vineri Street. There was no mistaking the huge menorah in the front. I knew from reading the history that the wall was decorated with names of those who had died during the holocaust and with righteous gentiles who had helped the Romanian Jews.

Despite it being so close to a main square on Unirii Bukevardul, the synagogue had been quite an effort to find. The taxi driver, who professed to know all of Bucharest, drove up one street and then another. Several dead ended or became one-way after only a few blocks. Mice in a maze had it easier.

I had been told that Bucharest was called the Paris of the East and having already been lost in Paris once, I could certainly understand it.

With relief we finally found it.

Greeting us warmly the assistant rabbi told us how pleased he was that we had come as promised.

"Promised?" Susan asked. "I didn't even write you."

The rabbi looked askance. "You are sure? I could swear it was listed on my calendar. Well, never mind. Come. I will show you the Jewish museum and then you will be my guests for dinner at the community center. Yes?"

"Yes," Susan said excitedly.

∽ ∽ ∽

If the synagogue had been hard to find, the community center or cantina was even harder. This way and that way we turned. Finally a roadblock we came to. At one end, the street was manned by uniformed guards.

"Oh, it's you, Rabbi." The guard ushered us through.

"It's necessary to have security?" I asked.

"Unfortunately, yes," The rabbi told us. "We always have to be *shomers*. If we guard against problems they are less likely to occur."

Rachel tried to take a photo of the nondescript brick building "for memory." But the guard put his hand in front of her camera. "I am sorry. We cannot allow that. Too much has happened lately."

"Like what?' I asked, ever curious.

The guard leaned closer and whispered. I could smell the garlic on his breath "Two deaths. Just last week. Their bodies drained of blood."

"Samuel, please." The rabbi pulled me away. "You will make

Mrs. Zindel think we are crazy superstitious." He shook his head. "Please pay Samuel no mind. For all our educating, some of the old tales still surface. Both men who died, although they were part of our community, did little to enhance it. But the deaths were natural." He pointed to a table near the kitchen. "The waiters are starting to serve. Come. You will have some soup, some stew, and some *mamaleka*."

"Oh, yes," I said and proceeded to ask for the recipe.

Mostly older people had come, those on pension and those seeking the company of their fellow Jews. Such a fuss they made over Rachel and Susan. Even more of a fuss when they found out that Rachel was adopting.

Just as we were leaving, a gust of wind blew the door open. Already outside was dark.

For all the chill, Baruch strolled in wearing only his fur *shtreimel* and long black *becksher* coat with *gartel* tying it off. His cheeks were rosy from the cold. He sat down next to us, nodding at the rabbi, who acknowledged the greeting.

I couldn't help but hear the undercurrent whisper. A shame I didn't understand Romanian.

"You had a productive day?" he asked us but directed his attention to Rachel.

She flushed, but not from the fire.

"Mr. Barr is dead," Susan piped up.

"Barr?" Baruch acted as if he did not recall who that was. "Ah, yes, the lawyer. A shame. You are all right, Mrs. Barr?" He addressed Belinda.

She nodded, but was obviously still in a daze. "Shouldn't I be sitting *shivah* or something, shouldn't I?"

The rabbi said, "His death is still being investigated, isn't it?"

She nodded.

"Then you must wait until the burial."

"Oh."

Rachel was looking uncomfortable. Could she have had something to do with the lawyer's death? Her favorite person he hadn't been.

∽ ∽ ∽

Baruch offered to drive us back to the apartment. He and Rachel were deep in conversation and oblivious to all of us in the backseat. Me, I could only think about the murder and mud on Rachel's shoes.

A message from Vivian on the door told us that we would be traveling to Brasov tomorrow to pick up the baby.

Rachel turned to Baruch. "Will you join us?"

He shook his head. "Sadly, my business prevents me from accompanying you for such a *simcha*, but I will be here tomorrow evening to welcome you and your son home and join the happy event."

"Son? No, Vivian said it was a girl."

He smiled. "You are mistaken, my dear one. The child destined for you is a boy."

Before I could ask how he knew this and what his business was, he disappeared much in the same vein he had the night before.

∽ ∽ ∽

There was no question in my mind that Rachel fancied herself in love with this Baruch character. He seemed to be the only thing she could think of. Not even the baby occupied her mind as much. I only hoped that he wouldn't hurt her too deeply.

Shortly after he left, the police came to again question Belinda and to ask what we knew of Mr. Barr.

"Not much," I had to say. It was then that I learned his body had been drained of blood.

"We think this is a prank," the police said, "what with the vampire legends and all." I wanted to ask them about the two men whom the guard at the cantina had mentioned earlier, but I didn't dare. No sense in bringing more notice to the Jews than necessary.

৩৯ ৩৯ ৩৯

The countryside was beautiful, even in the starkness of winter. Outside the modern city, very little was built up. Though I think I would have hated to be a gypsy or a peasant having to eke a living out of the woods. Into the Carpathian mountains we drove. Easily I could envision the scenes from *Dracula*.

The orphanage was a cold and unforgiving gray brick building. Only the director's room had heat. I wandered through one of the rooms on my way to the bathroom and saw crib after crib after crib. Like sardines they were, crammed two, three to a bed, lying there, not moving, not blinking. Had I been younger, I would have scooped up every one of those babies. How many got kissed and tucked into bed at night? How many even got enough food?

"I could swear that we had arranged for you to adopt a little girl. But the paperwork says this baby is yours." Vivian handed Rachel a small blue bundle wrapped in six layers of clothing.

"If you keep his name, Jonathan, you will not have to readopt him when you return to the United States," she told us.

Rachel starred at Vivian and then at the baby lying silently in her arms. "My father's name was Jonathan. How odd."

Odd indeed, I thought.

The baby smiled up at her as if knowing that this was his new mother, his rescuer from a life of cold poverty.

On the drive back to Bucharest, the baby slept soundly in Rachel's arms. "I can hardly believe this. My son." Her face glowed. "Fanny, thank you for coming with me. I can't tell you how happy I am."

I nodded. "I only hope that you will be able to take care of him and guide him into a good Torah life."

She nodded and pushed the nipple toward him as he rooted toward the bottle.

The next days were a haze of activity. To the hospital to check the baby's health. A palace this must have once been. So grand. And so many stairs. Oy, my feet.

Luckily, other than being a bit underweight, the baby passed his physical.

Baruch was a constant visitor but strangely enough only in the evenings. To such restaurants and museums he took us, yet he, himself, hardly ate. Looking and talking with Rachel seemed all that sustained him.

I thought it odd when he asked me to remove the garlic string from the kitchen. He said he had an allergy. People have allergies all the time. Still, garlic was . . . garlic.

The time for our trip was coming to a close.

Only thing left was the baby's American visa, which we would get at the consulate. A bit concerned I was since the Senate had not yet approved the next year's budget. Some of the overseas State Department agencies had closed their doors earlier for the Christmas holidays to cut costs.

"Vivian told me that the American Consulate is opening just for today." Rachel came home excitedly. "Isn't that a miracle?"

I nodded. "*HaShem* be praised." I wondered what Belinda would do now that everything was accomplished for us three. Would she come with us or stay here for the investigation to finish? We had heard nothing from the police.

It was almost as if they were watching. No sooner had we closed the apartment door and started to settle the baby in, to begin packing for the trip home, than we heard the knocking.

"It's the police," Belinda said, wide-eyed.

"So?" Susan asked. "You have nothing to fear. Do you?"

Belinda began to wring her hands Lady Macbeth-style. "I

wanted him dead. I wanted him dead."

"But you didn't do anything," Rachel said.

"I wanted him dead," Belinda repeated.

"*Oy vay.*" I shook my head. "So nobody's going to answer the door? Fine. I'll do it." Thus saying I walked over.

"So, officer," I said, opening the door. "You'd like a cup of tea, maybe? Some schnapps?"

"Madam, you cannot bribe an officer of the law." He turned to Rachel Fink still holding little Jonathan. "You are under the arrest for the murder of Harry Barr."

A good thing I was only inches from her. Now it was Rachel's turn to be wide-eyed.

"What are you talking about? I hardly knew the man."

"Madam, you were seen at the scene. Please come with us."

Rachel looked helplessly at Susan and me. Then she looked at the now mute Belinda. "Call the American Consulate. Deborah King in the State Department," Rachel said as she stood.

∞ ∞ ∞

It was five hours later that much to our surprise Rachel returned. With her was our now constant companion.

"Baruch talked to them," Rachel told us, smiling.

"And what of the murder charge?" I asked. "How do we get Rachel and the baby out of the country with that?"

"There is no more murder charge," Baruch informed us. "Harry Barr has ceased to exist. His passports and documents have disappeared. There is no indication that he was ever in this country. When Belinda wakes from the wine she has drunk, she will recall nothing of the events from the past two days. She will know only that she is free.

"As you have seen, the police and people here are superstitious. As well they should be. A few bribes, a bit of American goods goes a long way here to erase memories. If there are questions, they would rather not ask. You will be leaving on Delta Airlines tomorrow at dawn. I cannot be there with you."

"But Baruch, I thought you said . . ." Rachel's voice cracked slightly. "I am sorry. I am being silly. Of course you can't leave your country and I have no passport for you, no way to get you into the United States with us. I mean you have ways of dealing with this so that you can come, can't you?"

"I shall be with you but only in spirit. The child you have here, Jonathan. He will be your memory of me. He is of my blood and his mother is dead. He is an orphan."

"Jonathan is yours?" Now it was my turn to be astounded. Some intrigue I expected but not this.

"Jonathan means gift of God," Susan said.

He nodded. To both questions. It was clear I missed something.

"But how can that be? INS and the adoption committee here insist that there be no link to the parents," I said.

Baruch shrugged. "You may have guessed that something was strange about me."

"An ugly duckling, you aren't. But, yes," I said, "you have an explanation to tell us maybe?"

He nodded.

"Maybe you had better clean the plates," I said as I sat down and indicated for him to have a seat.

"I am not the person you think I am." He turned quickly around.

The face we saw not even a mother could love. But within moments he had resumed his handsome look. "You see, I am a vampire."

Rachel screamed and fainted.

"Don't you dare touch her, you cad!" I cried as I intercepted him going over to her.

"She will be fine. And no, I will not harm her. I would not harm any of you. I prey only on those who do *averahs*, evil deeds of the most heinous kind."

Rachel began to stir.

Baruch brought water to her and held her hand. "My love. I am sorry to have shocked you."

"It's true then?"

The vampire nodded. "Come. The hour is late and I have much to tell you before you leave tomorrow."

"I'll go make the coffee," Susan said.

"My ancestors were of the Khazars, who ruled southern Russia from the seventh to the tenth centuries. My family was from Satu Mare, in what is now northern Romania."

"The seat of the Satmarer Chassidic dynasty?" I asked. That explained his white stockings and the pants just above the ankles, the traditional dress of the Satmarer Chassid.

"You know of them. Good." Baruch nodded. "Only at that time there were no Chassids. Not until much later. I dress like the sect only because of my homeland ties. But it is the Marhal whom I will always follow.

"I grew up during the time of the Marhal of Prague." He saw the look of surprise on our faces. "You think I jest. I wish I did." He paced the floor, holding the crying baby in his arms as good Tate would do, hushing it until it feel asleep on his shoulder. Then he proceeded to tell us his story.

"My father, a prosperous wine merchant, was known throughout the land for his good wines and for his learning. I, his son, hoped to follow and take on our family business. I was but nineteen years of age. I had come home for the holidays to help my father with his work and wait on the many customers who flocked to us during this time especially.

"A match was to be made for me. You can imagine I was quite excited at the prospect of having a *kalleh*, a bride. I trusted whomever my father would choose for me would be the best.

"The day I was to meet my bride one of our major clients, the bishop of Prague, Anton Salarz, had come for his order. It was a known fact that His Holiness was a Jew-hater. Despite this, he said he would have only the wines of my father's vineyards for his tables.

"In a hurry to be ready for my bride's family visiting, I had rushed about preparing the orders. I had forgotten to mix the berries in the proper portion as he always required. When he came to complain the following day, my father was in town preparing for my wedding so I was left alone to deal with this great and terrible man. The bishop was learned in the Hebrew tongue, in kabbalah and in the Talmud, but only so much as he could use it against us. A master of the black arts."

"Yes, I have heard that name."

"The man who lives today is a descendant and equally as evil."

"I argued with him about the necessary ingredients for a good wine and told him that I did not think a half pint of berries would be missed in his wine this one time. What we did not also know at that time was that he dabbled in the black arts. I did not know that he used our wines to mix with his poison. I merely thought he was being rude and obnoxious merely because I was my father's son and a Jew. I told him that if he did not like our wines, he was more than welcome to go elsewhere.

"When he left that day, he was still in a state of anger and vowed his vengeance upon me.

"Away from my yeshiva, I was vulnerable if I did not learn on a daily basis. A *Talmud Hachum*, student of Torah, is only one so long as he is learning Torah. But anxious for the coming of my wedding, I was in no mood to learn.

"It was two days later. This night I had set out to purify myself in the ritual bath for our wedding the following the day.

"Just two short doors away from the synagogue, I was set upon by ruffians who belonged to the house of the bishop. They were his lackeys. Their plan was to leave me for dead, but knowing the Jewish dictate against the use of blood in our foods, the bishop set upon a crueler fate for me. He cursed and turned me into a vampire.

"At first seeing that I had survived their attack I was pleased. I thought I had fought them off until the first of the hungers came upon me.

"I begged my father to postpone the wedding and in the dark of the night I hurried to the Inn in Bacau where the Marhal, who had come to town specifically for my *chasseneh*, my wedding, stayed.

"It was all I could do to keep myself from laying attack to my beloved teacher. And yet I managed to keep my wits about me as we talked. He told me that in an effort to protect my family, my bride-to-be, and the town I would have to be sent to Harem, the hell of limbo where I would await the day of the cure."

"For seven generations I have been forbidden to have contact with our people, yet I have kept up with my learning such as I can do on my own and occasionally have found sparing partners in the nearby towns. I have followed our history—tragedies and happiness with mixed emotions—waiting for the time when I, too, can go into *Olam HaBa*. Only in the last one hundred years did I realize what the Marhal wanted of me.

"I was to search the land doing mitzvahs and protecting our people whenever and wherever I could."

"Like the Golem?" Susan asked.

"Somewhat. The only ones I permitted myself to feed upon were those who broke the commandments. Those with *averahs*, sins or crimes, that were so terrible that they could never be redeemed."

"You mean like Harry, who was a wife abuser?"

He nodded. "Wife abuser and user of the poor. And others like the man at the community center who pretended his righteousness and then was in league with Harry to sell the children for profit.

"Belinda was not the first whom Harry had dragged into his purgatory. I had come to the airport for you, Rachel. The Marhal had foretold of your arrival. I had been haunting the airport for weeks now like a man consumed. You were coming, but I did not know when. I became a familiar face to the guards there.

"When I saw the Barrs I knew I had to perform one last mitzvah for Belinda. Now finally I am sure a cure is near."

"What type of cure?" Rachel asked, gripping the glass of wine in her hand.

"My teacher, my mentor the Marhal, was not content to have me in limbo. He read, researched, and he prayed to the Almighty to release my soul from this bondage. As he lay on his death bed, he gave me the key to my future. Seven generations I would have to wait in limbo until I realized my mission. Now that I have, and my time is here, I need you to help me. With the coming of the *Moshiach*, I will be set free forever."

He closed his hand over Rachel's and met her eyes. "My bride-to-be, my *kalleh*, her name was Rachel bas Tzipporah."

"That's my name"—Rachel's voice a mere whisper.

The blood had drained from my face as I could see it did from Rachel's and Susan's too. "What are you saying?" Rachel asked.

"You are, were, my bride. The Marhal told me that when I found you, you would release my soul from this hell. Together we will dance to our wedding music with the coming of the *Moshiach*."

"Baruch, what of the baby? Is he . . .?"

"Completely human. He will grow up like any normal child."

"And what do I tell him of his father?"

"Whatever you would have told the child you adopted. But come. The hour grows late. You must release my soul from this torment."

"But how am I do that? I know nothing of black magic. I don't even understand *kabbalah*." He took her hand in his and kissed so tenderly, I wanted to cry.

"Fanny," he said, "you know what has to be done?"

I sighed. "My knitting needles you want, I suppose."

He nodded. "A *rebbetzin* you should have been," he told me. "A *rebbetzin* you will be," he told Rachel.

I brought out my everything bag with the wooden needles and the metal ones just in case.

"No. I can't." Rachel backed away.

"You must. It is the only way. I promise, my love, we will dance with the coming of the Messiah. Only *He Who Blesses Us* can tear us apart again. You will care for my son, our son, and raise him as a true Torah scholar."

The deed was no harder than checking the temperature on a turkey, I told myself. But in the end I could not do it. It was Rachel who performed the deed.

"When the *Moshiach* comes." They were the last words we heard from Baruch's lips. Like the dust he had come from, he disappeared.

As he said, the cab came to drive us to the airport just at the crowing of the cock. Not once did the guards glance at our passports. They waved us through the line as if not seeing us. From the plane, I looked down at the receding ground.

It was almost as if we had never been to Romania.

But we had and only the three of us knew we had been someplace else as well.

It was decided that Belinda would stay with Rachel for a while, help her with the baby and get her life together.

The baby started to cry. Rachel rocked him and sang, "*Moshiach, Moshiach*, we want the *Moshiach* now."

Jonathan quieted. Somehow I had the feeling that this child would be instrumental in leading us all to the *Moshiach*.